For Virginia

xxx Bill

5/06

UNDER CURRENT

UNDER CURRENT

Wayne Barcomb

Permissions, Hot House Press
760 Cushing Highway
Cohasset, MA 02025

Library of Congress Cataloging-in-Publication Data

Barcomb, Wayne, 1933–
Undercurrent/by Wayne Barcomb.
p. cm.
ISBN 0-9755245-4-2
1. Private investigators–Florida–Sarasota–Fiction. 2. Lawyers–Crimes against–Fiction. 3. Sarasota (Fla.)–Fiction. I. Title.
PS3602.A775U53 2006
813'.6—dc22

2005035644

Printed in the United States of America

Book design by DeNee Reiton Skipper

Hot House Press
760 Cushing Highway
Cohasset, MA 02025
www.hothousepress.com

And once again—To Susan, my wife,
my editor, my soul mate, and full partner
in the creation of all my books.

ACKNOWLEDGEMENTS

So many people have helped and advised me during the writing of *Undercurrent,* that it's hard to know where to begin. But here goes.

First, all along the way I have called on law enforcement people at the Sarasota County Sheriff's Office and the Sarasota Police Department for guidance and answers to questions. These include Detectives Jim Glover, Greg Grodoski, Kevin Churchill, Paul Richards, and a very special thanks to Detective Sergeant Chris Iorio for his ongoing insights and help.

State Attorney Earl Mooreland answered some key legal questions for me. Former prosecuting attorney and now judge, Phyliss Galen and Attorney Derek Byrd helped me sift through the legal complexities of wire tapping.

Private Investigator Roy Winkleman provided valuable insights on what a private investigator can and cannot do.

Famed pathologist Michael Baden provided me with the name and description of a drug I wanted to use on one of my characters. Dr. Baden gave me the information I needed to ascertain the credibility of an important scene in the book.

Parker Ladd, former Association of American Publishers executive, read the first rough draft of the manuscript and offered critiques that sent me on the right path.

Jerris Foote, formerly with the Mote Marine Laboratories educated me on sea turtles, who do indeed play an important role in *Undercurrent*.

And my thanks to all the help and guidance from my publisher, David Replogle and his editor, Sally Weltman.

And finally, every author should be so lucky to have a supporter like Steve Uchman. It's impossible to quantify the number of people who have been introduced to my books through Steve's boundless energy and enthusiasm.

Wayne Barcomb
Sarasota, Florida

1

Maggie Robbins awoke with a start. She sat on the dock alone, in near darkness, and shivered as a coarse wind swept across the bay.

A flock of pelicans soared overhead, flying in perfect formation. Maggie watched them flap their wings, gain some height, bank to the right, effortlessly glide over Neville Island and disappear behind the trees. A fisherman in a small outboard floated past her, nodded, and was soon out of sight.

Again she shivered and thought of the three break-ins on Siesta Key in the past few weeks. And here she was sleeping on the dock with the house unlocked.

Easing herself from the chaise, she stood for a moment listening to the rustling of the palm fronds, the distant hum of a boat's motor, and the ghostly tinkling of the wind chimes hanging from the porch. She turned away from the bay and looked across the lawn at her home, framed by stately oaks. Shrouded in the early evening shadows, it looked foreboding, and she felt an inexplicable sense of gloom. And then she noticed. The front door was wide open.

She hugged her shoulders and hurried toward the house. Had she neglected to close the door? Had she left it ajar and the wind blew it open?

After closing and locking the door she checked all the other entrances. The clacking of her sandals on the hardwood floors echoed through the front hall and up the open stairway.

She switched on a light in the dining room and stood in front of the picture window overlooking the yard, watching the intricate shadows from the sea grapes and schefflera dance across the garden to the rhythm of the wind. A tapping against the house startled her. She fixed on the moonlit yard. Nothing. Again the sound, coming from the butler's pantry.

In the pantry, afraid to turn on the light, she felt her stomach tighten. She held her breath and peered from behind a shelf. Nothing but an areca palm scratching against the pantry window. The sound she'd heard a moment ago.

Back in the dining room, she continued glancing at the wide curtainless window. She felt a chill, and the silence she normally found restful was now a discomforting stillness.

It had not been a good day and in a way, she was glad Paul was in Miami. If he were home she would only take out her troubles on him.

She put in a CD, hoping the sweet sounds of Sarah Brightman's voice would soothe her. Instead, the day's depressing events replayed in her mind. She had been called a bitch, had hung up on a friend, and just before leaving the courtroom, she learned that the thug she defended for murder had been paroled from prison. And finally, the perfect end to a perfect day. She'd tried to start the car to go to the store for some bottled water, and the damn thing wouldn't turn over.

All she wanted was to go to bed, fall asleep, and wake up to the Florida sunshine. She switched off the lights and trudged up the stairs to her bedroom, turned on the lamp and began undressing.

* * *

The man in the boat sat quietly and waited. He was a patient man and knew that his patience would soon be rewarded.

The water lapped softly against his skiff, tied to the mangrove, shielding him from the house. But the opening he'd found in the dense shrubbery allowed him enough room to view what he had come to see—just as it did whenever he visited his vantage point.

The wind picked up, bringing with it the smell and feel of rain. No matter. He had his poncho and it was a warm night.

He smiled when the light went on in her bedroom and she appeared on schedule. His eyes remained riveted on her windows as he picked up his binoculars and trained them on the woman. She began undressing in the slow, sexual rhythm he'd been waiting for. One hand found his pants zipper and he slid it open.

* * *

After undressing, Maggie, still in the nude, walked into the bathroom where she followed her nightly ritual, examining her face for wrinkles and other signs of aging, and checked the scale. Still a trim 115 pounds. She brushed her chestnut-colored hair, searching for the little strands of gray that had begun to show. After plucking the few she found and still seeing no sign of wrinkles, she put out the light, satisfied that she looked pretty damn good for a woman soon to turn forty-three.

Her bedroom was hot and stuffy. She put on a nightgown, opened the windows and listened to the water slapping against the sea wall. The moon lit up the bay, exposing white caps rippling across it. "God, what a night," she said aloud, startled at the sound of her voice.

Nine o'clock. Time to call Paul. It was their arrangement when he was away. Actually, it was more her arrangement. She reached for the phone and held it for a moment before punching the numbers. She preferred calling him. She thought of his outburst during a recent argument when he called her a control freak.

He answered on the fourth ring. "Hello," his voice barely a whisper.

"Hi, it's me. You sound like I woke you up."

"Um, oh, yeah. Maggie. Yeah, I was sound asleep. Everything OK?"

"Yes, I'm fine. I'm in bed."

"Yeah, well I'm still half asleep. Talk to you tomorrow. Love ya. Goodnight."

She listened to the click and frowned. That was short and sweet. Probably has one of his women with him.

She glanced at the collage of pictures of her and Paul on the nightstand and smiled—a wistful smile reminding her of happy days. Her favorite was the one of Paul at the helm of their sailboat and her standing next to him, her hair billowing in the wind. She remembered feeling safe and protected as he held her with one arm and steered with the other.

Raindrops began pattering on the tin roof. Within seconds the patter turned into a deluge, slamming against the roof like bullets. Then, just as quickly the rain let up to a sprinkle. She got up and partially closed the windows, put out the light, and climbed into bed. Snuggling under the covers in the warmth and comfort of her bed, she felt the tension slide away and feeling contentment for the first time today, drifted off to sleep.

She wasn't sure how long she'd been sleeping, nor what it was that snapped her awake. She lay still on her back, listening, her eyes staring into the darkness. The house was silent.

The rain had stopped but the rumble of thunder pierced the silence and lightning streaked across the sky. The air in the room was heavy. Her nightgown clung to her, held by the dampness of her body. She pushed the light blanket away, curled into a fetal position and drifted off.

She had been in a deep sleep, dreaming when something awakened her again. She sat up and listened—nothing, except for the harsh sound of her breathing. Her imagination was playing tricks on her, causing her to hear things that weren't there. She lay back, turned on her side, and closed her eyes.

A movement downstairs. She opened her eyes and sat up. Again, the same sound—like someone or something moving across the floor. She sat motionless, afraid to move.

The house was quiet again. Like a preying animal testing for sound, she pivoted her head from left to right, alert, listening. Was it the rain and thunder fueling her imagination?

Again the sound. A footstep—this time unmistakable—treading on the floor below. "Oh dear God," she whispered. "Someone is in my house."

She eyed the phone on the night stand, but remained frozen in place. The footstep creaked on the old floorboard at the bottom of the stairs. She grabbed the phone and held it to her ear. Nothing. She clicked it several times. Nothing.

As the realization that someone had deactivated the phone swept over her, she heard another footstep, this one on the stair. Her body began shaking and she felt the sour taste of bile coming from her throat. Another footstep sounded on the stairs. Whoever was creating this nightmare would be in her bedroom in a matter of seconds.

She forced herself to stop shaking and to think. Her cell phone. Where did she put the goddamn cell phone? Her briefcase. She tiptoed to the chair where the briefcase lay, her hands trembling so badly, she had trouble working the clasp.

She opened the briefcase, pulled out the cell phone, and punched in the numbers. In her haste she hit the six instead of nine. The footsteps moved faster.

As she started to redial, a bolt of lightning lit up the room. A monk-like figure in a raincoat and hood stood in the doorway.

Maggie screamed and the phone fell from her hands. The ghostly intruder moved quickly and struck her on the head with something hard. Her knees buckled and she felt the floor come up to meet her.

She rolled away and staggered to her feet when another blow hit her and she fell onto the bed. All she could think was denial that this was happening. It was only a nightmare.

She tried to scream again but nothing came out. The figure was on top of her. She fought to stay conscious, but something prevented her from breathing. A peacefulness settled over her, and the last thing she heard was the howling of the wind.

2

Paul Robbins finished his coffee and motioned the waitress for another. Paul was not a compulsive man, but if he did have an addictive personality, he could get hooked on the Cuban coffee in his favorite café, a block from his apartment. He got lucky, finding the small condo in a funky part of Miami's Coconut Grove. It suited his purposes just fine—a one year lease at a very decent price and *voila!* His home away from home.

He sat next to the large open windows, enjoying the cool breeze and watching the passing parade of people. He smiled and nodded at a woman, admiring her long legs and firm breasts. She walked with a self-assured confidence, arms swinging, hips rolling. "Lovely morning, isn't it?" he said.

She returned his smile. "Yes, it is," she replied, and allowed his glance to linger until she passed and disappeared from view.

Paul was still smiling when he looked toward the door and spotted Mark. His partner hurried over and hugged him. "We did it, buddy," Mark said before releasing him. "How do you feel?"

"I feel a lot better. Took a handful of aspirin, got a good night's sleep, and I think I may have broken this thing. Hey, we did, didn't we? Sit down and have some coffee."

Mark sat and sprawled his long legs past the table. "When I called you last night I was flying high."

"No kidding."

Mark grinned. "Sorry I woke you up, but you told me to call. You sure you're feeling OK now? I must say you look a hell of a lot better than you did yesterday."

"Yeah, I don't know if it was the drinks we had or what, but all of a sudden I felt like I was going to pass out. Anyway, you closed the deal, and did we ever need it."

"No, *we* closed the deal. You had it wired right from the start."

Paul sipped his coffee and eyed his partner, who was dressed as always when calling on customers: dark blue suit, white shirt, and conservative tie. Paul rarely wore a tie, preferring casual polo shirts along with his chinos and loafers. Their mode of dress matched their personalities.

They teamed up to start the sporting goods company three years ago. It had been a rough three years and the deal they closed last night could start to turn things around. Two hundred kayaks and 150 canoes to the biggest chain in the country. Good for 300 grand. They weren't out of the woods yet, but this deal was a major shot in the arm.

Paul was a natural salesman. His lean body and boyish good looks combined with his gift for gab about triviality like Florida college football—the Gators and the Noles—had served him well over the years. Mark was the financial brains of the team, more fastidious about facts and figures, which was necessary when the B.S. wasn't going to cut it with a new customer.

Paul had worked hard with Mark to teach him selling skills and took pride in Mark closing the deal on his own. "I didn't have it wired, Mark. I think I did a pretty good job leading him to the water, but you're the one who got him to drink."

Mark adjusted his glasses and ran his hand over the few strands of hair left on his head. "Hey," he said, checking his watch. "We let the time get away. It's ten after eight. We're going to be late."

"What time are we seeing Weldon?"

"Eight-thirty. We'll call him from the car."

A half-hour later, as they drove into the parking lot of Sports Warehouse, Paul's cell phone rang.

"Hello."

Mark parked the car and signaled Paul to hurry.

"Yes, this is he."

Mark opened the door and motioned to Paul that he was leaving. "I'll see you there," he said.

Paul nodded and waved him on.

As Mark headed across the parking lot, he turned to see if Paul was following. He was still in the car. "Goddamn it," Mark muttered, as he hurried back to the car and opened the door. "Come on, Paul. Let's go. We're late."

Paul sat, staring at the windshield, his phone on the floor. "Maggie's dead. She's been murdered."

3

Sam Wallace snapped the leash onto Henry and picked up his coffee mug. "Come on, Henry, time for our morning stroll."

Henry studied Sam, his tail wagging, waiting to spring out the door. On the porch, Sam inhaled the fresh sea air of a crisp February morning, while Henry's little legs churned to get going.

"Oops, wait a minute," Sam said and zipped up his fly. He did a quick check to make sure everything else was in order: Siesta Key T-shirt, sneakers, his Red Sox baseball cap. He was taking no chances with the Florida sun on the tiny bald spot beginning to peek through on top, which seemed out of place with Sam's otherwise thick mop of curly dark brown hair. "OK, Henry. Let's go."

Sam was not a large man—maybe a tad under six feet—but at forty-four, he still had the slender, athletic build of the second baseman he played on his college baseball team. The tan he acquired since being in Florida made his blue eyes deeper—more interesting—and his smile brighter. His ex-wife Lisa told him he had sexy eyes, which is what first attracted her to him.

In the short time that Sam and Henry had lived in the cottage, a block from the beach and two from Siesta Key Village, they'd gotten to know most of the locals, thanks to Henry. The women loved him. "Oh, he's adorable. What's his name?"

"Henry. Uh, I'm Sam."

Sam had met a dozen attractive ladies through Henry since moving to Sarasota from Boston, but he met Jennifer Belding all on his own. After a long walk along Siesta Key's white sand beach, his first full day in Sarasota several months ago, he returned to his blanket to find a new neighbor, a stunning woman with hair the color of a sunset. And she was reading a novel by Sam Wallace—his book. That started it.

When Henry finally succeeded in getting Sam off the porch, he paused in front of the hibiscus bush, lifted his leg while Sam waited.

"Hey Sam!" A familiar voice rang out.

Sam turned and waved at Peter Caruso, his neighbor across the street. Peter was pumping air into his bicycle tires and beckoned Sam to come over. Sam winced and nodded. Peter was a talker. Once he made eye contact, there was no escape. Maybe he just wants help with his bike, Sam hoped, and trudged across the street.

Peter, a retired career army sergeant, was dressed in his usual attire: khaki shirt and shorts, knee length tan stockings and sneakers. He also wore his bicycle helmet, causing Sam to hope he was about to pedal off. Peter, already moving his lips, put the pump down and waited for Sam.

Sam came into range and braced himself. "Hi, Peter. What's up?"

"Hey, Sam, I'm glad I caught you. I'm going to put together a meeting at Siesta Beach on Wednesday at 1900 hours to discuss the sea turtle problem."

Sam hesitated for a minute, trying to remember what the hell 1900 hours meant. Ah, military time. He nodded. "Yes, I—"

"This sea turtle problem has just come to my attention, and we gotta do something about these poor turtles. I'm going to see that we do. Sam, do you know that all five species of turtles here in Florida are endangered or threatened?"

Sam started to say something, but Peter talked over him.

"We got a lot of turtles to take care of here, Sam. We got the Hawksbill Turtle, the Kemp's Ridley, the Loggerhead, the Leatherback, and the Green Turtle. Course they aren't all here in Sarasota, but I've been studying up. And I bet you didn't know that they can live up to sixty years or more."

"Yeah, well—"

"Some statistics say that we lose up to 18,000 turtles a year. If that continues Sam, these babies could become extinct and that's why old Peter is going to see to it that these turtles have a better chance for survival and that's where we all come in."

"Peter—"

"I'm going to set up a work detail to clean up the beach. We're going to clear the beach of any trash that could be harmful to turtles. I'm gonna personally make sure nobody feeds them, I'm gonna reduce the amount of plastic garbage I produce, and I'm going to urge everyone else to do the same. I'm going to write letters to the editor informing people about sea turtles and what they can do to help and—"

"Peter—"

"That's only the beginning, Sam. There's a whole lot more we can all do, and that's why I want to see you at the beach meeting. I'll be in charge of this event and I know you'll want to be there. This first session is crucial to our mission."

Peter paused to take a breath and Sam grabbed his chance. "Peter, I thought my biologist friend, Jennifer Belding, told me that turtle nesting season is between April and October. This is February."

Peter stopped and flicked his eyes back and forth. Sam resisted a smile as a puzzled look crossed Peter's face. "Uh, yeah, well you know, it's not too early to start planning our campaign. I'll, uh, keep you posted."

"OK, thanks, Peter. Gotta go now. See you later." He and Henry broke into a trot and hustled toward Dog Beach a block away. Henry led the way, his back arched and his little fanny twitching back and forth in his cocky way. Sam was exhausted from the encounter with Peter. He did, however, know from reading recent articles in the paper that the preservation of sea turtles was a serious subject and made a note to ask Jennifer more about it.

The beach was little more than a small patch of sand less than a hundred yards long, but it was the only beach on the Key that allowed dogs. Sam removed Henry's leash and held him by the collar. "OK, kid, you're off and running, but you pick one fight and we're outta here. Get it?"

Henry bussed him on the nose and turned to face the water. Sam let him go and he headed for a cocker spaniel sitting obediently next to a middle-aged woman, wearing a hat the shape of a UFO. The woman was yelling at her dog and shaking her finger at him. The dog hung his head in the classic way dogs do when they're being scolded. Sam wondered what the little fella did to deserve such an ass chewing.

The cocker came alive when Henry bounded across the sand and the two dogs went off on a round of sniffing and chasing each other. The woman climbed out from under her UFO and waved at Sam. He recognized Brenda Green, who owned Donegan's Deck, one of his favorite watering holes in the village and waved back.

After a quick swim, Sam rounded up Henry who was busy sniffing the cocker spaniel's bottom while Brenda kept a wary eye on them. The cocker had nipped Henry a week ago.

The walk home was pure bliss. A soft breeze filled Sam's nostrils with fresh sea air and the white clouds reminded him of snow-covered mountain peaks, the closest to the real thing he would ever see in Florida.

The phone jangled as they entered the cottage.

"Sam, this is Jennifer."

He loved the way she said that. No matter how many times a day they might talk on the phone, when she called, she always began in that lilting, upbeat voice, "Sam, this is Jennifer."

"Hi Jennifer," he answered, mimicking her in the surprised way that sometimes made her laugh, sometimes pissed her off. "What's up?"

"Sam, don't you play tennis with Paul Robbins?"

"Yeah. Why?"

"His wife, Maggie was found murdered this morning. I just heard it over my car radio."

4

Sam sprang to his feet, not sure or not wanting to hear what she'd just said. "What? Where, how. . . ?"

"Sam, I just heard it. Apparently a lawyer who works for her came by her house to drive her to work, and found her. The police are there now."

"Where's Paul? Is he at the house?"

"I don't know, Sam. They didn't say a whole lot. Their house is on Siesta Key, by the way."

"I know. I'm going over there."

"Here's your chance to use your new P.I. license." She paused. "I'm sorry, Sam. I didn't mean to be flip."

"It's OK. Where are you? At work?"

"I'm in my car, heading for an appointment. I'll be finished around one. Maybe we can have lunch?"

"OK, I'll call you later."

Sam changed into a pair of jeans and a respectable shirt and stood for a moment gazing out the bedroom window. Jesus, he had just played tennis with Paul the day before yesterday. Why would anyone want to kill his wife?

He thought of the perky, attractive bundle of energy he'd met a couple of times, once when he'd driven Paul home from tennis, and once when he'd bumped into them on the street and they'd chatted for a while. He remembered her as being smart and witty with a confident self-assured way about her.

"Henry, I gotta go. Guard the fort."

Henry hopped into the armchair facing the window, sat at

attention, and peered out. Sam knew he'd be in the same spot when he returned.

His mind was still spinning with thoughts of a grieving Paul and his poor wife when he walked across the street and opened Peter Caruso's garage door. What a break, finding space for his car so close. No way could he leave the old convertible outside all the time. There were times, though, when dealing with Peter made him wonder if it was worth it.

The drive to the Robbins' house took ten minutes. Normally, he loved driving along Midnight Pass Road on the south end of the Key in his vintage 1969 Mercedes 280 SE convertible. With the Gulf of Mexico on one side and Sarasota Bay on the other, the drive was one of life's simple pleasures. But not today.

Crow Point was nearly hidden from Midnight Pass Road, the main thoroughfare that ran through Siesta Key. Sam shot by it and had to turn around. Part of exclusivity, he thought. Make it hard to find.

He pulled onto a shell road, flanked on either side by a row of stately royal palms mingling with majestic oak trees draped in pale gray Spanish moss. After about fifty yards the road opened to display a large, elegant house set back from Sarasota Bay.

The lawn and drive were covered with official vehicles—police cars, medical examiner's vehicle, forensic van, an ambulance, and vans from three different TV stations. Big news, murder in a small town. Yellow tape surrounded the house, and two police officers stood in front of it.

Sam approached one of them, held out his hand, and lowered his voice to an official sounding growl. "Hi, I'm Sam Wallace. I'm a private investigator." It sounded funny, hearing himself say the words. Less than a year ago he was a college professor. He hoped he sounded authoritative enough, the way his character, Dirk Flanders did in his novels.

The officer, who had to be at least six-five, ignored his hand and looked down at Sam as if a rodent had just crawled across his shoe. Sam started to show his credentials, but the cop waved him away.

"Sorry, but only authorized persons allowed inside."

Sam held his ground. "Yeah, well, I uh, I mean . . ." He shrugged and backed off. He would have to practice this. Dirk always made it look easy. "Who's in charge of the investigation?" he asked.

"Detective Lewis," the cop said without looking at him.

Sam straightened. "Would you tell Detective Lewis that her friend, Private Investigator Sam Wallace is here?" That was better.

The officer looked at him for the first time, but held his position. Sam detected a slight furrow in his brow and knew what the cop was thinking. Do I tell this guy to fuck off and not bother Lewis, who could be nasty in the middle of an investigation? But what if the guy is a friend and I later take some heat from Lewis for not telling her he's here?

Sam held his credentials in front of the cop's face.

"Wait here," the young officer said and went inside the house.

The cop's grim-faced partner eyed Sam, who nodded and smiled. The cop ignored him.

Sam stuck his hands in his pockets and leaned against a palm tree, trying to look inconspicuous. He hadn't seen Lewis since they got a little drunk together in her office late one night, celebrating Sam's role in helping to solve two related murders. They had talked on the phone a few times, but other than that, had no contact.

Still, he knew he had no business being here. He had no connection to this case—except that Paul was his friend. He shrugged. "I'm here now."

He checked his watch. Where was Lewis? Was she going to stiff arm him? She could be so goddamned unpredictable.

The front door opened and a tall African-American woman appeared, scanning the area. She was dressed in black pants and a black cotton turtleneck, looking better than even Sam had remembered. Her clear, cocoa-colored skin was the shade sun-worshipping vacationers seek in Florida.

He came out from under his tree, and she walked toward him, chewing up ground with long purposeful strides. When she reached him she stood eyeball to eyeball with him and held out her hand. No smile, only the formidable intensity he remembered well.

"Hi, Diane," he said, shaking her hand. He'd forgotten the first time they shook hands. Too late. The crunch nearly broke his fingers.

"Well, Private Investigator Wallace. Why am I not surprised that you would show up?" She looked him up and down, cop-like.

He checked her out the way he always did and wished he didn't. She was a police officer, his colleague now, so to speak. But goddamn. Anyway, he always kept his cool and they had developed a pretty good professional relationship. At least he thought so. But he never knew which Diane would show up—his colleague or the ball buster.

"Yep, I'm doing everything by the book now. No more ersatz detective." He noticed a slight smile cross her face, remembering the day she called him that. "Anyway, I know the victim's husband. He's a friend of mine. Is he inside?"

The smile he thought he noticed was gone. He waited.

"Mr. Robbins is not here. He's on his way from Miami."

"Miami?"

"Yes, he's been there on business. We reached him on his cell phone earlier this morning."

Sam nodded, wondering how a man would react to a phone call telling him his wife had been murdered. "How was she killed?"

Lewis turned toward one of the officers guarding the perimeter, now sitting on a tree stump. She shot him a look. He scrambled to his feet and resumed his position. "She was found with a pillow over her face and appears to have been suffocated. She also has lacerations on her head from apparently being hit with a blunt instrument. But no official determination has been made yet. How long have you known her husband?"

Sam thought of the attractive woman lying dead inside that beautiful house. Why would someone break into her house and murder her? Robbery?

"I met him several months ago at the Bath and Racquet. We've played a lot of tennis together and played golf a few times." He nodded toward the house. "Any signs of a break-in?"

Lewis waved her hand and shook her head. "I'll ask the questions, Sam."

He nodded. The ball buster was in charge. "Who found her? Can you tell me that?"

She hesitated, studying him before finally shaking her head. "Sam, Sam. You'll snoop around and find out anyway, so I guess I can tell you. A woman named Jean Booth found her. She worked with Mrs. Robbins and came by to drive her to work. So, you've played tennis and golf with Paul Robbins."

"Yes."

"Have you spent any time with him other than that?"

"Well, a couple of weeks ago, Paul couldn't make it in the morning, so we changed it to six that night. After tennis we went up to the restaurant and had dinner together."

"So you know him fairly well."

He shrugged. "Yeah, I guess you could say that. I like him. I consider him a friend."

"Did he talk about his wife at all, you know, the way spouses sometimes do?"

Sam took his hat off and ran his fingers back through his hair and reversed direction. "Hmm. Let me think about that for a minute." He looked out across the bay and watched a sailboat under full sail come into view from behind one of the small islands.

"Come on, Sam, I haven't got all day." His colleague was not being very collegial.

"As a matter of fact, Diane, now that I think of it, I don't remember him talking about her. He may have mentioned her in passing."

Lewis' cell phone rang. "Yes, Lewis here. Good. And did you get Baumert's address in Bradenton? OK, get right up there and question him. Call me when you arrive." She glanced at Sam, turned her back, and walked out of earshot.

Sam looked around the yard and spotted a woman, dressed in a navy blue suit, white silk blouse and heels standing by a car, looking in his direction. Even from the distance Sam could see she'd been crying.

"Has to be the woman who found Maggie," he thought. She's dressed like a lawyer and her car is parked just outside the front door. No way the cops would let any other civilian car get that close.

He wandered over toward her and was about to say something when she addressed him. "Excuse me, Detective, but is it all right if I leave now. I've answered all of Ms. Lewis' questions, and I'm very tired and upset."

Sam got the picture. She'd seen him talking with Diane and assumed he was one of the cops. "You'll have to check with Detective Lewis." He motioned toward Diane. "But since I've just arrived, there is one question I would like to ask you."

The woman sighed heavily. "Yes, what is it."

Sam sneaked a quick glance in Lewis' direction. She was still facing the other way, talking on the phone. "Did my colleagues ask you about this Baumert fellow?"

"Yes, and I told them all I know."

Sam stroked his chin. "Yes indeed, we definitely will want to talk with this . . . Oh God. I've drawn a blank on his first name. It's . . . " He searched her eyes for help.

"Frank, Frank Baumert."

"Ah, yes. Thank you," Sam said and stole another look toward Lewis who was putting the phone in her purse. He edged away from Jean Booth and nodded toward Lewis. "Thank you, ma'am. You can ask Detective Lewis if it's OK to leave now."

5

Larry Gump sat in his double-wide trailer, sipping a beer and watching television.

There it was—big story on the local station. "Prominent local attorney found murdered in home." Larry took three long hits on his beer and drained the can. He listened to each word carefully, not wanting to miss any details. His hands shook with excitement, making it difficult to focus on what he was hearing. Another beer would calm him down.

After downing half his new beer he got his hands under control and resumed listening. He glanced at the clock. Almost time to go down and sign up with Labor Ready for a day's construction work. No rush. This was too important. Gettin' tired of that shit anyway.

"Jesus Christ." He couldn't believe what he was hearing. The Robbins' broad murdered. He was there. He saw the killer. If it hadn't been for the rain pounding so hard, making him afraid to untie the skiff and leave, he never would have seen the car.

Larry turned off the television with the remote. He got up and walked around the trailer from the kitchen to the living room, into the bedroom, and back to the kitchen where he finished off his beer.

He pulled his T-shirt up and wiped the sweat off his forehead. The AC was on, but he couldn't stop sweating. "Jesus Christ," he muttered again.

Stay cool. Think this through. Larry knew he had something big by the tail, and he had to be smart, figure how to deal with it, handle it right.

Hot damn! He knew something was fishy the way that vehicle came up the driveway with no lights, and the driver gets out and tip toes along the bushes, so's not to be seen.

And there's Larry in his skiff in his favorite spot for night fishing off the Robbins' dock, tied up to the mangroves. And the minute he sees this car drive up with the lights out, he stayed hidden and kept his eyes on the driver walking toward the back yard. With the hat and long coat on, he couldn't tell if it was a man or woman, but he knew goddamn well they was up to no good.

But then old Larry got real smart when the person disappeared behind the house. He secured his boat, made his way over to the vehicle, and wrote down the license plate number. Back in the boat, he waited.

Twenty minutes later, the driver comes out from behind the back, looks around, and takes off. Pretty slick.

Larry had heard about the robberies on the south Key and figured maybe that's what was going down. But Jesus, murder?

No question that was the killer he saw. And Larry's got the license number. All he's gotta do now that he's in the catbird seat, is figure out what to do with it. Larry nodded and grabbed himself another beer. Man's gotta have somethin' on his stomach before goin' to that shit job.

6

After leaving the Robbins' house, Sam stopped in Siesta Village to pick up a few groceries. Within a small three block area, everything a person could want was available: groceries, hardware store, post office, drug store, fire department, police, clothing stores, a range of bars and restaurants, and plenty of local characters. And, like all tourist areas, the main drag was lined with small shops selling Florida beach souvenirs.

Unlike most resort areas, however, Siesta Village had managed to retain its simple, funky charm. The center was a hodgepodge of architecture, consisting of 1930's beach style cottages painted in a mix of Caribbean colors standing alongside 1960's square concrete boxes and low lying ranch type buildings.

Tourists enjoying a week or two of sunshine away from the frozen Midwest and Northeast strolled the streets in shorts and sandals. Sam easily spotted them. They were the ones with the suntans.

Back at his cottage, he found a yard sign and a stack of brochures about sea turtles resting on his porch. Peter had struck again. Inside, he turned on the local TV station where they were still talking about the murder and the rash of break-ins on the Key, but offered nothing new. He turned off the TV and poured himself what was left of the coffee.

He wondered if anything of value was taken from the Robbins' house. There was no indication that anyone was hurt during the other robberies. According to the papers they'd all taken place in the middle of the night when the occupants were asleep. He doubted Lewis would shed any light for him, but Paul would have some insight on the break-ins.

He settled in front of the computer and pulled up his manuscript while Henry lay on his feet, his favorite napping spot since moving to Florida. The move had unnerved him, and the new position had become his security blanket.

He was almost halfway through his third Dirk Flanders book and been on a roll. His second book had been out for a couple of months, was getting good reviews and selling well.

Private Investigator Dirk Flanders was not only Sam's character, he was his hero, his inspiration for getting his own P.I. license. But this morning he was getting nowhere. Curiosity about Maggie Robbins' murder gnawed at him, leaving his fingers hovering haplessly over the keyboard.

After ten minutes of frustration, he got up, grabbed his baseball glove and ball and paced around the living room, pounding the ball into his glove, a ritual he'd developed to jump-start his mind.

Maggie was not a large woman, small enough for someone reasonably strong to suffocate her, especially if she'd first been hit on the head. If it wasn't a burglar, it shouldn't be too hard to determine if she had any enemies. From what they said about her on the television she was well known in town.

He threw the glove and ball on the couch. What the hell was he doing, thinking he was involved in the case? He wasn't crazy about getting his ass reamed by Lewis, which is what would happen if he snooped around too much.

A car's horn honked three times followed by a man's voice. Sam looked out the window and saw a car nosed up to his porch, with Jimbo Conlin easing his 300 pound bulk out of it.

7

It was the car that held Sam's attention—an old Cadillac convertible the length of a football field with flaring rear fins and a pair of steer longhorns perched on the hood. He went out to the porch and ran into Jimbo's bear hug.

"Sam, you old reprobate. Where you been? I miss m' buddy."

Sam slid out of the big man's grasp and nodded toward the Caddie. "Jimbo, that has to be the ugliest car I have ever seen. Where the hell did you get it?"

Jimbo jerked his head back to the car like he'd forgotten it was there. "I dunno. It's been around for a long time. I think it's kinda nifty myself."

"Every time I see you you're driving a different car," Sam said. "How many do you have?"

Jimbo shrugged. "Shit, I don't know."

"Come on, you must have some idea. It's not like I'm asking you how many pairs of socks you have."

Jimbo plopped down on one of Sam's webbed lawn chairs, snapping the middle webbing. "Well, if you're gonna get chicken shit about it and pin me down, I'd say—"

Sam smiled as he watched his friend stick out one finger at a time until he used up both hands and started over, mumbling numbers and car makes. "I'd say about fourteen or fifteen, give or take. Hey Sam, you got a beer for your buddy?"

Sam looked at his watch: 11:15. "You want a beer now?"

"No, I'll come back next week. Fuck's a matter with you, Sam? Course I want it now. Man works up a thirst fightin' them bureaucrats. County's givin' me a rash of shit about some candy-ass code violations on one of my new buildings."

Sam brought Jimbo a Corona and a Coke for himself. He settled into a chaise and winced as another part of Jimbo's chair snapped.

"Haven't seen you in a couple of weeks, Sam. Where you been?"

Sam eyed the chair and Jimbo, who now looked like he was sitting on a toilet. "I've been here and there, working on my new book, playing tennis." He turned and winked at Jimbo. "Won a tournament last week."

"Hey, Sam, you been playin' with those girls again?" Jimbo looked around. "Where's Henry?"

"He's back in his room napping."

"How is the little feller? Thunder's taken kind of a shine to him, you know."

Sam nodded, but said nothing, not wanting to tell Jimbo that Henry wanted nothing to do with the hundred-pound rottweiler who had "taken a shine" to him. Nor did he have the heart to tell Jimbo that Henry had fled to the rear of the house when he spotted him.

He was glad Jimbo stopped by. Not only did he enjoy the big guy, he also knew more about Sarasota than anyone Sam had met. "Jimbo, do you know the Robbinses, Paul and Maggie?"

Jimbo took a deep slug of his beer and drained the bottle. He set it down and nodded. "Yeah, I know 'em, and I know she was murdered last night. Heard it on the radio. Been a number of break-ins around their house. Maybe she walked in on one of them." He got up and the aluminum chair frame came with him. He turned and swatted at it but it refused to let go.

Sam helped him out of it and into a wooden chair. "What do you know about them, Jimbo?"

"The Robbinses or the break-ins?"

"The Robbinses."

Jimbo got up again, walked across the porch, and turned back to Sam. "She's a lawyer and he's been in and out of half a dozen cockamamie deals since I've known him. I think he sells sporting goods now. He's an OK guy, but he's got a big, fragile ego. Likes to have people think he's a lot smarter than he is. It's important to him.

"I've known Maggie a long time. When she first started out she was doing some real estate law, and I used her on some of my deals. Smart lady. Also tough when she had to be."

"What do you mean?"

"I mean she was tough, not in a nasty way. But she had a sharp mind and a quick wit and was always prepared. You damn well had better be also, if you were going to tangle with Maggie Robbins. She eventually branched out into criminal law. She was a defense lawyer for a while, but decided she wanted to prosecute the bad asses instead of defending them. She'd been in the prosecutor's office for several years where she was considered to be kind of a rising star."

"Was she still tough?"

"Sure she was, or she wouldn't have been as good as she was. Actually, I always liked her. She could turn on the charm when she wanted, and when she did, ol' Maggie could charm a bear out of a tree."

"She have any enemies that you knew of?"

Jimbo went to the kitchen and helped himself to another beer. Sam watched the untied laces of his black high top sneakers trail across the floor, which fit in with the frayed shorts he wore. Hard to believe Jimbo was one of the wealthiest men in the county.

Jimbo returned to the porch and leaned against the railing, took a pull on his beer and eyed Sam for a moment. "Enemies?"

"Yes. She sounds like she might have had a few run-ins with people." It was more a question than a statement.

Jimbo nodded. "Hell, Maggie could piss off the Pope. But you know, underneath it all, she was a caring person and dedicated to the community. She was committed to fighting over-development here and not letting it destroy the character of the town. And strangely enough, that's the part of her that pissed off one person the most."

8

"Who's that?" Sam asked.

Jimbo closed his eyes and took a long swig of his beer, swirling it around his mouth before swallowing it. Sam smiled. Jimbo could make drinking a beer from a bottle look like pure ecstasy.

"Her brother, Bryce," Jimbo said, opening his eyes.

"What do you mean?"

"Well, it's a long story, Sam, and I ain't got the time to go into it all. But the short of it is Maggie was the apple of her dad's eye. The old man was one rich dude." He slowly dragged out the last three words. "I knew her father, met him when I first came to town a lot of years ago. Like I said, he was a very wealthy guy. Tough as nails. That's probably where she got it."

"You say was. Is he dead?"

Jimbo returned to the wooden chair and sat. "Yeah, he died about a year and a half ago."

"Tell me more about Maggie and Bryce."

"I told you it's a long story, Sam." He looked at his watch. "Oh, Jesus, I gotta run now. I was drivin' through the Key and I just wanted to drop by and say hello and cadge one of your beers. I'll come over again when I got more time."

Sam walked with him toward his car. "What's your impression of Paul."

Jimbo stopped and chuckled. "Different story there. Like I said, he's a nice enough guy, but not in her league when it comes to smarts. He's always been sensitive about that. He got pissed at me one day after tennis when I kidded him for screwing up a deal he was working on. I told him it was a no brainer, said he had to be pretty dumb to fuck that up."

"In your inimitable tactful way," Sam said.

"Yeah, I never saw him get so mad, so I just backed off and apologized.

"I never had any dealings with him, though. We played tennis a couple times, and I had a few pops with him one night when I ran into him at Coasters bar." Jimbo shook his head as if just now realizing Maggie's tragic death. "Jesus."

Sam watched a car full of kids cruise by in an old Chevy, two sets of bare feet hanging out the back windows, radio blaring with the sounds of an unrecognizable rock group. They turned left toward the beach and the throbbing bass gradually faded away. Carefree kids who would eventually have to grow up and face life. But not today.

"You know Paul, don't you, Sam?" Jimbo said. "I see you playin' tennis with him a lot at the Bath and Racquet," Jimbo said as he eased himself into the Caddie's stained seat.

"Yeah, I know Paul. I was just wondering about your impressions, that's all."

Jimbo nodded. "Yeah, he likes the ladies, too. And they seem to like him."

"How do you mean?"

"I see him at the club, always talking, flirting with good lookin' women. And they give it right back. Hey, doesn't make him a bad person."

It was Sam's turn to nod. "Yes, I've seen some of that, but so do a lot of other guys. Usually doesn't mean much." He thought for a moment. "Is there any one in particular?"

"Naw. He spreads himself around pretty good."

Jimbo looked at his watch again and threw up his hands. "Hey! I gotta go, Sam. Got a meeting with the head of the building department about my medical complex. Could be a make or break on whether they let me continue." He threw a pair of old sneakers from the front seat to the back, where they joined a couple of two by fours, some carpet and tile samples, a pair of muddy boots, two bags of fertilizer, and some rusty golf clubs.

Sam held onto the car's window as Jimbo started the motor. "Jimbo, how big is this medical complex?"

Jimbo made a face and pulled a baseball cap out from under him. "Sixty thousand square feet. It'll be the biggest facility of its kind in the county, depending how I make out in today's meeting and they let me build it. You never know," he said and drove off, his Texas Longhorns leading the way.

Sam went inside. Henry came out of the bedroom, looked out the window and peered up at Sam.

"He's gone, Henry. Thunder wasn't with him, anyway."

Henry barked at the window, a parting shot to let Sam know he wasn't scared.

9

After pouring more coffee, Sam went back out to the porch, folded Jimbo's mangled chair, and set it out for trash pick-up. It had taken him a while to figure out his buddy, but he really was a very smart, sweet guy. He liked Jimbo and he liked the casual lifestyle of his neighborhood. After living in soulless apartment buildings in Boston, the funky charm of the cottage as well as the whole village had completely seduced him.

He thought back to the day Jimbo sold it to him. Sam had been instrumental in solving a murder case in which Jimbo had been the chief suspect and when Sam found the real killer, he and Jennifer Belding and Jimbo had celebrated over champagne in the cottage Jimbo owned.

He had insisted on giving it to Sam but Sam refused to take it without paying him for it. Sam smiled, remembering the scene: Jimbo saying, "You're bein' a prick, Sam. Jennifer, tell him."

"You're being a prick, Sam," said Jennifer.

After some more haggling Jimbo finally agreed to take some money, and the deal was done. Jimbo made out a bill of sale, and they popped open another bottle of champagne.

There wasn't a lot to the cottage. The biggest part of it was a kitchen-dining-living space, with two wide windows overlooking the small, tree-lined street. The interior was bright with beachy colors, and the only change Sam had made was to have bookcases installed, which were filled to capacity.

Sam's favorite part was the broad front porch, sheltered from the street by mature oleander and a large citrus tree, now laden with oranges, their fragrant bouquet filling the air. The silhouettes of pink flamingos that surrounded the porch were a nice touch. Just tacky enough to be cool. The smell of the sea drifting through the neighborhood was a constant reminder to Sam of how lucky he was to have the Gulf of Mexico just around the corner.

He decided to take another crack at his novel and went back inside. There were two messages on his answering machine.

"Sam, this is Jennifer. I finished a little early, and I'm back in the office. Call me."

The other message was from Diane Lewis. "Sam, sorry if I was less than cordial this morning. It was good to see you. Drop down to the station if you can. I'll be there after three."

Good sign. The ball buster was gone—at least for the moment—and his colleague was back. After calling Jennifer and making a date to meet for lunch in a half-hour, he called Diane and said he'd be at the station between three and 3:30.

Looking forward to seeing Jennifer, he selected a dapper outfit, his new pink polo shirt, a spiffy pair of white chinos, loafers with no socks—all capped off with his brand new Panama hat. He probably looked like a tourist, but the hell with it. In a way, he still was.

The nastiness of Maggie Robbins' murder faded as he thought of seeing Jennifer. He cruised along Bayfront Drive, past the park and Marina Jack's Restaurant. The collage of sailboats and yachts at the marina and the glistening waters of the bay reminded him of why he'd fallen in love with Sarasota, especially in February. He stopped at a red light and from the corner of his eye he watched a guy pull alongside him and lower his window. He knew what was coming.

"That's a beautiful car you have there, friend. What year is it?"

Sam smiled. "It's a '69."

"She's a beauty," the man said and pulled away as the light changed.

"Yep, she is a beauty," Sam said aloud to himself and turned left to head over the bridge to Lido.

Since he'd been living here, the new high fixed-span bridge was completed and replaced the old drawbridge. Off to his left, the view was spectacular toward Bird Key and beyond to the drawbridge carrying cars and people onto Siesta Key. A breeze drifted across the bay and into the car. Sam wished the bridge were ten miles long.

To the right and behind him the city loomed. Sam was startled to see so many tall construction cranes dominating the skyline. He counted at least eight of them, dramatically confirming the complaints he'd heard from several people about the over-building taking place, changing the flavor of the town forever. Progress?

The soft breeze abruptly accelerated into a sharp gust of wind. Sam's hand flew up to his head. Too late. He turned and watched his fifty dollar Panama hat sail gracefully over the railing and slowly flutter into the water. He turned again for a final look at it, floating serenely out to sea.

As his car descended onto the road, Sam watched the windsurfers effortlessly glide across the water, powered by the same breeze that drifted into his car. In the distance a sloop under full sail knifed across the water. Winter in Florida.

A few minutes later he pulled into the yard of the Old Salty Dog, a rustic place befitting its name, tucked behind a large boatyard and sitting smack on the open bay. He spotted Jennifer sitting at an outside table, gazing at the water. When she turned and greeted him with a broad smile and wave, his legs wobbled.

Jennifer Belding did things like that to him. She was on her feet, still smiling as he made his way across the deck, wondering how a woman could look so sexy wearing khakis and a polo shirt. With her hair, the soft red-yellow of a classic strawberry blonde, drawn back in a pony tail, she looked more like a college student than a thirty-four year old Ph.D. scientist.

When he reached her table, the smile still glistened on her lips. And the freckles on her nose were more pronounced in the sun.

"Hi Sam," she said in that breathless way like she hadn't seen him in months. She reached out and softly ran her hand down his upper arm. "You look nice. Where's your new hat you told me about?"

His hand went up to his head. "Oh, I—uh, forgot it." He kissed her and sat down. "Hey, where's your water bottle?"

"Come on, Sam. I don't carry it into restaurants."

"How's my favorite marine biologist?"

"She's OK. How's Dick Tracy?" She sat and beckoned him to do the same.

Sam smiled at her nickname for him. "He's fine," he said, sitting and putting his hand over hers.

She squeezed his hand and motioned for the waitress. "We'd better get some food. I have to get back soon."

After ordering, Sam got around to the Robbins' murder. "You knew Maggie, didn't you, Jen?"

"Yes, a little. She was in my running club. That's how I first met her in fact. She was friendly and inquisitive about what my job entailed so I took her on a tour of the Galt and she became one of our most active supporters. She was very impressed with the research and public education we do there."

"Yes, I also heard from Jimbo that she was . . . tough is the word he used, I believe."

Jennifer smiled and slowly nodded. "Yes, she could be a little outspoken at times, but people respected and admired her commitment to various causes. She was always very supportive of the programs she believed in, both with her time and with her money.

I always got along fine with her. I thought she was a very nice person." She bit into her grouper sandwich and pointed to it. "Hmm, delicious."

Who couldn't get along with Jennifer? Sam thought. She could find some good in Atilla the Hun. "Did she have any friends that you knew of?"

"Of course she did."

"Who?"

"Come on, Sam. She had plenty of friends. Actually, she was very social and involved in a lot of community work." Jennifer said. "I know that she and Sarah Hastings were close. They were involved in sea turtle protection, especially Sarah. She has a public relations firm and one of her clients is the Sea Turtles Protection League. I think she works pro bono for them.

"Sarah is passionate about saving the turtles and she and Maggie were very involved in fighting high rise construction along our waterfronts, particularly on or near beaches where sea turtles nest. I've seen them together several times."

Sam started to speak, but she held up her hand. "Sam, that's all I know about it. By the way, she said Paul really looked up to you."

"Me?"

"Yes, you being a former college professor and novelist and all that."

Sam looked out across the water and softly drummed his fingers on the table. He looked back at Jen who grinned and nodded.

"OK, what do you want to ask me now?"

Sam shook his head. "You're scary, you know that? As a matter of fact, Jimbo Conlin mentioned to me that Maggie had a brother. Bryce Hanson, I think he said. Did you know him?"

"Yes, I do know Bryce," Jennifer said.

"You get around. You know everybody."

"This is still a small town, Sam, and I've been here for nine years. Bryce Hanson is a real estate broker, and when I was looking around for a place to buy he was one of the people who showed me some properties. I bought my house through another broker, but Bryce keeps in touch, hoping I might someday buy something through him." She frowned. "I actually went out with him once."

"Why the frown?"

She hesitated before replying. "I don't know. There was just something about him I didn't care for. Frankly, I thought he was a pompous jerk and he had an edge to him. Definitely not a relaxing person." She smiled. "Not like you, Sam."

He nodded. "Thank you, Jennifer."

"Why do you ask?"

"Well, Paul mentioned him to me once when we played tennis. I've forgotten the context now, but the mention wasn't what you'd call an objective comment."

"What do you mean?"

"He referred to him as 'Maggie's asshole brother.'"

"Oh. Definitely not objective."

"Exactly. So I asked him why Bryce Hanson was an asshole."

"What did he say?"

"He didn't. A guy we both knew came by and joined us so we never got back to it."

Jennifer looked at her watch. "Oh, oh. Gotta get back to work. You can give me a ride. I walked over."

Sam nodded and made a mental note to look up Sarah Hastings and Bryce Hanson.

10

Sam paid the check and silently cursed himself for wasting a nice lunch in a beautiful setting with Jennifer, talking about a murder. "What are you doing tonight?" he asked on the way to the car. "You're working too hard. You need a Sam fix."

She screwed her face into a frown. "I know, but I've got to finish a report on some research we're doing on the impact of red tide on sea turtles that's due tomorrow. Remember I told you, Maggie and Sarah were active members of the Sea Turtles Protection League. A lot of people are."

"Hey, that's exactly what I wanted to ask you about. A neighbor of mine is all worked up about them. What can you tell me?"

When her eyes lit up, he knew he had touched a chord and maybe bought some additional time with her. Inside the car, instead of starting the engine, he probed some more. "I know the turtles are among your favorite projects, but you've never really talked much about them."

Jennifer turned to him, her time constraints now forgotten. "Oh, Sam, it's so sad what's happening."

"What do you mean?"

Jennifer brushed her hair back and leaned toward Sam, into it now. "Sea turtles have been on earth 155 million years, and because of humans, they are now struggling to survive, facing extinction."

"What are we doing to them?"

"They're suffering from polluted waters all over the world, ingesting debris like plastic which they mistake for their favorite food, jellyfish. People steal eggs from the turtles' nests, and turtles are hunted for their meat and their shells are used for jewelry. One of the biggest problems they face is the artificial lighting in the houses and condos facing the beaches, which disorients the turtles and they become stranded."

"What do you mean?"

"Turtles are attracted to beaches, which is where they lay their eggs and when they mistake artificial lights for the shimmering reflective light of the Gulf, they get disoriented, wander away from the water and die of dehydration. The biggest danger though is to the hatchlings. When they crack out of their eggs and dig their way out of the sand, they are immediately attracted by light. If it's artificial light from houses or cars, they head toward them, and never make it to the water."

"I thought I read somewhere that taking turtles' eggs and or killing them is against the law."

Jennifer vigorously nodded her head. "It is, but people ignore the law."

"What's the Sea Turtles Protection League?"

She continued nodding, into it big time now. "It's a group of volunteers who patrol the beaches, conducting nesting surveys and relocating nests when necessary. They look for stranded turtles and guide them to the water. They also educate people about them. Maggie, by the way was very active, she went into local schools to talk to students, to heighten their awareness."

Sam watched her eyes, animated, darting about the car, impressed and respectful of her passionate concern. "Guess I hadn't really given that much thought to them," he said. "You are a learning experience, I must say."

She looked at her watch and motioned for him to start the car. "I have to get back, Sam, but there is so much more I can tell you about sea turtles. They're marvelous creatures."

Sam started the car. "OK," he said, but decided to take another shot at keeping her talking before driving away. "Continue."

She gave him the funny look she used when telling him she knew what he was doing. "Well, I just have enough time to tell you the most fascinating thing about them. As I said, the females nest on beaches twice a year, and they will travel hundreds and even thousands of miles away from the beach where they first nested. Miraculously, although they can only lift their heads a few inches out of the water, and have poor eyesight to boot, they eventually not only migrate back to the same beach where they previously nested, but often within a hundred yards of the same spot."

"How do they do that?" he asked.

"Nobody knows, Sam. There is one fairly new interesting theory that scientists all over the world are working on, including us. And that is that turtles can detect both the angle and intensity of the earth's magnetic field. Using these two characteristics, they may be able to determine its latitude and longitude, enabling them to navigate virtually anywhere. It's one of the most remarkable acts in the animal kingdom." She motioned for him to get going. "Gotta go."

Sam put his hand on her cheek. "Come on. You don't have to do that report tonight?"

She nodded. And touched his hand. "I do, Sam. Promised my boss I'd have it on his desk in the morning. It's overdue, and he let me know it."

"So, this was a good warm up. I'll feed you again. We'll have an early dinner."

"Can't do it."

It was his turn to frown.

"Don't pout, Sam." She leaned her head back and took a deep breath of the salt air. "Actually, if I had my way, I'd say let's drive the car for a couple hundred miles in any direction—with the top down."

"Good idea. Let's go."

"Nope. Take me to the Galt and step on it."

Less than a minute later, they pulled up to her building. Sam had never heard of the Galt Marine Laboratory before moving to Sarasota. He quickly learned that it was one of the foremost marine labs in the U.S. And Jennifer Belding was one of its stars. Jennifer hopped out, blew him a kiss, and hurried inside.

He took his time driving downtown, enjoying the view, which was always changing. Somebody behind him honked, and a kid in a pickup with wheels higher than Sam's car roared by on the bridge. Sam shook his head. Drivers here represented two extremes, red-neck cowboys like the guy who had just passed him and the very elderly, hunched over the wheels of block long ten year old Lincoln Continentals, chugging along, oblivious to the rest of the world.

Nearing the sheriff's headquarters, he kicked his mind back into gear about Maggie Robbins' murder. Given what he'd heard about her so far, he wished he'd had the chance to have known her better. He also had a feeling that the list of people who might have wanted her dead might grow. Whether any of them could turn into legitimate suspects was another story.

He pulled up and parked a half block from the station—just like in the movies. The chances of that happening in Boston were somewhere between no way and never. And if you did find one, they'd find an excuse to tow your car. He opened the door and headed toward the building, wondering which Diane Lewis would greet him.

* * *

Frank Baumert stabbed out his cigarette and lit another. He got off the bed, emptied the nearly full ashtray into the toilet and flushed it.

"Where the fuck is he?" he muttered and began pacing the

small motel room. He tripped on the frayed rug and nearly fell, bringing on another round of cursing.

Frank wanted to make the deal and get out of this fucking dump. The room smelled of perspiration and urine, reminding him of his prison cell. But he used the place for his drug deals because it was off the beaten path away from traffic, and he'd known the owner for years. He would never be bothered or hassled here. Another plus was it was only fifteen minutes from the bar where he worked.

He checked his watch again. In twenty minutes he was due to begin his shift, and he couldn't afford to lose this job—at least not for a while. He would give Chuck five more minutes.

The pint of whiskey sitting on the table had about two shots left in it. He drained the bottle and threw it in the wastebasket.

Twenty thousand dollars worth of cocaine sitting on the bed and he gets twenty percent of it. Four grand which he desperately needs.

He looked at the door. "Come on, you fucker," he yelled. As if in response a knock came on the door.

"Yeah?"

"It's me, Chuck."

Baumert opened the door and two men entered the room. A small white man not more than five and a half feet tall with a wispy goatee wore sunglasses, and a black man towering a foot over his companion trailed behind him. He shut and locked the door.

"Sorry we're late," said the white guy. "Believe it or not we had a fucking flat tire." He looked at his friend who nodded.

"It's OK, it's OK," Baumert said, eyeing the large black man. "But I gotta get my ass out of here and go to work." He reached for the plastic bag and held it up. "Here's the coke, Chuck. Now gimme the money."

The little guy took the bag and walked to the table lamp. He poured some of the coke into his hand and held it under the light, taking his time examining it.

Baumert followed him. "Will you hurry the fuck up? I told you I gotta go."

Chuck ignored him, wet his finger, dipped it into the coke and tasted it. "Luther, come over here and taste this and tell me what you think."

"Give me the fucking money," Baumert hissed.

Luther glared at Frank and pushed his way past him to the cocaine bag. He went through the same routine as Chuck and nodded, "It's good."

Chuck smiled and handed the bag to Luther who placed it in a large briefcase. They continued to ignore Baumert.

Frank watched the two men exchange glances. He had dealt once before with the little fuck but had never seen the big jig. Mean lookin' dude. "Uh, you boys want to give me the money now so I can get going?"

Chuck reached into a satchel he carried. Baumert held his breath and waited.

"You're pretty antsy today, Frank. I guess that's what prison does to you, huh?" He looked at Luther who responded with a smile that was not pleasant.

Chuck pulled out four packets of bills from the satchel and handed them to Baumert. "Here you go, Frank. Count it."

Frank took the money and riffled through each packet containing fifty 100 dollar bills. He placed the bills in a paper bag and left.

11

Waiting for Diane Lewis in the reception area, Sam thumbed through a copy of *Sarasota Magazine* and was startled to see a picture of Maggie Robbins in a section called "People to Watch." Interesting coincidence.

He'd read most of the magazine by the time she came out to get him. In spite of her gracious phone message, he couldn't help wondering if it was the ball buster keeping him waiting.

"Sorry, Sam, but I was on the phone with the sheriff, and the conversation doesn't end until he says so. Anyway, come on in."

He smiled, taking the apology to be a good sign, nodded and tagged along behind her. In spite of his determination not to, he slipped into the routine of watching her body, hips undulating, and her tight ass moving sensuously under the dark pants she wore. She was a very competent professional, a disciplined, smart cop, but no matter how hard he tried, he hadn't yet learned to see her as a cop first and a woman second.

Lewis sat behind her desk and beckoned Sam to a chair in front of it. He noticed her shoulder holster hanging on the coat rack and thought back to the first time she summoned him to her office months ago. She'd kept it on that day, looking very intimidating. He assumed that was why she left it on. Maybe not wearing it now, she no longer felt a need to intimidate him, that they were maybe, colleagues?

Lewis sat erect, arms resting on the desk, hands folded, staring at Sam. He shifted in his chair. When she finally smiled, some of the tension seemed to go out of the room. She nodded toward him. "Are you going to a costume party, Sam?"

He looked down at his outfit, squirmed in the chair, and braced himself to deal with the ball buster. He started to respond but she cut him off.

"So. You have your license now, Sam. Sarasota's newest private investigator."

He ran his hand through his hair, not sure if she was being straight, or if there was a little jab behind her remark. Hard to tell with her.

"Yes, and we both know I owe it to you. You do know how to slice through red tape. Thanks again."

She smiled and shrugged.

"Don't shrug it off," he said. "I would have had to wait for seven or eight months and even then I'd have had to work for an agency before I could get an A license. I don't know how you did it, but you cut through it all, and bingo, I got the license in two months."

"Well, the fact that you already had your 2000 hours requirement made all the difference. You've come full circle, Sam. Three years a cop, graduate school, college professor, and here you are a cop again—sort of.

"But I'm curious as to how you can do justice to two careers. You're a writer and a good one. As you know I read your first book and liked it a lot. Now you want to be a private investigator. Can you handle both?"

"I think so. The P.I. work can only help me with the kinds of books I write. And I have the liberty of only taking cases I believe I can handle and still keep up with my writing. But I appreciate your point. It's a good one. I'll just have to see how things go. All work and no play makes Jack a dull boy—and I don't want to be like Jack."

She cocked her head, raised her eyebrows, and studied him for a moment. "Anyway," she continued, "my helping you wasn't altruistic. I'm a pragmatist. That was good police work you did butting into our case last year. I was impressed, even though you're . . . shall we say, unorthodox, and you can be a loose cannon. But you do seem to get from A to B, and I can always use good help."

"Yep. That's me, Diane. Good help."

She stiffened her back at his little joke and he cursed himself for misreading her compliment and body language.

"Having said all that, I need to remind you Sam that you can't go off half-cocked on this case. No one has hired you, at least that I know of, so if you do start poking around, be circumspect and make me aware of anything and everything you do."

Sam's head jerked down each time she slapped her hand on her desk on the words *anything* and *everything*. "OK, I get the message. Anything you want to tell me before I'm dismissed?"

She pushed the chair back and got to her feet. "See. There you go again with the wise-ass stuff." She came around the desk and faced him.

He stood his ground, inhaling the intriguing mixture of perspiration and cologne. Neither said anything for a moment, until Sam backed off and said, "Sorry."

She waved her hand as if dismissing the whole thing and leaned against her desk. "We believe the autopsy will confirm that Maggie Robbins was suffocated. What can you tell me?"

"Do you know how the killer got in?"

She hesitated for a moment before replying. "Whoever it was used a glass cutter to cut a perfect square in the french doors."

"A glass cutter. Same as the break-ins. And I hear the phones had been disabled. Do you think it was a break-in and she confronted the intruder? Could you tell if anything was taken?"

"Slow down, Sam. Don't get carried away." She walked across the room and adjusted the blinds on a window, turned and tented her hands in front of her.

Sam stood, wondering what would come out of her mouth now. He hated the way she had of keeping him off balance.

She surprised him. "The drawers had been ransacked and Mr. Robbins tells us some of her good jewelry is missing. He's not sure of anything else at this point. We haven't formed any conclusions, yet. That's all I can tell you. Now what can you tell me?"

Sam walked to her desk and took a jellybean from a dish. He held it toward her and nodded, asking permission.

She ignored him. "Come on, Sam. I haven't got all day."

He relayed the information he had gleaned from Jimbo and Jennifer and thought for a moment. "I suppose you know that Maggie and her brother, Bryce didn't get along."

"Interesting." She pondered what she had just heard for a moment, before walking to the door and opening it. "OK, thanks for coming down."

Sam started for the door and stopped. "Speaking of Paul, how is he doing? How is he handling all this?"

"He's badly shaken, as you might imagine. He's been very helpful."

Sam moved slowly toward the door and stopped. "Did you ever hear if Maggie had had any run-ins with developers?"

Lewis stood at the door and beckoned him toward it. "If I do you'll be the first to know."

Sam smiled and saluted. "See ya," he said and left, convinced that as usual, Diane knew a lot more than she shared with him.

12

Sparky Waters greeted Bryce Hanson at the door of his office. "Go on in and make yourself at home, Bryce. I gotta run down to the can. Oh, uh, sorry to hear about your sister. Damn shame. Help yourself to some coffee, Coke, water . . . whatever."

Bryce nodded, but said nothing. He'd gone over to Maggie's house when he heard about her death, talked to the cops, expressed his concern, and since there wasn't anything else he could do, he left. But now life goes on and he wasn't about to cancel his meeting with Sparky.

He walked over to the wall mirror, checked his teeth and straightened his tie before settling into one of the Baroque sofas facing the bay. Bryce himself would soon have an office like this high atop Sarasota's most prestigious building. Sparky was his hero, the kind of wheeler-dealer, big-picture guy Bryce could identify with. His story was an inspiration to Bryce.

Sparky's rags to riches rise was to Bryce what made America great—a hand-to-mouth electrician's assistant who became one of the county's wealthiest developers and patron of the arts. Sparky had gone from nothing to multi-millionaire in a little over two years. As an alert electrician apprentice doing some work in Sunny Skies Assisted Living Facility, he'd noticed an extensive list of names and addresses of people who had recently been accepted to the highly sought after facility. The list was qualified by the fact that their acceptance was dependent upon their moving in by a certain date.

Attached to the list was an internal memo stating that these people were in the process of putting their homes on the market so they could move into Sunny Skies by the required date. Sparky made a copy of the list and moved swiftly from there.

He enlisted the aid of a cousin who had a real estate license and a little money. They began snatching up the properties of the folks desperate to sell at fifty cents on the dollar, offering favorable terms and quickly flipping the properties. Within two years they had bought and sold 200 dwellings netting themselves nearly fifteen million dollars. Sparky was on his way. Yes sir. Sparky was Bryce's kind of guy.

Bryce got up and returned to the mirror where he ran a comb through his hairpiece and straightened it. He scurried back to the sofa when he heard Sparky coming down the hall.

Sparky returned and sat at his desk, an ornate colossus that looked like it had been hand carved from ebony. He loomed over Bryce, causing him to squirm and silently curse his insecurity. He had hoped Sparky would join him on the couch.

Bryce waited respectfully as Sparky signed a stack of papers and looked through several other documents, ignoring him. Bryce knew better than to start the conversation until Sparky was ready.

Sparky finally looked up from his work and gave Bryce a look as if spotting him for the first time. He frowned and glared over his glasses.

"Bryce, we're getting a little concerned about those fucking do-gooders. They keep causing these delays and meanwhile we're losing money." His eyes narrowed. "I don't like to lose money, Bryce."

Bryce bobbed his head up and down. "Damn right, Spark, neither do I."

"Yeah, well that Hastings' broad and the rest of her crowd are fucking us up. You know what I'm sayin' Bryce?"

Bryce focused on Sparky's necktie. He had seen one like it at Saks. Two hundred bucks. He made a note to get one like it.

"You listenin' to me, Bryce?" Sparky barked.

"Course I am, Spark. Don't worry about Hastings. I keep telling you, Spark, I'm on top of things. Don't worry."

"Yeah, you keep tellin' me that but I'm still worryin'."

Bryce nodded his head, unable to think of anything else to say. He silently cursed Hastings.

"All this bullshit is aggravating," Sparky said. "Hastings and the rest of those nuts are causing trouble, and I don't like trouble any more than I like losing money." Sparky peered over his glasses at Bryce. "You hear what I'm sayin'?"

Sparky opened his desk drawer and pulled out a cloth and buffed his shoes. "I don't need to tell you how much we've got at stake here, Bryce. I'm getting fed up with these goddamned environmental freaks giving us a hard time. I mean, Jesus Christ, what the hell is the world coming to when a man can't make a decent living?"

"You got that right, Spark," Bryce said, admiring the sheen on Sparky's custom made Italian shoes and the sparkling diamonds in his watch. He leaned forward and started to speak but Sparky interrupted him.

"Let's get together with the boys and discuss all this. They're concerned, too. I'll set it up and call you."

"Sure Spark. Good idea. But don't you worry about Hastings and the rest of those clowns. You know I'm tight with the right people."

Sparky grunted and put the cloth away. He looked at his watch and got up. "My tailor's coming in to fit me any second." He took Bryce by the arm and guided him to the door. Bryce turned, took a final look at the office and left.

13

Sam stood in the lobby of the Alhambra Arms condominium waiting for the concierge to ring Sarah Hastings' unit, admiring the ornate Moorish and Spanish décor.

"Mr. Sam Wallace is here to see you, Miss Hastings. Yes, Ma'am," he said and hung up. "Go right up, Mr. Wallace."

A minute later Sam rang her doorbell. He was gazing at the artwork on the walls of the hallway when a voice said, "Mr. Wallace?"

Sam turned to face an attractive woman, about five-five, late thirties, early forties, wearing a black sheath dress, revealing slender, but well-defined arms. The rest of her body had the lithe, graceful look of a woman who took very good care of herself. Her close cropped highlighted hair, large expensive-looking designer eye glasses, and a broad smile displaying a mouthful of perfect white teeth combined to give her an appearance you would notice in a crowded room. Instead of looking at him, she scanned the hallway and quickly ushered him inside.

"Yes," he said. "I'm Sam Wallace. Thank you for agreeing to see me."

The woman extended a well-manicured hand. "Of course. I recognize you from the photograph on your book jacket," she said as she led him into her apartment.

"Really?" he piped and immediately felt like a jerk. He should have simply smiled, raised his eyebrows, and said something like, "Oh?" in that cool way he'd seen other writers do. But at least it was a sign that he was gaining recognition.

"Yes," Sarah said. "I know Jennifer Belding, and Jennifer told me about you and your writing, so I bought a copy of *Jeopardy* and liked it a lot. I loved the twist at the end when the cop's ex-wife turned out to be the killer. Jennifer told me you might call."

He raised his eyebrows and thanked her. Better, he thought. "Again, it's good of you to see me. Let me tell you why I wanted to come by. As I said on the phone, I'm a friend of Maggie's husband, Paul, and since I am also a licensed private investigator, I'm trying to gain as much insight as possible into Maggie in hopes that I might be of some help." He got it all out without taking a breath and waited for her reaction. "I understand that you and Maggie were friends."

"Yes," she said softly. "Maggie and I had been friends."

Neither said anything for a moment. Sam used the silence to check out the rest of Sarah Hastings. The subtle make-up she wore was barely noticeable, and her only jewelry was an understated pearl necklace highlighted against her black dress. He also noticed that, although she was cordial, she seemed tense, fidgeting with a ring on her finger, her eyes darting about the room.

She offered him a seat, but before sitting he took a moment to enjoy the view from her condo. The floor to ceiling glass walls facing the bay had the effect of bringing the water inside. The view had it all: the waterfront park, marina, and the view of the Gulf through the pass. The apartment's stylish decor reflected Sam's image of its owner.

Sam wondered if he should take off his shoes before walking on the elegant white carpet and warily eyed the white furnishings before sitting, being careful not to touch the snow white walls. He sat on the sofa to which Sarah directed him. "I see you like white."

"How did you guess?" she smiled and joined him.

Sam continued to study the woman, impressed with the way she handled herself, sitting angled on the edge of the sofa, legs crossed, toes pointing toward the floor, hands with the perfect nails resting on her knee. The subtle scent of expensive perfume hung in the air.

"So you're a private investigator," she said.

"Uh, yes, that's right. It sort of fits in with what I write about," he said nodding, hoping she would see his point and agree.

"Oh, absolutely. I think that's a great combination. It probably makes you better at both. Would you like something to drink?"

He declined. "Well, I'm a little too new at the P.I. thing to know about that part. But that's what brings me here." He grinned. "Maybe you could grade me when we're finished."

She let go with a bawdy laugh, inconsistent with the rest of her. Sam decided that he liked this lady.

"So, tell me Ms. Hastings, how long had you and Maggie been friends?" Sam asked.

She gazed out toward the bay, and Sam sensed that talking about Maggie would not be easy for her. "We'd been friends for about two years," she said, still looking straight ahead.

"When was the last time you saw her?"

She turned and faced him. "Are you working on this case, Mr. Wallace?"

"Please call me Sam. No, at least not officially. I guess I have a more than passing interest since Paul is a friend. Why?"

She removed her glasses and set them on a table. "Sorry, I guess I'm a little sensitive about people asking about Maggie. I cared a lot for her, and I thought she was a good person." She looked away again, and Sam saw moisture glistening in her eyes.

"I know you did, and I didn't mean to be prying."

"How did you know?"

Her question seemed odd to him, but even more so was the aggressive way she asked it. "Well, as I said, Jennifer told me that you and Maggie were friends, so I assumed you cared for her." He smiled and said, "I'm practicing my powers of deduction," hoping his little joke would loosen her up.

When she smiled, her entire demeanor changed again, and he felt like maybe he'd broken through the tension he'd felt ever since he walked in.

"Not bad, Sam. I can see a promising future for you in your new career. And by the way, please call me Sarah."

"Sarah, I'm planning on talking with Bryce Hanson, Maggie's brother. Do you know him?"

"Yes."

Sam waited, but she offered nothing further. "Uh, anything you can tell me about him?"

"I don't really care for Bryce Hanson, Sam. Can we leave it at that?"

"Sure," Sam said, a little puzzled by her response. He went silent for a moment.

Sarah seemed to sense his discomfort.

"Sam, I know Bryce well enough to know he's like two people. One is a pompous, arrogant ass, and the other is a sycophant who toadies up to people he thinks are big shots and can help him."

"Hmm, definitely not a ringing endorsement."

Sarah laughed again, a warm, infectious sound that filled the room.

"Now you've got me really curious. You sure I can't coax a little more out of you. That's what P.I.'s do, Sarah, and I'm trying to impress you with how good I am."

She studied him before responding and then smiled. "You're pretty good, Sam. "Let's say Bryce and I are on opposite sides of the fence."

"How do you mean?"

"Well, he's in bed with some big time developers to build a fancy

Club Med type resort on the last piece of undeveloped beach front property on Siesta Key. I'm surprised you haven't heard about it."

Sam nodded. "Yes, I have read a little about it. Where is the land?"

"It's five acres just south of Siesta Beach. It has over 600 feet of beach frontage. When Bryce's father bought it way back when, it was zoned for commercial use and the county never got around to changing that zoning, so at the moment the land is grandfathered as commercial. And what makes it even worse, it's going to be right in the middle of one of the largest turtle nesting areas on the West Coast of Florida—not to mention the glut of traffic the thing will bring to the Key."

"And you are very active in the Sea Turtles Protection League from what I hear. In fact I'm told your PR firm represents them."

"Yes, we do it pro bono," Sarah said. "And Bryce, owns the land where they're trying to put that resort." She leaned in closer to Sam and half-whispered. "Well, they're not going to succeed."

"Why not?"

Sarah took a deep breath, readying herself for what Sam figured to be her favorite topic. "Billy Hanson, Maggie and Bryce's father, bought the land thirty or forty years ago and never did anything with it. Seems he always had too many other big deals going on.

"Anyway, now that Bryce has his hands on it he and his cronies have been trying to move quickly to get the necessary permits to start construction on their resort before the zoning is changed."

"And you are not happy about that."

"I love Sarasota, Sam. I love its beauty and it pains me terribly to see what has happened to so much of that natural beauty. Some of us need to take a stand to, at least, slow down the growth. I don't mean only here. I mean everywhere that it's happening. But here is where I live and I want to do everything I possibly can to preserve what open land we have left—before it's too late. We have a group called CAPPS, which we formed to combat the growth and greed of some developers.

"This is an emotionally charged issue. Last week we had two nights in a row of debate and public testimony before the county commissioners about this project, without any resolution. As of eleven o'clock the second night, there was still no word as to when they would vote. Things got very ugly."

"And Bryce was there?"

"Of course he was there with his cronies."

"I admire your tenacity, Sarah."

"It isn't just mine. Maggie was every bit as tenacious. She and I have been the biggest thorns in Bryce's plans."

"His own sister."

Sarah snickered. "Bryce and 'his own sister' were not exactly close. In fact, rather than mourning her death, celebrating might be a more appropriate word."

Sam had watched her expression throughout her speech, impressed by the intensity and conviction and a little put off by the fierceness. "What are your chances of prevailing? Heck, if everybody's against the project, I would think your chances are very good."

"Everybody's not against it. Most of the merchants are for it because of the influx of tourists and the money they spend. From that standpoint it'll be a shot in the arm for the Key. Anyway, we've been lobbying everybody from the County Commissioners to the building commission to the zoning board, and as you might imagine we're getting mixed reactions but I think we're going to prevail at the zoning hearing next week."

"You think you can actually prevent them from getting the building permit?"

She fidgeted and Sam sensed a quiver in her voice when she next spoke.

"I don't know, but I must have them scared."

"How do you mean?"

Her demeanor suddenly changed as she looked around the room and moved closer to him. "Because I've been violated."

14

"What do you mean, 'violated'?" Sam asked Sarah.

She took a deep breath and her lower lip puckered again. "Somebody broke into my apartment."

Sam waited while she sniffled and blew her nose. "I'm sorry to hear that, Sarah. When did this happen?"

"Three nights ago, Saturday night."

"Saturday night. That was two nights before Maggie was murdered."

Sarah nodded.

"You want to tell me about it?"

She straightened and seemed to pull herself back together. "I wasn't going to say anything, since I don't really know you. But I like you, and . . ." She paused and took a deep breath. "I walked into the apartment at about ten P.M. and the place had been trashed. My desk had been ransacked, some of my personal papers were taken, and the bastards cut most of my wardrobe up into pieces."

"Who are 'the bastards'?"

"I know it's those developers. That Bryce. They're trying to scare me off."

"Were any valuables taken?"

"Not that I know of so far."

"Do you think it had anything to do with Maggie's murder?" Sam asked.

"I don't know. It's very possible."

"What do the police say?"

She threw her head back and fluffed her hair with the long,

elegant fingers he'd admired earlier. "The police! They've been more interested in questioning me about Maggie's murder than investigating who broke into my home."

"What do you mean?"

"Forget it, Sam. Let's just say my break-in doesn't seem to be high on their priority list. They took a statement from me, dusted for fingerprints, and left."

"Do you have any idea how they got in? Your building seemed pretty secure to me."

"Um . . . no. I have no idea, except that when the concierge leaves his post to go to the men's room the entry and foyer are unattended."

"Have you talked with him?"

"Yes, I called him right away. He did go to the bathroom about an hour and a half before I got home. Said he was gone for about five minutes."

"Did he notice any strangers leaving the building?"

"He said he didn't. Doesn't surprise me. The jerk spends most of his time sitting there, reading porno novels."

"But how would anyone get into the foyer?" Sam asked.

No response.

"Sarah, did you hear me?"

"Yes, I heard you. I don't know—unless they came in when another resident entered the building."

"Yes, but—"

"I don't know, Sam," she said with a firmness that suggested he'd best not stay too much longer.

"Has the lock been damaged?"

"No."

"Did anyone besides you have a key to your place?"

"Absolutely not."

"Sarah, how can you be so sure the developers were behind your break-in?"

"Who else could it be? Who else would break in, cut up my clothes, and rifle through my papers?"

Sam nodded, not sure what to say next.

"Sam, they think they can scare me, but they're wrong. I'm going to keep at this. We're going to cause delays, delays, and more delays until they get fed up and look elsewhere to build their resort. We're going to get those bastards, Sam."

Sam nodded, seeing an entirely different side to this stylish woman. "I wish you well, Sarah," he said.

"We've got plenty of money and we're going to take back our town." She abruptly brightened. "Hey Sam, how about a glass of wine? It's almost cocktail hour."

"Sure," Sam said. "Why not?"

Sarah poured the wine and they touched glasses. "How long have you had your firm?" Sam asked.

"I started it a little over seven years ago. In fact, Paul Robbins' company was once a client."

"Was? Are they no longer a client?"

"No, they moved on and so did I."

She checked her watch. "Sam, I have an appointment later, and I want to catch a little nap beforehand. Let's do keep in touch." She got up and walked toward the door.

That was abrupt, Sam thought, setting down his glass of wine and following her. Just when things were getting interesting. His appetite was whetted to learn more about CAPPS, not to mention Bryce Hanson.

* * *

On the way home Sam reflected on his conversation with Sarah. Something just didn't ring true about the break-in. He couldn't imagine any resident in that very upscale residence letting just anyone waltz into a high security building like that.

But if the person or persons could pick Sarah's lock they could probably pick the front entry as well. And yet the timing of such a thing would have had to be perfect.

And she sure was quick to throw the blame on the developers and connect them with Maggie's murder. He would definitely keep her on his radar.

Thirty minutes after Sam arrived home, Jennifer's Jeep pulled up. Sam walked out to greet her. "Hey, what are you doing here?"

"Oh? Is that any way to greet a lady who drops by with lascivious thoughts on her mind?"

"Uh, excuse me? Did you say lascivious?"

"I did."

"Hmm. You've come to the right place, lady."

She got out and hugged him. "Sam, I felt like such a jerk, turning you down for dinner. And when I got back from lunch my boss informed me that he wanted me to join some of the other scientists on the research boat going to the Keys tomorrow. Gave me a grace period for my report." She hugged him again and kissed him. "If your offer is still on, here I am."

Something about the kiss and the way she looked at him told him he doubted they would get to dinner. Not if he could help it.

Inside the house, he discovered he was right when he took her in his arms. She responded with a passion that put dinner on the back burner—way back.

Without breaking their kiss or embrace they maneuvered into the bedroom and slowly, gently undressed one another, savoring the anticipation of each moment, allowing the craving each felt to continue building. They stood naked for a moment, letting the heat intensify before falling onto the bed where they began a slow dance of touching and feeling followed by the passionate melding of their bodies.

They were insatiable until simultaneously they reached that moment of bliss when the reins of final restraint fell free and they entered into that ecstatic place reserved for lovers.

They lay motionless, basking in the afterglow of their sex, talking softly until they slowly drifted off to sleep.

15

Larry Gump sat at his kitchen table and pulled on his work shoes. He winced at the stink of his own feet. But who wouldn't get smelly, diggin' in all that filthy mud on that fuckin' construction site.

They got all their fancy equipment, but they still need suckers like Larry to do the dirty work. He popped open a Bud and smiled. Well, Larry's days are numbered doin' any more of that shit.

Yessir. Larry had a plan. Got it all figured out right down to a gnat's ass. Just handle this nice and cool.

Larry grabbed a mud-caked T-shirt off the pile in the corner and put it on. He thought about them fancy polyester sport shirts he saw at Wal-Mart. Maybe get himself a couple—get some new jeans, nice new pair of shoes. Start lookin' like a man with some style now that things are startin' to break for him.

Funny how things happen. Just a matter of bein' in the right place at the right time. Lotta guys wouldn't have the guts or the smarts to deal with this. But old Larry does. He's been waitin' a long time to better himself. Ain't no way he's gonna let this one pass him by.

* * *

In the morning after a reprise of last night's performance, Jennifer left. Sam dialed Diane Lewis' office. "Diane, this is Sam. Any word on the autopsy report yet?"

Silence from the other end, except for what sounded like a sigh. He braced himself.

"The autopsy report?"

"Uh, yes, I've been curious since you and I talked."

Again the uncomfortable silence. The woman was beginning to piss him off.

"Sam, Sam." The patronizing tone that he hated. "You can be a bit of a pest, you know that. Yes, we do have the results. As we suspected, the cause of death was asphyxiation through suffocation. By the way, Sam, do you have a client involved in this case?"

"No, why?"

"Just wondering. Is there anything else?"

"No, and thanks a lot, Diane."

She hung up without saying goodbye. He made a face into the phone and put down the receiver.

He settled into his leather swivel chair in front of the computer and began working. His small u–shaped work space just off the kitchen faced out a window giving him a sliver of Gulf view. To the left of the window, his built-in bookcases were filled with fiction, non-fiction, and reference books, including an extensive collection dealing with the criminal mind. To the right of his computer, he'd managed to squeeze in a two-drawer filing cabinet that held his phone and answering machine.

He was soon in a zone, his fingers flying over the keys. His gut told him that this book was going to be his best yet. The plot was complex and sophisticated, and he had become friends with his characters—always a good sign.

Four hours later he shut off the computer and closed his eyes. He was just starting to doze when the phone rang.

"Hey Sam! You going to the memorial service for Maggie Robbins tomorrow?" Jimbo's voice boomed through the phone.

"Yes, of course I'm going. Two o'clock, right?"

"Right, and the reception at the house to follow. Jennifer coming with you?"

"No, she's going off to the Keys for a couple of days on the Galt's research boat. Duty calls."

"OK, see you there. By the way, you talked to Paul since the murder?"

"No, I called him and left a message. He called back and got my machine and said he'd see me at the reception. Hey, how'd your session with the building department go?"

"Aw, them yokels are still jerkin' my chain, but we're workin' through it. I should be breakin' ground in another few weeks. Gotta go."

Sam thought about the service and who would be there. Certainly her brother and Sarah Hastings. Paul, of course, and most likely his partner. Probably most of the town given Maggie's high profile. And who knows who else? He hoped to mingle and talk with as many people as possible.

* * *

The next day he shut the computer down at one o'clock, shaved, fed Henry, and headed for his car. He stopped and groaned. Peter stood near the garage, attired in his khakis and bush hat, watering his small patch of grass.

His back was to Sam, who edged behind him, slipped into his car, and started it. He was halfway out when Peter turned and spotted him. He rushed over and leaned on the open car.

"Hey Sam, good to see you. Where you heading?"

"Downtown. I'm in a bit of a—"

"Let me tell you about our meeting. Sorry you couldn't make it, but we had a good turnout. Annie Zaleski was there. Just out of the hospital a few weeks, but she made it. Had her gall bladder taken out. You know Annie, don't you? Lives over on Treasure Boat Way. Lives alone now since her husband died. Charlie. Terrific guy. Great big fella. Used to work for the city. He—"

"Peter," Sam interrupted. "I'm running real late. I gotta go. I'll talk to you when I get back." He backed the car further out of the garage and slowly headed down the street. Peter jogged along beside him, still talking, as Sam picked up speed and outdistanced him.

* * *

The church on Main Street was nearly full, and people were being seated in the balcony when Sam arrived at 1:45. He took a seat in the last row, looked around and spotted Paul sitting in a front row pew next to a man about Maggie's age who was probably her brother. Both men sat stoically staring straight ahead.

Sam tried to imagine what it would be like attending a memorial service for a loved one who had been murdered. Bad enough to lose someone in the prime of her life, but mourning one who had been brutally murdered would have to be excruciating.

Looking around, scanning the intelligent looking, stylish people in the church, he realized that the Robbinses were even more well connected than he had thought. He wondered if there was any measure of comfort in that.

The murmur of the crowd stopped and a hush fell over the church as the service began. Sam found it odd that the two people who delivered eulogies were colleagues rather than family members. One was the lawyer, Jean Booth, who found Maggie's body when she went to pick her up for work. The other was a woman who referred to Maggie as her mentor, as had Jean Booth.

After the service, the minister announced that everyone was invited back to Paul Robbins' house for a reception. Sam wasn't sure of the protocol for a reception when the deceased has been murdered. Fortunately, he'd never had to deal with anything that horrible.

Outside the church Sam waited to speak to Paul and offer his condolences, but, since Paul was surrounded by people, he decided to wait until he got to the house. He spotted the man he assumed to be Maggie's brother heading for the parking lot, looking more grim than sorrowful.

He started to turn toward his own car when he noticed a scruffy looking guy in dungarees, a sweatshirt, and sneakers coming out of the church. No big deal, but the guy looked out of place among the well-dressed, well-heeled crowd. Maybe an ex-client, he thought.

"There you are, you old fart." Sam felt a heavy hand on his shoulder and turned to face Jimbo.

"Jimbo, you look positively elegant. I wouldn't have recognized you."

"Hey, Sam. I don't think that came out right."

Sam eyed his friend, decked out in a handsome blue blazer, white shirt and maroon tie, slacks that could use a pressing, and shiny new black wingtip shoes. "Sorry. What did you think of the service?"

"Very nice. And what a turnout, huh?"

"Yeah. See you at the house."

Jimbo shook his head. "Can't make it, Sam. I forgot that my brother's coming into Tampa Airport in," he looked at his watch, "an hour and a half. In fact, I gotta haul ass outta here now. See ya."

Sam listened to Jimbo's shoes squeaking across the sidewalk toward a dusty, fairly new Mercedes sedan parked on the street. The man does have an eclectic taste in cars, he thought, and headed toward his own.

16

Sam pulled into the Robbins' shell driveway, parked in the yard, got out and for the first time, studied the house. When he'd gone there after Jennifer told him about the murder, he was so stunned, he'd hardly noticed the house. The size of a small hotel, it looked like a cross between *Gone with the Wind*'s Tara and a Mediterranean villa. He wondered if it had been designed by a committee, with size being the only guiding principle.

He stood for a moment admiring the view of Sarasota Bay and the sculptured landscaping before making his way across the manicured lawn to the open front door. He joined a small line of people standing on the columned porch waiting to get in. As he got closer, he saw Paul Robbins greeting each visitor.

Sam and Paul spent most of their time together on a tennis court or golf course where he had paid little attention to Paul's physical appearance, except to notice the obvious. He was a good looking guy. Now, watching him greet the guests, he was impressed.

The tailored dark pinstripe suit he wore draped elegantly over his trim body and the white shirt and blue silk tie accentuated his coal black hair. He greeted each guest with a polite smile, that, even with the sadness in his eyes, lit up his handsome face. He exuded the kind of casual sex appeal that reminded Sam of a young Paul Newman. If he was the womanizer Jimbo claimed, Sam figured he must be good at it.

All the men were in fact, dressed in expensive suits. Sam's, an off the rack number, paled in comparison to the designer suits of the high rollers present. Probably all lawyers.

When it was Sam's turn to enter, he and Paul embraced. "Very sorry, Paul," he whispered as they greeted. Up close, Sam could see the fatigue and sadness in Paul's face.

"Thanks, buddy. Come in and help yourself to some food. I'll see you inside."

Sam nodded and eased his way through the crowd toward an elaborate spread on the dining room table where a line of people waited while a chef carved slices of roast beef and ham. Sam nibbled at a small triangular shaped chicken salad sandwich, trying to spot a familiar face in the crowd, hoping to dispel the awkward discomfort he felt. Everyone seemed to know everyone else—except him, who knew nobody.

He searched the house for a friendly face and was about to give up when a voice said, "Excuse me, but aren't you Sam Wallace?"

He turned to face an attractive blonde woman with a warm, upbeat demeanor who appeared to be about his age.

"Uh, yes, I'm Sam."

She acknowledged his puzzled look with a broad smile. "We haven't met but I recognized you from your picture on the jacket of your book." She gave him a thumbs up. "Good likeness."

"Really?" Sam piped, instantly realizing his reaction was not cool.

She extended her hand. "I'm Carol Scherer. I know your friend, Jennifer Belding. We've done some volunteer work together, and she's mentioned you."

"Oh sure," Sam said. "You're the lady who does creative things with glass. Jennifer has shown me some of your work. In fact she gave me one of your wine bottle lights."

Carol acknowledged his comment about her work with a laid back smile, the kind of reaction he would have to practice.

"I liked your book, Sam. Can't wait for the next one. Whoops! There's my husband Bob over there. He must have just arrived. It's been a pleasure meeting you, Sam."

"You too, Carol," he said watching her disappear into the crowd. Nice woman, he thought, admiring her choice of books.

A prosperous looking middle-aged man and woman stood next to him, talking. He cocked his ear, thinking he might introduce himself and join them.

"Oh God, I know what you mean," the woman was saying. "We're out just about every night of the week at one function or another. I promised my husband we would start staying home at least one night a week, but we haven't managed it yet. It's just one gala after another. Charles has worn out three tuxedoes since we've lived here."

Sam decided not to join them.

He glanced through the dining room door and spotted the man he assumed to be Maggie's brother in a corner of the foyer talking with a woman, who was holding his hands, looking sorrowful. He offered her a thin smile as she released him and moved away.

Bryce Hanson headed toward the bathroom at the rear of the front hall, relieved to be rid of the clinging woman and her inane sympathy. Inside the bathroom he fluffed his hairpiece and arranged a few locks to drape casually over his forehead, giving him the rakish look he liked.

He turned sideways, pulled in his stomach, and tightened his belt a couple of notches—not very comfortable but it gave him a more streamlined look. Holding his hand up to his mouth, he exhaled and grimaced. He pulled a small canister of Binaca from his pocket and squirted a dose into his mouth.

After checking himself in the mirror from a variety of angles, he left. In the hallway he spotted two women, both of whom he had dated, and turned to avoid being seen. Too late. They waved and one of them giggled.

He headed away from the women, but watched them out of the corner of one eye, both laughing, looking in his direction. Bitches. Like he's the only guy who's ever suffered from erectile dysfunction.

Sam spotted Hanson and maneuvered his way through the crowd toward him. "Hello, I'm Sam Wallace. Are you Bryce Hanson?"

Bryce eyed him before answering. For a moment, Sam wondered if he was going to reply. "Yes, I'm Bryce," he said, his eyes questioning Sam as if he were an intruder. "And you are . . . ?"

Sam shifted his weight from one foot to the other. The coldness emanating from Hanson was palpable. Although they had never met, he gave Sam the distinct feeling that he didn't like him. His bulbous nose was just red and veiny enough to give the impression of one who might have a drinking problem. He appeared to be trying—without much success—to look imperious. Rude was the word that came to Sam's mind. The two were about the same height, but Hanson somehow managed to look down at Sam, making him feel smaller. He thought back to Sarah's description of the two Bryces and had no trouble figuring out which one he'd encountered. "I'm Sam Wallace," Sam said, acknowledging Bryce's question. I'm a friend of Paul's. We play tennis together, and I met your sister a couple of times. I'm terribly sorry, Bryce." He wondered if he'd been too forward, immediately calling him by his first name. Bryce Hanson did not strike him as a warm fuzzy guy.

"Thank you," Bryce said, without returning Sam's smile.

Sam watched Hanson's eyes darting about the house. He seemed wary, uncomfortable. His body language signaled that his encounter with Sam was finished, and he was preparing himself for the next well-wisher.

Sam plowed ahead. "You live here in town don't you, Bryce?"

Hanson's head snapped back toward Sam, as though surprised he was still there. "Uh, yes, I do." He tucked his necktie into his suit jacket and buttoned the jacket. Not a good idea, thought Sam, eyeing the button ready to break away from Bryce's ample stomach. Bryce's glance dropped to Sam's shirt front and remained there.

Sam checked his shirt, removed a small piece of chicken salad, dropped it into his coat pocket and gestured toward the crowd in the same movement. "It must be gratifying to you and your family to see such a turnout for your sister. That beautiful church was packed."

Instead of smiling and agreeing as Sam suspected most people would, Bryce frowned and said, "Yes, she knew a lot of people." With that he excused himself and walked away.

Pleasant guy, Sam thought, scanning the room, hoping to find someone a tad more friendly. But in Hanson's defense, he realized this was hardly the occasion for him to entertain a person he'd never met before.

He spotted three men standing by a large picture window overlooking the bay and wandered over to them, hoping he might join the conversation. He drifted closer, but they ignored him.

"Four acres," he heard one of the men say. He wore a three-piece suit, the first time Sam had seen anyone wearing one in Sarasota.

"Yeah, and right on the bay," another said. "Some piece of property." He ran his hands through the thick gray hair along his temples.

The third man, his Guccis glistening under his tailored trousers, spoke up. "Knowing Paul, I doubt he'd want to stay on in this mausoleum alone. He never liked the place, but Maggie inherited it from her father. She wouldn't budge from it."

Sam noticed that all three wore blue-striped shirts, each with a pure white collar, which seemed to be a uniform for the professional men here.

"Well, she's out of the picture now," the vested one said. His head swiveled from left to right as he gestured outside. "Look at this. Can you imagine what we could do with this place?"

The thick hair guy nodded. "Level the house, and all those gardens and trees and shit. Put up a high rise with forty, fifty units, start 'em at a million and go up from there. Get up a few floors, you see not only the bay on one side, but the Gulf on the other. Do the numbers."

"Yeah," Gucci said. "You know how big Maggie was on that environmental crap. Be just like her to leave this fabulous property to the town for a flower garden like that Selby woman did. What a waste!" He leaned in closer to his friends and spoke softly, barely loud enough for Sam to hear. "Think it'll be too early to talk to Paul in the morning?"

Sam decided he didn't want to join these guys either. He drifted around the house picking up dribs and drabs of conversation, people shaking their heads, looking mournful.

Sam went into the dining room and helped himself to some grapes. Two middle-aged women stood near him, sipping tea. Sam munched on the fruit and looked around, hoping to spot a familiar face.

"I didn't know you knew Maggie Robbins," one of the women said.

"Oh, I didn't really." She touched the other's arm and leaned in closer to her. "I knew that all the important people in town would be here so I came to pay my respects. I mean, it's just one of those events that you simply can't miss. Look, there's Cynthia

Mayfair over there. I'm sure she'll have something in her column. I'm going over and say hello."

Sam watched her cross into the hall and sidle up to Cynthia, Sarasota's society columnist. He remained near the food, eyeing the jumbo shrimp when a man wearing a black blazer with some kind of emblem on it, headed in his direction. He walked up to Sam and stuck out his hand. "Jack Stinson."

Sam shook his hand.

"Say, didn't I meet you at the Berger's party on Longboat Key? I'm sure you remember that one. My God, it was the party of the year. Everybody who was anybody was at that one."

"I wasn't there," Sam said. "I don't know the Bergers."

"Oh," the man said. He sounded offended. "Aren't you Victor Hulse from the Sarasota Yacht Club?"

"Afraid not," Sam said.

Jack Stinson grunted and walked into the foyer, leaving Sam feeling somehow guilty that he wasn't Victor Hulse.

"Excuse me, Sam." Sam turned around to face Sarah Hastings.

"Sarah." He couldn't help staring at her. The dullness in the clear, bright eyes he had admired, was accentuated by heavy, dark circles under them, changing her entire face.

She made a stab at rearranging her hair. "I know I look terrible, Sam. That's why I need to talk with you." Her eyes darted around the room. "But I can't do it here. Can I come by your house and see you later? It's important."

"Uh, when did you want to come by?"

"How about later on tonight?" She thought for a moment. "No, tomorrow morning would be better. Would that work for you?" Again her eyes shifted away from him, exploring the house as if looking for someone.

"Hmm, yes, that should be OK. Say about nine?"

She took his hand with both of hers. "Thank you, Sam."

Sam watched her hurry to the door and leave.

17

Sam eased his way back through the crowd and walked into the large stately room which overlooked the bay. In a corner stood an easel filled with photographs of Maggie. They represented all stages of her life—a little toddler in a pink dress holding her mother's hand; a grade school girl soaring on a back yard swing; her blond hair flying behind her; a shapely teen in a cheerleader's uniform; and the graduate walking across the stage in a cap and gown. Others as an adult, playing tennis, skiing, holding hands with Paul on the beach—a rich, full life in perspective.

"She was quite a woman," a voice behind him said.

He turned to see Paul standing alone with a wistful smile on his face. They hugged and Sam could feel the tension in his friend's shoulders. He was struck by how different Paul now appeared from the man greeting his guests earlier. He looked tired, the color drained from his face.

Paul put his arm around Sam and led him across the hall into a room and closed the door. "This is my study, Sam," Paul said beckoning toward the room lined with rich mahogany paneling and floor to ceiling bookcases. "It's also where I keep my good booze. How about joining me in a drink of some of the best Kentucky bourbon made?"

"Sounds good to me," Sam said.

Paul poured the bourbon and motioned for Sam to sit. "I'll have to get back out there in a few minutes, but I just wanted to thank you again for coming."

Sam lifted his glass toward Paul. "Hey, we're friends. How could I not come?" He leaned over and gently gripped Paul's shoulder. "If there's any way I can help, Paul, just let me know. I'm here for you."

Paul settled into a leather chair and held the bourbon up to the light before closing his eyes and drinking from it. "Sam, the note you sent me was beautiful, and I can't tell you how touched I was by it. It got me thinking how much I've enjoyed our friendship. And I hope we can see more of each other."

"I do too, Paul, and we will."

"You know, Sam," Paul said, "Maggie and I were pretty social. We had a lot of acquaintances and we were often invited out. But I've never really considered any of them as friends. I enjoy your company, Sam. I think you and I hit it off well. I think of you as a good friend."

"Thanks, Paul," Sam said. "I feel the same way."

Paul leaned back and closed his eyes. "Been a long three days," he said.

Sam said nothing, letting Paul relax and catch his breath for a moment from what had to be a *very* long three days. After an awkward silence Paul opened his eyes. "I saw you talking with Sarah Hastings. Did you just meet her or have you known her?"

"I've met her just once before. She knows my friend, Jennifer Belding. I gather that Sarah was a good friend of Maggie's." He noticed Paul frown ever so slightly.

"Yes, they were, uh, friends. What else did she say?"

"Not a whole lot. She told me about the environmental activities that she and Maggie were involved in."

Paul formed a mirthless smile and nodded. "What did you think of Sarah?"

Sam shrugged. "She seems all right. Why? What do you think of her?"

"Let's just say I'm not terribly fond of her."

These people don't beat around the bush, Sam thought. "Any reason?"

Paul put down his glass and got up. "I'd better get back. Please call me, Sam, and we'll play some tennis or have dinner, or something. I want to try to resume some semblance of life again reasonably soon. OK?"

Sam sat savoring his drink, thinking about Paul's comments. Maybe Paul was feeling an emptiness with Maggie gone and was reaching out. In any event, he liked Paul, enjoyed his company and looked forward to their continuing friendship.

He was still thinking of Paul's remark about Sarah as he went to the dining room in search of more goodies and spotted Brenda from Donegan's Deck. She wore a flowing kaftan adorned with beaded Indian jewelry, her long hair twisted in the back and held with a round clip the size of a hula hoop, and she had a ring on every finger.

"Hi Brenda!"

"Sam!" she took his hand and placed both of hers over it. "What an awful thing, isn't it?"

Sam agreed that it was and asked Brenda how she knew Maggie.

"It's mostly through our involvement in CAPPS," she said. "You know about CAPPS, don't you?"

"What does CAPPS stand for and what's the difference between CAPPS and the Turtle League?" Sam asked.

Brenda inhaled and said, "OK, but let's go out on the porch and sit. I don't get much of a chance to talk with you, Sam honey."

They settled into rockers on the porch and Brenda began. "OK, CAPPS. First of all, it stands for Citizens Actively Planning Park Sites. The Turtle League and CAPPS both fight against the building of high rise developments and resorts on beach front property where turtles nest. As Sarah probably told you, the goal of the CAPPS people is to raise enough money to buy up property in general to prevent over-development and to turn these properties into parks. The two groups often combine their efforts as they're doing now regarding this proposed resort on the beach. Sarah and Maggie have been the driving forces behind both efforts—Sarah's zeal and Maggie's money."

"Maggie's money?"

"Well, yes. What we're doing is expensive and a good chunk of our money comes from the Hanson Family Trust that Maggie administered. I don't know what's going to happen now with her death. You may not know this Sam, but Florida is a national leader in land conservation, having purchased and preserved more than two million acres in the last fifteen years."

"No, I didn't know that, but I do know about the battles going on between parts of the citizenry and the developers and the developers' pressures to get zoning restrictions changed. There are articles in the paper every day."

Brenda nodded and continued. "And the state's land buying program is being squeezed by Florida's sizzling real estate market. Developers are grabbing every square foot of land they can get their hands on. In fact many large tracts that are highly desirable for their ecological value are being dropped from the state's priority list because it can't compete with the developers."

"Interesting. And that's where people like Sarah and Maggie with her money come into the picture."

"Exactly."

"And the Sea Turtles Protection League?"

"Oh," she said, like she'd forgotten that part. "The Sea Turtles Protection League is a watchdog group for turtles. Like I said, they work closely with CAPPS."

Sam thought for a moment before phrasing his next question. "Uh, Sarah mentioned to me that she doubted Bryce would be mourning his sister's death. 'Celebrating' would be a more appropriate word, I believe she said. Any thoughts on that?"

Brenda laughed and slowly nodded, like she wasn't surprised at the question. "Well, Maggie was very passionate about all this." She looked back toward the house and moved her chair closer to Sam. "And she had an additional motivation."

"What was that?"

"She always wanted to win wherever her brother was concerned."

"What do you mean?"

"Sam, the private investigator in you is showing."

"You're probably right. But continue."

"Well, Maggie, Bryce and I all grew up together. As they got older the two of them didn't get along at all. Mostly, it was because of their father."

Sam nodded and waited, but nothing more came. Brenda appeared to be enjoying herself, throwing out provocative statements and letting them hang there. "Their father?"

"Yes, he was extremely wealthy, you know. Started investing in real estate all over Florida fifty years ago. His biggest coup was in huge tracts he owned in Orlando where Disney World is now. And he was a powerhouse here in Sarasota County. Anyway, he always favored Maggie over Bryce, and as they all got older Bryce felt that Maggie manipulated the old man to her advantage.

"It was no secret around town. Both Bryce and Maggie have been well-connected here for years, and the animosity between them was pretty much common knowledge." She paused. "Especially since the business with the will."

"The will?"

Brenda turned and pointed in the direction of a small woman who appeared to be in her late fifties talking with an elegantly dressed woman about ten years younger. "Oh look! There's Nancy Potter, one of our County Commissioners talking with Congresswoman Katrina Harrington. We need their help. Sorry, Sam, but I've been trying to reach both of them and here they are together. See ya later."

Sam watched her hurry away in a flurry of rustling silk and jangling jewelry. He strolled inside the house and noticed Paul talking with Jack Stinson, who spotted Sam and pointed in his direction. A few minutes later Sam saw Stinson heading toward him.

Too late for him to get away, he waited as Stinson moved close to him and scolded, "Why didn't you tell me you were somebody?"

Sam gave him a puzzled look.

"Paul Robbins just told me you write novels. Are you famous?"

"No, I'm not, Jack, but I hope we can still be friends. Excuse me, I'm looking for someone I have to see before I leave." He hurried away to a spot out of his new friend's vision.

He decided it was time to go and as he headed toward his car he noticed the trio from inside, now standing on the dock, pointing and gesturing across the property.

Driving home, he puzzled over his conversations at the reception, and particularly Brenda's comment about the will. And why was Sarah so eager to see him again?

Without warning the sun disappeared and the temperature dropped. The blue sky of moments ago was replaced by dense gray clouds and for a moment an eerie silence fell, as all sound seemed swallowed into a black hole. And then the wind picked up and the clouds darkened. He watched the tree leaves turn inside out and heard the distant rumbling of thunder. He was about to be caught in one of Florida's sudden late afternoon rains.

The sky was now black and an ominous darkness settled over everything. He stepped on the gas harder, hoping to reach Peter's garage before the storm hit.

Bolts of lightning crackled through the darkness followed by more thunder, closer and angrier. Driving past the South Bridge toward home, he got a glimpse of the bay now churned into a snarling sea of whitecaps.

He and his open convertible were about to get very wet. There was no time to pull over and remove the car's boot, pull up the top and fasten it over the connectors. He watched in envy as the top of a modern convertible rose automatically and closed over the car, the joys of modern technology.

In spite of his predicament, he was fascinated by the abrupt change in weather. The heavy, tropical feeling in the air was not unpleasant. It was actually rather sensuous.

Another explosive burst of thunder growled across the sky as he reached the village and turned onto his street. Just as he pressed the remote, opening Peter's garage, the deluge came. He managed to get inside avoiding most of it.

Rather than risk facing Peter, he dashed across the street into the haven of his cottage. After a quick shower and some dry clothes, he made notes on a legal pad of everything that had transpired at the funeral service and the reception. Perception was one of his strengths and no detail was too small. He even wrote down the scruffy looking guy at the church, because he looked so out of place.

He listened to his messages. There were three, one from his editor reminding him of his deadline, one from Jimbo: "Just checkin' in."

But it was the third message that floored him.

18

Larry Gump popped open a Budweiser and rolled back the top of a sardine can. He picked one out with his fingers and dropped it into his mouth, absorbing the gamey, salty taste before washing it down with the beer. Goddamn! Larry loved them suckers.

After a few more sardines he finished off the Bud and got another. He'd worked up a thirst sitting in that stuffy church, and it felt good being back in the double-wide with his shoes off.

All those boity-toity big shots sitting there in their fancy clothes and their fancy cars parked outside didn't have a clue about anything. But Larry knew.

He downed another sardine and picked at a toenail. All them people in that church, all wondering who the fuck could have killed that lady. Nobody in the world knew, except the person who did it—and Larry Gump. That's why he had to go to that service, just to sit there and feel superior to all them assholes who wouldn't give Larry the time of day.

What goes around comes around. All those years of letting Sid Nassif come fishing with him and putting up with him trying to act like such a big shot because he works for the state. Fucking clerk in the Department of Motor Vehicles.

Well, it paid off this time. Sid gets him the name of the car's owner and bingo! Larry's got himself smack in that old catbird seat. Just a matter now of how to best go about it. How to handle this whole deal.

* * *

Sam stared at the answering machine. What could his ex-wife Lisa possibly want? After all this time.

He played the message again. "Sam, this is Lisa. I very badly need to talk with you. Please?" She gave her number, and that was it.

Almost a year and one adulterous incident later, her voice still did funny things to him. He wished that it didn't. He thought he had managed to drive her out of his mind and make a totally new life for himself. She had become a part of his past, and suddenly one call on a message machine, and memories came flooding back.

Well, he had more important things to do, other more pressing calls to return. He picked up the phone to make his calls, hesitated, and dialed Lisa's number.

"Hello."

The voice tentative, but familiar. Achingly familiar. His stomach tightened. "Lisa, this is Sam."

"Sam. Thank you for returning my call. I . . . I wasn't sure."

Everything about her voice told him something was wrong. "What is it, Lisa?"

She began to sob. "I don't know where to turn, Sam. All I could think of was you."

"That's me, good old Sam. Court of last resort."

"That's not what I meant. What I'm saying is that you're the first and only person who came into my mind. Funny, huh?"

Very funny. But he needed to get her to the point. "Tell me what's wrong, Lisa."

She started to cry again. "It's Walt, Sam. He's a monster. I had no idea. He has an insane temper. He's beaten me because he's crazy jealous. I left him six weeks ago, but he won't leave me alone. I've told the police, but they say there's nothing they can do. I'm afraid of him, Sam, and I don't know where to turn."

Sam tried to picture the Walt Piro Lisa was describing, the mild-mannered, nerdy Walt Piro, his former colleague at Whately College. It didn't fit. "Is he still teaching at the college?"

"No, he resigned under pressure shortly after you left. He was OK for a while, but then he started to get weird, and when he turned violent, I left. Sam, I'm so sorry to intrude in your life like this. I know I have no right to, but I just don't know who else to turn to."

"What do you want me to do, Lisa?"

There was a pause while Sam heard her blow her nose. "I don't know. I just wanted to tell you. Whenever I had a problem, telling you about it always helped and usually made it go away."

In spite of himself, Sam smiled. She was right. Whatever her problem, he seemed to have had a magic way of solving it. That was part of the good marriage he thought they had—until Piro. They had problems, but who didn't? The thing with Piro dwarfed everything.

Later, when she tried to tell him why, he didn't want to hear it. He'd been too devastated. If there was a problem, why didn't she come to him and discuss it instead of jumping into bed with Piro? Walt Piro, of all people.

Now, hearing her voice again, he found himself focusing on the happy times, all the things he had loved about Lisa. And in spite of the past, he couldn't ignore her call for help. "Do you really think he's capable of doing you serious harm?"

"Oh! God yes, Sam. He's a violent man, and he's already threatened me."

"What do you mean, threatened you? What did he say?"

She began sobbing again and he waited for her to compose herself. "He came over late in the afternoon yesterday. The back door was unlocked because I had been in and out doing different things. I was in the kitchen, looked up and there he was. He'd been drinking, and his eyes were wild and crazy looking. Without a word, he walked over and hit me in the face."

"What?"

"I fell to the floor, and he kicked me twice. I looked up and asked him why he was doing this. He said, 'That's just a sample of what you deserve and to give you something to think about until I come back.'"

"Lisa! You have got to call the police and file a complaint. Get a restraining order now."

"I'm afraid. He told me if I said anything to the police, he would kill me. I'm afraid, Sam. I believe him. He's not the Walt Piro you remember. You should see him."

Sam let the enormity of what she had just told him sink in. He thought about Piro, a man he'd worked with for six years, a wimp, afraid of his own shadow. He was also a coward, and it didn't surprise him that a coward would pick on a woman.

How many times had Sam seen him back down in faculty meetings? His colleagues referred to him as Walt the Wimp. He would try to throw his weight around with younger colleagues, but when they stood up to him, he always caved in and shut up.

"Lisa, do you know anyone you can stay with for a few days?"

"Not really."

"OK, then check into a hotel and call me. If I'm not here, leave a message."

"What good are a few days?"

"Lisa, please do it. I have an idea." He hung up and after calling Sarah and changing their meeting to tomorrow night, he called and reserved a flight for Boston in the morning.

19

Sam's neighbor, Peter Caruso and Brenda Green sat drinking diet sodas in Brenda's kitchen. "Missed you at the reception for Maggie today, Peter," Brenda said.

"Yeah, I was sorry to miss it. I was at the church service, but I had another commitment after that I couldn't get out of." He kept a wary eye on the macaw sitting on his perch in the open cage, while the bird stared at Peter. Peter blinked. "What do you think's gonna happen with things now that Maggie's out of the picture?"

Brenda sighed. "I don't know, but we're sure going to miss her money." She frowned and shook her head. "Oh, I didn't mean that the way it sounded, Peter. We're all going to miss Maggie for a whole lot of reasons. And it wasn't just her money by any means. Her brains and leadership will be missed every bit as much."

"Yeah, well we still have Sarah, and she's a fireball. Heck, I always considered Sarah to be our real leader."

Brenda smiled. "So did Sarah. And I agree that her drive and guts are a big part of what has kept us going. She's also a classy lady who knows how to charm people around to her side. Actually so was Maggie, but she wasn't as aggressive as Sarah."

Peter went quiet and looked away for a moment.

"What's the matter, Peter? What are you thinking about?"

"Well, last week, I went to the CAPPS office to pick up some more fliers and I heard Maggie and Sarah talking in the conference room. I didn't want to disturb them, 'cause you know, sometimes they tell me I talk too much. So I was about to leave when they started to argue. I was curious, so I kind of hung around for a couple of minutes."

"Oh? What were they arguing about?"

"I don't know exactly, because I only heard dribs and drabs, but they sure seemed to be going at it. Sarah called Maggie a bitch and Maggie fired back that she didn't want anything more to do with Sarah. Next, I heard a loud slap. One of 'em slapped the other. I'm not sure which."

"What happened next?"

"I heard Maggie say, 'I'm leaving' and that's when I took off."

"That's interesting."

"Yeah. I wasn't going to say anything about it, because I don't like it when people say I'm a gossip and stuff like that, but I figured I'd tell you, Brenda, 'cause you and I are buddies."

Brenda nodded and made a mental note to mention this to Sam.

* * *

Jimbo Conlin was on his way to a meeting when his cell phone rang. "Yeah?"

"Jimbo, my boy. This is Sparky. How ya doin'?"

"Sparky, you old warhorse. Evict any widows today?"

"Come on, Jimbo. This is a serious call."

"Oh, oh, let me put my hand on my wallet."

"Jimbo, these CAPPS people are givin' me a lot of crap over my new resort on the Key. I know you've had dealings with 'em. I remember way back when you wanted to build those condos on what's now the park at the North Bridge. Seems to me they raised enough money to not only block it, but they actually bought the land and built the park. That right?"

Jimbo let out a Jimbo sized guffaw. "You got that right, Sparky."

"How'd you let 'em get away with it. Nobody's got better connections than you. I can't imagine you letting that happen."

"Well, you know, Sparky. You win a few and you lose a few. To be honest with you, I didn't mind losin' that one. Right is right sometimes, and I think those folks had right on their side. And those CAPPS people are tough."

"So am I," Sparky said.

Jimbo chuckled. "Yeah, well you're not dealing with some celery farmer out east of I–75 like the time you slipped those bucks under the table to the guy who had the agricultural tax exemption. Got him to bulldoze vegetation off all them parcels so you could dodge the preservation rule and buy his land and build all those big ticket condos. You remember that, dontcha, Spark?"

"Come on, Jimbo, you know that was just good horse trading."

"Sure, Sparky, sure it was. Anyway, these people you're up against now are gonna hand you your head. And it couldn't happen to a nicer guy."

"Fuck you, Jimbo," Sparky said and hung up.

20

Walt Piro lived in a working class neighborhood of Boston's North End. He had never strayed far from his roots and after his second divorce the heavily Italian North End provided the solace and comfort he needed. His place wasn't much, but the lawyers didn't leave him with much. Sam had been there only once before to drop off some work Piro wanted when he was home sick.

Sam landed at Boston's Logan Airport at 2:35, hailed a taxi and gave the driver Piro's address, which was a short distance away. He had no idea if the bastard was home, but knowing him and his lack of any outside interests, he was probably watching soap operas.

The cab went quickly through the tunnel and into Piro's neighborhood. The leafless trees hovered like gaunt spindles against the gray sky, and the drab three-decker tenements looked as lifeless as the weather.

His taxi pulled up to a dilapidated triple-decker, not much different from the other houses on the street. Sam pulled up his coat collar against the harsh wind, walked onto the porch and rang Piro's doorbell. Other than a dog barking in the distance, the street was quiet and empty.

He tried the doorbell a second time and waited. He would wait all day if he had to.

The door opened, and Piro stood in his stocking feet, emitting a stench of alcohol and body odor. The sweatshirt he wore was too short, and his gut hung over his belt like a stack of pancakes. His eyes looked like two small pieces of coal pressed into a lump of dough. Piro was never any prize, but the guy facing Sam looked more like a felon than the college professor Sam knew.

"S-Sam," he stammered. "What are you doing here? I heard you were living in Florida."

"Yeah, I am, but I'm up here visiting, and I thought I would stop by and say hello." He pushed past Piro, walked into the living room and turned off the TV.

Piro shut the door and hurried after him. "Good to see you Sam, but, uh, I'm pretty busy right now. Maybe we could get together later for a beer or something." He looked around the room like someone looking for a place to spit.

Sam eyed the pathetic creep facing him and wondered how in the world his beautiful Lisa could have possibly been attracted to this slug. Although in truth, he sure used to look a lot better.

"Naw Walt, I think we ought to have a little chat now. I've been hearing things about you, like you get your kicks beating up on women. That right, Walt?"

Piro backed away, putting as much distance between him and Sam as the small room would allow. "Now look, Sam, if you've come here to start trouble, you'd better leave." He looked at the phone.

"Oh, you want to call the cops?" Sam picked up the phone and held it toward Piro. "Here, call them, and then we'll get Lisa over here, too."

Piro shook his head and waved the phone away. His expression changed, and his flaccid features came alive. "I don't know what that bitch told you, but whatever she got, she deserved. Fuck you and her, too." His expression changed again to one of wide-eyed fear, as if he couldn't believe what he just said.

Sam grabbed him by the shoulders and flung him against the wall. He bounced off and came at Sam, who side-stepped and watched him lumber past, lose his balance and fall to the floor. He sat there, holding his hands up. "Please don't hit me," he whimpered.

Sam pulled him to his feet and held him against the wall by his shirt. "Listen to me, you bastard. You ever, ever touch Lisa again, you ever come near her, and I will find you. No matter where you go, I will find you, and I will beat the living shit out of you. I swear. Your own mother wouldn't recognize you." He shook Piro hard with both hands. "Do you understand?"

Piro nodded.

"Say it! Say, 'Yes, Sam. I understand. I will never go near Lisa again.'"

Piro's eyes glistened with fear and tears. He choked the words out. "Yes, Sam. I understand. I will never go near Lisa again."

Sam twisted the shirt and cocked his fist. "Say it again, you scumbag."

Piro repeated it, and Sam let him go. He slid back to the floor and sat there, sobbing.

"Cry, you fucking coward. Is that what Lisa did, when you beat her? Remember what I said. Go near her just once, and you're a dead man, you piece of shit."

He left Piro, sitting on the floor, took out his cell phone and called a cab. Two hours later he was on a plane back to Sarasota.

21

By the time his plane landed, Sam had mixed feelings about the long day. He hadn't shown that kind of violence since he was a rookie cop and collared a rapist running from the scene.

He did what he had to do. It was the right thing to do. He knew Piro well. Once a coward, always a coward. He wouldn't bother Lisa again. Still, he wasn't proud of the ugly scene back there.

Lisa had called him back last night and told him she was staying at the Park Plaza Hotel on Park Square. The Park Plaza was a short cab ride from Piro's place, and while waiting for the cab, he debated whether to take it to the Park Plaza or to the airport. He chose the airport.

It might have been nice to go to the hotel and see her, tell her what happened, and take it from there. Sure, and undo all the progress he'd made over the past year. No, he had been right to come straight back, and call her from the safety of Sarasota.

He picked up Henry from his new neighbor, Brewster Larrymore, and carried him home. Henry was too worked up to walk. He wrapped his paws around Sam's neck and hung on, licking and lapping Sam's face all the way.

Once inside, having some quiet time with Sam, Henry calmed down, curled up, and went to sleep. Sam knew he'd been in good hands with Brewster, an elderly retired actor, who having met Henry, insisted on taking care of him while Sam was gone.

"I shall be forever indebted to you, Sam, for providing me with the opportunity of caring for this splendid little canine." Sam had a feeling he was going to enjoy having Brewster as a neighbor.

He opened a beer and picked up the phone. Lisa answered on the first ring.

"How's the Park Plaza treating you," Sam asked.

"Sam, where are you?"

"I'm home. How are you doing?"

"Oh." Her voice dropped an octave.

"Yes, I just got back."

"From where?"

"I went up and paid a visit to Walt Piro."

"You were here in Boston?"

"Yes. The bottom line, Lisa, is that Piro won't bother you again. You can go home now."

"Sam . . . I . . ." she stammered and went silent.

He waited.

"How long were you in Boston?"

"Probably an hour. I went right to Piro's from the airport and then back."

"Why didn't you call me?"

He knew that was coming. What he didn't expect was the seductive tone of her voice.

He took a long pull on his beer before responding. "I thought it best not to."

"Oh?"

What did she expect? He would take care of her problem and then come running into her arms like nothing had ever happened? "I needed to get back here."

"I see," the seductiveness gone.

"Anyway, the important thing is that Piro won't bother you again. He's a coward, Lisa. I threatened him, and he reacted predictably. Go home and chalk him up as a bad experience."

"Thank you, Sam. It was a bad experience, and I was a complete fool. We all make mistakes, and that was the biggest one of my life."

"Don't beat on yourself, Lisa. I don't think anyone who knew him ever saw the truly ugly side of him."

"That's not what I meant, Sam. The mistake I made was hurting you, cheating on you, the most decent man I'd ever known."

Oh, Jesus Christ! He didn't need this. Not now. He finished the beer, stalling for time, not sure how to respond to what she had just said. His first reaction was to say, "If I was so decent, then why did you screw another man?" But that was ancient history and he had moved on.

"It's OK, Lisa," he said simply. He heard her sniffling the way she always did when she was emotional and trying to hold back tears.

"Sam, I'm just so sorry. I've thought about you constantly since that awful day. And . . . and I've missed you."

Should he tell her how many nights he lay awake missing her? How many nights he reached across the bed, looking for her? How many days he went through the motions of his life in a fog, his mind numb from thinking of her—missing her?

If he said those things, it would be so easy to drift back, looking for something that could never be the same again, something he'd lost, pieces of himself that had been chipped away. And now when he has himself patched back together, she tells him she has missed him.

"Lisa, I missed you for a long time, but I've moved on. I'm glad I could help you when you needed it, and . . . I don't know what else to say."

"Have you met someone else?"

Goddamn it. What gives her the right to ask that? Things are starting to come back in his life—good things. Things he thought he might never have again. "In a way."

"In a way?"

"Yes, I've met someone. I've met a lot of people. But that's it at the moment."

"OK, Sam. I'll let you go. Can I call you in a few days, just to let you know everything is all right—or if I've heard from Piro?"

He hesitated before answering. "Sure, that'd be fine."

22

Sam checked his watch: 7:30. He'd been on the go for over twelve hours, and he was exhausted. But he'd promised Sarah he would call her. "Sarah, sorry to call so late. I had a bit of an emergency. Do you want to come over now?"

Sarah agreed and fifteen minutes later she arrived. She didn't look any better than when he last saw her. If anything she looked worse.

He motioned toward the writing table while he grabbed a yellow pad from a drawer. "Step into my office. Would you like some coffee?"

"No thank you." She still hadn't sat.

Henry came over to check her out, but she seemed not to notice. Sam hauled him off to his room, returned to Sarah, and gestured again to the table. She moved tentatively toward it and sat. The self-confidence she exuded the day they met at her condo was replaced by a timidity and a voice he barely recognized as hers. He sat back and waited for her to begin.

"Sam, I want to hire you." She blurted it out and gave him a tentative look, as if expecting him to turn her down.

"You want to hire me?"

"Well, yes. You're a private investigator, aren't you?"

"Uh, yes. But . . . I mean, why do you want to hire me?"

"Because I'm being persecuted by the police about Maggie's murder, and I need you to help find the real killer. The cops seem to think they've found her." She pointed to herself. "Me."

Sam sat quietly for a moment, watching Sarah squirm in her chair, her eyes darting about the room, looking out the window like she was expecting someone.

"Sarah, tell me why the police think you killed Maggie Robbins," Sam said. "Tell me everything you think I need to know."

She took a deep breath and cleared her throat. "The police found evidence at the Robbins' house which they say incriminates me. They found footprints leading to the back door. Size ten. I wear size ten. Large feet run in my family."

"Is that it?"

"No, there's more. They found a fake fingernail on Maggie's body—like the kind I wear. OK?"

He nodded, acknowledging that he was still with her.

"They found tire tracks from an SUV. They say the tire tracks match mine."

Sam waited for more, hoping there was nothing else. What she'd already told him was enough to convince him she was in trouble. "You drive an SUV?"

"Yes. There's still more, and this may be the worst. When they found the body there was still a scent of perfume on it. It's a very strong perfume, one whose scent would linger for twelve hours or more. It's Joy. Been around for a long time and it's still one of the most potent fragrances. But it's not all that widely used, because it's very expensive."

"And you're going to tell me that's the kind you wear."

"Yes."

"Well, to be honest with you Sarah, it's not hard to see why the police have zeroed in on you."

"That's why I'm here, Sam," she said softly.

Sam leaned back and looked over the notes he had taken. "Shouldn't you be hiring a lawyer rather than a private investigator? From what you've told me you need an attorney more than you need me."

She was nodding her head before he finished. "I have, but I want someone to dig into this whole thing in a way the police won't, now that I've become their primary focus." She paused and her voice broke. "I won't be surprised if they arrest me any day now."

"What about the fingernail? Did Maggie ever wear false nails?"

"I never saw her wearing any."

He watched her face, not sure what he was looking for. "Why have you come to me, Sarah? I'm a rookie at this."

"Two reasons. I liked you when I first met you and secondly, you had a lot of publicity for your involvement in those murders here last fall. And I know about your police background."

"You've done your homework."

"Yes, I have. My life is on the line here. Where do we begin and when?"

They agreed upon his fee and she handed him a check as a retainer. She gave him the name and phone number of her attorney.

"Tell me more about yourself. Ever been married?"

"No. I think I've told you most of the rest." She thought for a moment. "I've lived here for thirteen years. Came from New York. As I told you I've had my own PR firm for seven years. Worked for another for a few years before that. I work hard but I also devote a good share of my time to environmental concerns." She stopped and leaned toward Sam. "I'm a good person, Sam. I don't kill people."

Sam studied her and thought how he would hate to discover that this person—even now, when she was looking anything but her best—could be a murderer. He glanced over his notes. "Is there anything else you haven't told me that you should?"

Sarah gave him a sheepish look, began fidgeting again and turned away. Sam tried to make eye contact but she avoided it. Her discomfort was palpable.

"Sarah, if I'm going to help you, you must tell me everything, no matter how difficult or painful it might be. Otherwise I'll return your retainer now, and we'll forget it." He held the check toward her.

She pushed the check back to him. "I've told you everything, Sam."

The look on her face and her body language told him she was lying, but he accepted her denial for the time being. "Do you know anyone else with an SUV—someone who might have had a motive for killing Maggie?"

"Yes! Her brother Bryce has one. Mine's a Toyota, his is a Lexus. Same company, as you know, and I think the tires may be the same. I'm not sure, though."

"We can check that out. Who else do you know—again same category—who wears a size ten shoe?"

"God, I don't know. Who knows people's shoe sizes? Check Bryce, check Paul, check this Baumert, who threatened her years ago and is back in the area. I know Maggie was very nervous when she heard he was paroled. Oh, by the way, Paul has an SUV. Seems like everybody in this town does."

"What kind is his?"

"I think it's a Nissan. I'm not completely sure, but I do recall that it's another Japanese car."

Sam nodded and went quiet for a moment. He rubbed his eyes and checked his watch. "The perfume is the tough one, Sarah—although I'm sure you're certainly not the only woman in town who wears it. Did Maggie wear it?"

"To be honest with you, I never knew Maggie to wear Joy. It's possible she might have started using it. I know she liked mine."

"What do the police say?"

"They say there was none in the house."

"What about Paul? He should know."

"I don't know. I haven't talked with him, and the police didn't say."

"So, you hadn't seen Maggie in a week. Had you had any contact? Had you called her?"

She hesitated again, but held up her hand and nodded, when she saw Sam's expression. "Yes, I tried calling her a few times but always got her machine. She screens her calls."

"Why wouldn't she call you back? You were friends, weren't you?"

"I don't know, Sam. I don't know." Her voice cracked on the second I don't know.

Sam looked at his watch again. "I think we've covered enough for now, Sarah. I'll get started on this tomorrow." He got up and walked to the door.

Sarah followed him "We'll talk soon?"

"Yes, I'll call you in a day or two." After Sarah left Sam reviewed his notes on their conversation. Size ten shoes. Not a typical woman's size but certainly a common size for a man. The perfume, the fake nail, the tracks that fit her tires, all very incriminating. Hiring him could simply be a ploy to show people that she's innocent and trying to prove it.

Why would Sarah kill Maggie? What else do the cops have? Are they looking at anyone else? Paul? Bryce? Baumert? Then again, it could be a common thief, who just happened to hit the Robbins' house. Maybe Maggie woke up and caught him taking her jewelry. And the developers. Could Sarah have been throwing him a red herring? Did someone really break into her place?

He called information to get a number for Frank Baumert, knowing he wouldn't be in the book yet. He got the number and B.S.ed his way into getting the address in Bradenton. He would get up there soon. But first he needed to find out more about Mr. Baumert.

23

Paul Robbins called the next morning. "Sam, I was wondering if you might like to hit some balls. I need some exercise to let off a little steam. What do you say?"

"When did you want to play?"

"They have a court available at eleven. Is that a good time for you?"

"Yeah, sure. See you then."

Sam hung up wondering if he would be up for playing tennis so soon after his wife was murdered. After his marriage came apart, he could barely get up in the morning, let alone play tennis. He shook his head hard, trying to dislodge those desolate thoughts that had almost destroyed him. Now almost a year later, he was living a second life, a simpler life, and he was happy again.

Actually, Paul wanting to play tennis again was probably a healthy sign. And Sam was pleased that Paul would turn to him.

* * *

At one o'clock Sam served an ace that ended the second set. They were both sweating like pigs, and Sam hoped that Paul would not want to play a third set.

"What do you say we call it a draw, one set apiece and go have a drink?" Paul asked, to Sam's relief as they shook hands at the net.

They sat outside on the balcony of the Bath and Racquet's second floor restaurant, drinking Cokes. As usual in early afternoon, even at the height of tourist season with perfect weather, the club was nearly empty. Neither of them said anything as they wound down from their two sets. Sam looked out at the vacant courts below and heard the *thwomp-thwomp* sound of a tennis ball being hit on a distant court. He remained quiet until Paul broke the silence. "Thanks for agreeing to play on such short notice, Sam. Appreciate it. I needed this."

"I'm glad you called," Sam said. "Sometimes exercise can be the best antidote for grief. That was a lovely service by the way, and half the town must have shown up at the house. A real tribute to Maggie."

Paul nodded and looked away. Sam spotted some flecks of gray in Paul's hair that he hadn't noticed before. Had the gray slipped in since the murder? It's been known to happen.

Paul's rugged good looks made him appear younger than his forty-three years. Sam remembered their once getting on the topic of age and Paul asking him to guess his. Sam said thirty-seven and Paul triumphantly announced his real age. It seemed important to him.

"Yes, it was a nice service, wasn't it?" Paul said and lapsed back into silence.

Sam waited until it was obvious that Paul was not going to say anything more. He seemed preoccupied, swirling the Coke around in his glass. "Paul, I can only imagine how hard all of this must be for you." He hesitated for a moment, groping for what to say next. "How long had you and Maggie been married?"

Paul nodded like he was glad Sam asked the question—like he wanted to talk about Maggie. "It would have been eleven years in June," he said.

"Where'd you meet her?"

Paul echoed Sam's question with a smile as if recollecting the event gave him pleasure. "Where did I meet her? I met her at a Tiger Bay Club meeting. The Tiger Bay Club is a social–political organization for professional people to meet and discuss issues of importance to Sarasota and since I had recently moved here, I joined it.

"Maggie was on a panel discussing growth in Sarasota—its pros and cons. I thought her presentation and comments were the most impressive and passionate of any of the participants and went up and told her so at the end.

"We chatted, hit it off, and I called her a couple of days later, asked her out to dinner. She accepted and we were married seven months later. It was a first marriage for both of us—seemed like each of us had finally found the right person." The muscles in his face contorted and he swallowed hard, studying the tennis courts below.

Sam searched Paul's face, looking for a flaw in his sincerity. He found none. "Where did you move here from, Paul?" Sam asked.

"Atlanta. I had been in the real estate business there and heard that the Sarasota market was red hot. So I moved here and got my Florida license."

"Was it as hot as you'd heard?"

Paul hesitated. "Well, not really. I went to work for one of the big real estate companies, but as luck would have it things kind of died down and—well, I just got bored with it. I knew I could do better. Real estate just didn't seem to challenge my intellect. Anyway, I hear you're now a P.I."

Sam couldn't help notice the abrupt change of subject. "Yeah, how'd you know?"

"This is a small town," Paul said.

It was Sam's turn to change the subject. "Is Maggie's brother, Bryce taking her death hard?"

"Probably not."

"You don't pull any punches, do you?" Sam paused for a moment. "How are you doing, Paul?"

Paul hesitated before answering. "How am I doing? I'm dealing with it, and I guess I'm doing OK, except for the fact that the police have been questioning me."

"Oh dear." Sam said.

"Yeah, nice, huh?" Paul said. He shrugged. "Actually, I guess I shouldn't be surprised. They say the first person the police generally turn to in a murder is the victim's spouse."

Sam nodded. He knew that. "Yes, but—"

Paul interrupted him. "I know. I was in Miami at the time, but they still wanted the whole story. They talked to my partner, Mark, twice. Wanted to know all about Maggie and my marriage. Got right down to questions about my fidelity, made some cracks about her will."

"Oh? Has the will been read?"

"No, but the lawyer is back in town and he's in the process of setting it up now."

"What do you mean, cracks?" Sam asked.

"You know, things like 'Well, you're going to be a very wealthy man soon.' Bullshit like that."

"Are you?"

Paul crinkled his eyes and shrugged, and let it go at that.

Sam was dying to ask who might get what, but wisely kept his mouth shut. "Who's been interviewing you?"

"Which cops?"

"Yes."

"There are two of them. They're actually from the sheriff's department, since our house where the crime took place is located in the county. The one doing most of the talking and who appeared to be in charge is a woman. Homicide detective named Lewis. You know her?"

Sam nodded. "You want a beer? I'll get them."

When Sam returned, he said, "Yes, I know Detective Lewis. She's a tough cookie."

"No shit."

Sam chuckled. "Yes, I'm sure you've already discovered that. Do you know if they're talking with anyone else?"

Paul took a hit on his beer and poked at the bowl of chips Sam bought. "No, I don't, but they asked me what size shoe I wear, which leads me to think they may have some footprints."

Sam, remembering Sarah's comment about the size ten footprints, instinctively glanced at Paul's sneakers. "Did they tell you that?"

"No. I asked them, but they wouldn't say. By the way, now that you're a private investigator are you going to get involved in this?"

Sam loosened his sneakers and put his foot on the railing. His back was starting to hurt, and he needed a shower. He thought about Paul's question before answering and decided—for the moment, at least—to say nothing about Sarah hiring him. "Well, I want to help in any way I can. Did the police ask you about Maggie's perfume?"

Paul shot Sam a quizzical look. "Yes, as a matter of fact. They asked if she wore Joy perfume, said the scent was on her."

"Did she?"

"No, never."

"Do you know any women who do?"

Paul thought for a moment before answering. "Can't say that I do."

"Do you know the woman who found Maggie? Jean Booth, I believe is her name."

"Of course I know Jean. She and Maggie had been friends for some twenty years. She's a lawyer, worked with Maggie. Jean's a good lady."

"How about a man named Baumert, Frank Baumert."

Paul gave him a quizzical look. "Frank Baumert! Bet your ass I know who Frank Baumert is and so do the cops. Obviously you do or you wouldn't have asked."

"I've heard a couple people mention his name. That's all. Who is he?"

Paul's expression changed. "I'll tell you who he is. He just might be the son-of-a-bitch who killed my wife."

Sam winced. "Tell me about him."

"Maggie defended him on a second-degree murder charge ten years ago when she was a defense attorney. He was convicted and blamed her. Said she didn't like him and gave him only a half-hearted defense. He called her a bitch and threatened her."

"How do you mean?"

"When he was sentenced, he turned to her and whispered, 'You bitch, you'll be sorry for this when I get out.' He was paroled a month ago."

"Did anyone else hear him say this?"

"No, only Maggie, but she told me and several other people. We didn't give it too much thought, because he was sentenced to fifteen years in prison, and that was a long time away. We only heard last week or so that he had been paroled after serving ten years."

"Who did he kill?"

"He killed two people. Got into an argument with two guys in a bar and it erupted into a fight. Baumert went berserk, and killed both of them. Broke one guy's neck, knocked the other one down and stomped him to death before anybody could stop him.

"Actually, the two were all over Baumert at first, so he claimed self-defense, and it looked like he'd be tried for manslaughter. But after the bartender and others told the cops, Baumert was a time bomb, always looking for trouble, and starting fights and what a nasty guy he was. They went for second degree murder. That's what they got him on. The bartender is still around by the way and I understand he's scared shitless since Maggie was killed."

"And you told the police all of this?"

"Of course I did."

"Where's Baumert now?"

"I understand he's living somewhere in Bradenton. The cops know all about Baumert and I know they've been talking with him."

"From what you've told me, it doesn't sound like he has reason to hold enough of a grudge against Maggie to kill her," Sam said, watching Paul finish off his beer.

Paul screwed his face up and shook his head. "Hmm, I don't know. Baumert was pushing her to fight for the self-defense angle and at least get him the manslaughter charge. She knew it couldn't be done and tried to convince him to plea bargain. He refused and went nuts when they convicted him and sentenced him to fifteen years. Said she gave him a half-assed defense."

It was Sam's turn to ponder. Might as well see what he could find out while Paul was in a talkative mood. "Who else would the cops want to interview?"

Paul looked at his watch. "I should be going, but I must say it feels good to relax and talk to someone." He paused and touched Sam's arm. "A friend."

"How about another beer?" Sam said.

Paul gave him a quizzical look and hesitated. "Oh, what the hell, one more's not going to hurt. I'll get them."

While he waited, Sam tried to analyze their conversation. He was surprised at how much Paul was sharing with him, but his partner was back in Miami, and he knew that Paul didn't have a whole lot of friends in Sarasota—many social acquaintances, but not friends. From what Paul had said at the reception Sam was probably as close as any.

The noise volume picked up below, interrupting Sam's thoughts. He peered over and watched three mixed doubles groups now playing on the courts below them. He smiled at the contrast in attire. The women wore chic tennis outfits, each color coordinated from their stylish sneakers to their matching visors. Most of the men wore oversized cotton shirts hanging out of their baggy shorts. Only one wore his cap backward, a dying fad for which Sam was grateful.

Paul returned with the beers and sat. "You're a good tonic, Sam. I'm glad we got together. Where were we?"

"I asked you who else the cops would want to interview," Sam said.

24

Paul smiled. "Ah yes, who else? Well, speaking of wills—as we were—Maggie and her brother, Bryce, were involved in an ugly pissing contest over their father's will."

"Oh?"

"Yes. Maggie was always her father's favorite. She was in fact, a lot like him. Billy just more or less tolerated Bryce. He left everything to Maggie except for a token pittance to her brother. Bryce contested the will saying that Maggie had unduly influenced their father, said Billy had promised him a piece of land on Siesta Key—actually the largest piece of Gulf front left on the Key. Apparently, he'd made the promise to Bryce in front of a couple of witnesses."

"Did she unduly influence their father?"

"Ah, that's bullshit. She handled her dad's legal and financial affairs and as such she had complete access to his money, the same as any financial advisor would."

"Which Bryce did not."

"Which Bryce did not. Christ, if he did, the money'd been gone in a year. Anyway, the will got held up for about fifteen months before Bryce prevailed and the will was overturned. Bryce got his land.

"Here's what happened. It's true that the old man told Bryce he would get the piece of land—even had it in the will. However, as the years went by he became more and more disgusted with Bryce's half-baked schemes and had lost all respect for him."

"So he changed the will."

"Exactly. Toward the end of his life he decided to change it, which he did, leaving the land to Maggie. The old man had been pretty ruthless in a lot of his dealings and I think toward the end he wanted to atone for some of his past by leaving the land to Maggie. He knew she would make better use of it."

"Like what?"

"I'm not sure. She was active in CAPPS, the Nature Conservancy and the Turtle League, but I'm not sure what she would have done with it. I do know it would have been better than anything that idiot Bryce will do."

Sam thought it odd that Paul would not know what his wife would do with the land, but let it pass. "How did Bryce wind up with it?"

Paul untied his sneakers, put his feet up on the railing, and began rubbing them. "Old Billy was apparently pretty sick at the time he changed the will. And that's the basis on which Bryce ultimately prevailed."

Sam eyed Paul's feet again.

"But here's where it gets interesting," Paul continued. "As I'm sure you've heard, Maggie was a dedicated environmentalist. Among other things she was a nut about sea turtles."

Sam nodded.

Paul looked away for a moment before continuing. "Anyway, as you've probably also heard, Bryce is in bed with some big time developers to build a Club Med type resort on that piece of property and Maggie was very upset about the impact that would have on the sea turtles. She saw the whole scene as a nightmare for the turtles with people running all over the beaches, doing the kinds of things day and night that they do at a resort like that."

"And?"

"Maggie was in the process of challenging the judge's decision in a higher court where she had some tight connections. Normally, it's very difficult to get a will overturned a second time and the thing went on for almost another year, but with Maggie's connections, the word was that she was about to win."

"And if she did?"

"If she did, Bryce would have been ruined. He had already put most of his cash into the project with the understanding that the land would constitute the rest of his investment to make him a full partner in the endeavor. Of course without the land everything was down the tubes."

"I understand that Sarah Hastings worked closely with Maggie on these environmental concerns. In fact, I'm told that Hastings has been the real spearhead." Sam said.

An expression came over Paul's face like he'd bitten into a lemon. "Sarah Hastings is another story."

"Oh?"

"The woman is not worth discussing," Paul said and started to get up.

Sam gently guided him back to his chair. "Anyway, getting back to Bryce, I gather from what you're saying, Bryce might have had a motive for wanting to see his sister dead?" He floated the thought like a question, not a conclusion. The words hung in the air.

Paul raised his eyebrows and shrugged, as if to say, 'What do you think?' He finished his beer and fixed his gaze on Sam.

Sam ran his fingers around the rim of his glass, waiting to choose his words carefully. "Paul, it's pretty obvious that Bryce isn't one of your favorite people. But do you think that he's capable of—"

"Of murder? Who knows?" Paul rose again and pointed to his watch. "Gotta go, Sam. You want to play next week, same time?"

Sam agreed and Paul got up and started to leave. He turned and grinned. "By the way, I wear size nine shoes."

It was mid-afternoon when Sam headed over the Siesta Drive Bridge onto the Key. Paul sure wasn't subtle with his innuendoes about Bryce and his blunt dismissal of Sarah. There was much more he wanted to discuss about Hastings, but Paul cut that off, for now. And this guy Baumert.

How much did the police know by now? Probably a lot more than he did. What about the footprints Paul alluded to? How hard are the cops pursuing the break-in possiblity?

25

Bryce Hanson and his new partners sat in the bar of the Ritz-Carlton Hotel sipping scotch. The Ritz would now be Bryce's new hang-out—his kind of place—drinking Macallan Highlands single malt scotch at twenty-five bucks a pop. Bryce liked the feel of the Ritz, liked being around the movers and shakers who frequented it.

Sparky Waters raised his glass. "Gentlemen, I believe a toast is in order. Here's to Club Siesta, the classiest, most elegant resort this area will ever see."

Bryce looked around the room, recognizing some of the heavy hitters in town, watching Bryce and his colleagues, probably wondering what they were toasting. He sensed a buzz in the room with all eyes on Bryce and the power table.

Waters turned to him. "And here's to Bryce Hanson, who has made it all possible." Sparky's eyes focused on Bryce.

The other two joined in the toast and gave themselves a round of applause. Bryce raised his glass higher than the others, basking in the moment which was the highlight of his life.

Sparky interrupted his reverie. "And Bryce has assured us that he's got all this turtle and CAPPS' bullshit under control, haven't you, Bryce?"

Bryce's eyes darted around the table and he nodded vigorously. "Oh, you bet, Spark. You bet I do. Not to worry. I got everything under control. All this noise those nuts are making is a tempest in a teapot. It'll all blow over. I'm on top of it. You know that, Spark."

Sparky's eyes narrowed, causing Bryce to wiggle in his chair, crossing one leg over the other, then switching legs. He smiled and nodded at the others, trying to look cool, relaxed. They just ignored him.

"Just so we understand each other," Sparky said. "You know what I'm sayin', Bryce?"

The others nodded and sipped their scotch.

"Sure do, Spark. It's all under control."

The table went quiet while Bryce tried to hold his fading smile.

"Bryce, those fanatics are still causing trouble, especially that Hastings' broad. And now I hear she's got some detective snooping around," Sparky said. "We've got nothing to hide but all this shit that's going on is still bothersome, you know what I mean, Bryce?"

"Damn right I do, Spark, but like I said, I'm on top of everything. Don't you worry. You know you can count on me." He felt a trickle of sweat slide out from under his hairpiece, and dribble down the back of his neck. "Spark, how do you know she's got a detective snooping around?"

Sparky sipped his scotch and motioned the waiter for another. He gave Bryce a patronizing look. "Bryce, there's very little that goes on in this town that I don't know."

Bryce nodded and hung his head like a school boy who'd just been scolded. It bothered him to see Sparky upset.

Bryce had been preparing for a deal like this since he left college. He was finally in the big time—no more kissing asses to sell condo units to people quibbling over commissions, too cheap to pay the full rate a man deserved.

He had risked everything for this opportunity—mortgaged his house way over his head and sold his stocks to raise the money needed to join the project until he had the land to put up for his full partnership. He was a gambler but on this deal he held a royal straight flush. When the doctor confirmed his father's pancreatic cancer and gave him six months to live, Bryce was thrilled. It was the go ahead for Bryce. He could then safely put up the money to secure his partnership in the project until he was ready to provide the land.

And then came the curve ball that almost ruined him. He couldn't believe his ears when the will was read. It took over a year, fighting to get that goddamned will overturned. His money had been tied up for that long year, legal fees were piling up and he couldn't have lasted another month. Relations between him and his future partners had become strained to the breaking point. They had begun looking around for another piece of land for the project. Anyway, that was all behind him and the land was his.

The turtle people and those other creeps were an inconvenience like little gnats nibbling at him, making noises about disturbing nestings and that bullshit. And that bitch Hastings. But they had no real clout, and he was pretty well wired into the right people in town, and they're not going to let the do-gooders hold this up forever. No way.

He knew he would have to deal with the innuendoes about Maggie's untimely death just when it seemed she was about to get the will changed back to the original. Well he could handle it. Yes sir, he could handle it. He finished his Macallan and ordered another round. On him.

26

After his tennis with Paul, Sam went home and listened to Brenda's phone message relaying an argument between Maggie and Sarah that Peter Caruso overheard a few weeks ago. He showered, and left again.

He took his time driving along pristine Longboat Key where the condominiums were so much more glamorous and lushly landscaped than those on Siesta Key. The exquisitely manicured Longboat Key Club golf course meandered along the side of the road, enhancing the beauty of the drive. Everything about Longboat smacked of exclusivity and money. And yet, in Sam's view, the place had no charm, unlike Siesta Key with its funky, laid-back lifestyle that was more to his liking.

Once over the bridge in Bradenton, he was in a different world. Bradenton Beach was a far cry from Longboat Key, but the Gulf of Mexico played no favorites. The turquoise water was just as glorious here as the toniest parts of Longboat. And to Sam, Bradenton Beach looked like a hell of a lot more fun.

He drove along a mixed bag of buildings lining the street, directly across from the Gulf. There were small vacation cottages, rickety looking two and three decker buildings of indeterminate nature, souvenir stores, and restaurants. Sam found the street he was looking for and drove about fifty yards past a medley of small houses that appeared to have been placed in a hodgepodge jumble by a drunken surveyor.

He finally spotted Frank Baumert's street sign and pulled up to his house number. A pickup was parked in front of the house on what was once a lawn. Sam assumed it belonged to Baumert, who must be inside. Maybe luck was still with him.

He got out of the car and walked onto the porch. The rotted boards bent under his weight. He rang the doorbell several times with no response. If it was anything like the rest of the place, it probably didn't work. He knocked on the door. Nothing. Twice more, same result. He tried the door. Locked.

As he was about to leave, a man came out from behind the house next door. "You lookin' for Baumert?"

"Yes, I am."

"He ain't home. He's at work."

"Oh." Sam pointed to the pickup. "That his?"

"Yep."

Sam looked at the man and back at the truck. The guy picked up on his confusion. "He don't need his car. He works across the street at the Water's Edge."

Sam thanked the neighbor, backed out, and pulled into the parking lot of the Water's Edge. The bar and restaurant sat only a few yards from the sand, facing directly on the Gulf. The exterior of the place had a rustic, inviting kind of beachy look to it, and when Sam walked in, his eyes were drawn to the blue-green waters of the Gulf, framed against the glass walls.

The bar smelled of cigarette smoke and stale beer. It was also empty. "Hello," Sam called out.

A man stood up from where he'd been kneeling behind the bar. "We ain't open yet, buddy. Another half hour." He went back down to whatever he had been doing.

Sam walked to the bar and leaned over. "Are you Frank Baumert?" He watched as the man continued filling a cooler with beer bottles.

The guy finished with his task and stood, facing Sam. "Who wants to know?"

Sam took a step back. The man was about Sam's height, maybe five-ten or eleven, but he had a massive neck that vibrated with muscles when he spoke. His biceps looked like they'd been carved out of oak. He wore a tank top that accentuated the size of his arms and the tattoos adorning them. One struck Sam as particularly gross—that of a coral snake slithering down his left arm. The top of his head was tightly wrapped with a red bandanna, and a dirty blond pigtail trailed down his back. His expression was not friendly.

Sam smiled and offered his hand. "Hi. I'm Sam Wallace."

The guy ignored his hand. "So what?"

This is going to be fun, Sam thought. He forced another smile and asked again if the gentleman was Frank Baumert.

"I'm Baumert. Who the fuck are you?"

Sam eyed Baumert's muscles and wondered why prisons allow inmates to build their bodies to the point where they become human weapons, capable of crushing a person's skull with one mighty flex. And they walk around in those bodies with the kind of hostility Baumert was displaying.

"Mr. Baumert, I'm a private investigator who has been hired by a client who has asked me to talk with anyone and everyone who might have known Maggie Robbins. You may have read that Mrs. Robbins was murdered Monday night."

The air in the bar was close, and Sam wished he could offer Baumert some deodorant. Not a good idea.

Baumert turned and moved toward the other end of the bar, walking with the rolling gait, arms out from his sides, the way body builders do. He grabbed an ashtray and returned to Sam, who waited while Baumert lit a cigarette.

"I don't have to talk to you. I've already been questioned by the cops, so why the fuck should I give you the time of day?"

Sam moved away from the puffs of smoke coming from Baumert's mouth as he talked. "You don't have to talk with me, but I'm involved in the case, working closely with Detective Lewis." He bit his tongue for that bit of bullshit, but he doubted Baumert was going to call the cops to check on him.

Sam plowed on. "Everyone else I have talked with has been very cooperative, making it clear they have no reason not to be. The police are aware of what you said to Robbins when you were sentenced. That's of course why they came to talk with you. Right? And I'm sure you're smart enough to know that you're a suspect because of that."

Baumert looked at him with eyes that had narrowed to ugly slits. Sam felt a sudden longing for sunlight and fresh air.

Baumert stabbed out his cigarette with a series of pecking motions, taking his time before responding to Sam. "Look pal, what I said to Robbins was a long time ago. I got over it, and I'm tryin' to move on with my life. I don't need this shit." He took the last cigarette from the pack, lit it, crumpled up the pack and held it in his fist.

Sam sensed a crack in the guy's bravado. "Where were you the night Robbins was killed?"

Baumert blinked several times and rubbed his hand over his mouth. "I already told the cops I was home watchin' TV." He threw the cigarette pack into a trashcan and walked across the room, setting place mats on the tables.

Sam followed him, looking at his feet. He wore sneakers that appeared to be medium size. "What did you watch?"

"Fuck, I don't know. That was almost a week ago. You remember what you watched on TV a week ago?" He kept moving from table to table laying out his paper mats. Sam stayed with him.

"I know what you're saying, Mr. Baumert. But since you don't really have an alibi and since you're a two-time loser, the cops are going to keep on you. There is going to be a lot of pressure on them with this one. You know, Robbins being a prominent citizen of the community, key member of the District Attorney's office. They're going to want to put this to bed fast. And right now, you are a prime target." He waited, letting it all sink in. "It would help your situation if you could remember what you watched that night. That's all I'm saying."

Baumert set his last mat down and turned to face Sam. He sat down heavily at the table and Sam joined him. Sam could only imagine what was going through the guy's mind.

"I hear you. I told the cops I thought I watched some kind of animal show. But you know, it could have been a basketball game."

"What basketball game?"

Baumert thought for a moment. "Knicks and Celtics." He snapped his fingers. "Yeah, I remember now. Came on at nine o'clock."

"Mr. Baumert, I follow the Celtics pretty closely. They didn't play Monday, Tuesday or Wednesday of that week."

"Fuck you!" Baumert roared. "I told you I don't remember. I was drinking. What do you want from me?" He got up and pushed the chair back, sending it clattering across the room, stormed up to Sam, and stood inches from Sam's face. "I oughta bust your fucking head open."

Sam stared him down without flinching. "I wouldn't do that," he said, eyeing Baumert's bulging neck veins with a calmness he didn't feel, trying to forget why Baumert had been sent to prison. "You lay one hand on me and you'll be back in prison so fast you'll think you never left."

Baumert pulled his arm back and held his cocked fist for what seemed to Sam like twenty minutes. He stood his ground.

The ex-con dropped his arm and turned away. "Get the fuck outta here. I got work to do."

Sam decided not to press his luck and left. He drove out of the parking lot, but instead of turning right to head back to Sarasota, he pulled across the road and into Baumert's yard.

It was empty and quiet. Sam got out of his car and inspected the tires on Baumert's truck. Little pieces of crushed shell were imbedded in the tires. No big deal, but he extracted a few and left without noticing Baumert's neighbor watching him from inside his house.

Frank Baumert hunkered onto a stool behind the bar and punched in a familiar set of numbers on his cell phone. The phone rang four times before a voice answered.

"Yeah?"

"Norm, this is Baumert."

"Frank, my boy, how you doin'?"

"I'm OK, but I need some cash. I know some guys in Tampa who would be happy to buy what you have to sell. I think they'd go for at least twenty-five grand."

"Twenty-five-grand. That's a nice number. What makes you think they want to spend that kind of money?"

"Because they have it. They're mid-size distributors and they are good at what they do."

"You trust them?"

"Yeah, I've never had a problem with them." The silence on the phone stretched itself out. Baumert fidgeted and wiped his brow with his shirt sleeve.

"I wouldn't mind moving some of my product. Set it up and get back to me. Same deal as before."

Frank finished tidying up the bar, getting it ready for his shift to begin. It would be his last.

* * *

After leaving Baumert's place Sam pulled out his cell phone and called the prosecutor's office for Jean Booth. It was nearly five on a Saturday afternoon, but he remembered Paul saying Jean was a workaholic. Maybe he would catch her. It was worth a shot. To his surprise, she answered.

"Ms. Booth, my name is Sam Wallace, and I'm a private investigator. I have been working with the sheriff's department on the murder of your friend and colleague Maggie Robbins, and I wonder if I might chat with you for a few minutes." Not bad, he thought except for the line about working with the sheriff's department. If that gets back to Lewis, he's dead meat.

The long hesitation was not a good sign. "What is it you want to talk with me about, Mr. Wallace?"

Her voice sounded surprisingly friendly, given the nature of his call. He remembered Paul's description of her, and pressed on, encouraged. "I know you and Maggie were close friends, and I was hoping you might be able to provide some insight into who or why someone would want to hurt Maggie. I know you must have talked with the police, but another perspective never hurts."

After some polite verbal sparring, Sam finally prevailed and they agreed to meet in a café across the street from her office. Still new to the P.I. business, Sam wasn't sure what he would accomplish, but he would give it a try. If she recognized him from the brief encounter at the Robbins the morning after the murder, no big deal. He never identified himself as a cop.

Sam had been sitting at a table in the restaurant for five minutes when Jean Booth arrived. Even though she wore jeans, the briefcase, scholarly eyeglasses and inquisitive look told him it had to be her. He got up. "Ms. Booth?"

"Yes. I don't have a lot of time, Mr. Wallace, but I'll be happy to help in whatever way I can," she said as she joined him. She showed no sign of recognizing him from their previous brief encounter. The entire morning was probably a blur to her.

Sam immediately liked her polite, gentle demeanor. "Thank you for agreeing to meet with me, Ms. Booth. I promise I won't take much of your time. I understand you and Maggie had been friends for a long time."

Her wistful smile did little to mask the sadness in her eyes. "Yes, Maggie and I were friends for twenty years and we worked together for the past eight years. In fact, it was Maggie who helped me secure the position in the prosecutor's office. Maggie was a very giving and caring person."

Interesting, Sam thought, the different perspectives he was getting on Maggie. "Did she have any enemies that you knew of?"

The waitress brought the Cokes Sam had ordered. Booth sipped hers before answering. "As you must know, the police asked me that question and I'll give you the same answer. The only negatives I can tell you would concern that man, Frank Baumert, who as you may know by now, threatened Maggie when he was sentenced. And I know she was concerned when she heard he'd been paroled."

"Did she tell you that?"

"Yes. She was frightened. And Maggie didn't frighten easily."

Sam went silent for a moment, thinking how to phrase his next question. "So, other than Baumert, Maggie got along OK with people—as far as you know?"

Sarah, frowned as if resenting the question. "Maggie got along fine with everyone. People respected her intelligence and abilities."

"How about her brother, Bryce?"

"That's a different story. Maggie and Bryce, never really got along. Actually, I shouldn't say never. I think it all began when he started to build that nightclub."

"When was that?"

She smiled. "I remember very well. It was the year my first child was born, eleven years ago I even remember the time of year. It was June."

"And what was the trouble?"

She finished her Coke and glanced at her watch. "Bryce was building a nightclub on some land he owned. The club was apparently going to feature exotic dancers. The townspeople began to raise hell and put pressure on the planning commission to stop it. Well, the commission had already given the OK, but Maggie, who opposed it on moral grounds, enlisted the aid of their dad, who had tremendous clout in this town—probably more than anyone. Their father, who agreed with Maggie, stepped in and caused roadblocks and delays that lasted for three years.

"Bryce had a lot of money tied up in the project and all the delays were killing him financially. He eventually had to give up and sell the land. He blamed a lot of people, but especially Maggie for bringing their father into the picture."

"Were there other problems between them?"

"I assume you're referring to the will."

Sam smiled and nodded. "Did you like Bryce?"

"I think that's a rhetorical question, Mr. Wallace. Let's just leave it that he was not my favorite person."

28

The conversation with Jean Booth had whet Sam's curiosity to further pursue the business about the strip joint, and to learn more about Bryce. He called the *Herald Tribune* and was told that although he couldn't himself have access to old issues of the paper, he could tell the information marketing people what he wanted, and they would provide him with what he needed.

He learned that in the month of June of the year in question there were three articles dealing with Bryce's nightclub project—one devoted to the groundbreaking ceremonies and the controversy connected with it. The other two were devoted to the increasing outcry from the community. Sam decided to start with those issues, got the dates and went to the library.

He scrolled the library's microfiche reader until he got to the pieces about Bryce's project. He began with the article and pictures of the groundbreaking ceremony, which told about the project and mentioned the controversy surrounding it.

The second article dealt with the increasing complaints about the project and included a photo of a few protesters with placards yelling at some of the laborers. Sam was about to move on when something in the photo caught his eye. One of the laborers had a distinctive tattoo on his left arm.

* * *

The next day Sam reached Bryce Hanson at his office.

"Yes, I know who you are, and yes, I do remember meeting you at my sister's house. What is it that you want?"

Sam was not looking forward to another encounter with Hanson. But business is business. "You may or may not know that

I'm a private investigator, Mr. Hanson. I've been retained by a client to help in the investigation of your sister's murder and—"

"I know that," Bryce interrupted. "Sarah Hastings has hired you and I know you've been snooping around. I thought I would hear from you."

Tight little town, Sam thought. "Well, yes as a matter of fact, I was hoping to talk with you. Can I buy you lunch today?" He wasn't sure if Hanson's long pause was a good or bad sign.

"I have a lunch appointment today, but tell you what. We're eating at Marina Jack's. Stand in front of your car at the end of the restaurant's parking lot, and I'll pick you up at two sharp. I'll be driving a black Lexus SUV." He hung up without saying goodbye.

At 1:55 Sam stood next to his car at the edge of Marina Jack's parking lot, waiting for Bryce Hanson. He thought it an odd way of meeting, but it seemed to fit what little he knew of the man.

Actually, he enjoyed the wait, looking out across the water at the boats moored in the harbor. Most were sailboats of all shapes and sizes, some looking sturdy enough to take a crew to far off lands.

Several cars drove past him, lots of Mercedes and Jaguars, Sarasota's Fords and Chevys. At a little after two a black Lexus SUV pulled up. Bryce Hanson opened the passenger's door and beckoned Sam in.

"Nice car," Hanson said, nodding toward Sam's Mercedes. "What year is it?" Before Sam could reply, Bryce looked into the mirror and checked his teeth and picked out a piece of food.

"Sixty-nine," Sam answered as Hanson drove out of the lot, turned right into another parking area that faced the bay, and stopped.

Sam studied Bryce Hanson for a moment. His face was flushed, the smell of alcohol on him probably the reason. He wore a cashmere blazer over a black silk T-shirt, and even sitting down, the cuffs of his charcoal slacks curled over a pair of black loafers in need of a shine. Sam wasn't sure what image Hanson was trying to create. If he was trying to look cool, he didn't, particularly with his ill-fitting toupee. He wondered if Hanson knew how obvious it was.

"We can talk here, and the view's not bad." Bryce said, opening the windows. A soft sea breeze drifted through the vehicle, bringing with it the smell of marine life. Sam welcomed it as an improvement over the alcohol and Hanson's cologne.

"What's on your mind, Mr. Wallace?" Hanson asked in a tone that implied he was a very busy man.

Sam shifted in his seat to face Hanson. "Well, the reason Sarah hired me is—"

"Is because the cops think she did it, and she wants to use you to divert their attention elsewhere," Hanson interrupted. "Tell me something I don't know, sir."

Sam was prepared not to like the guy, and Hanson was making it easy. "I wouldn't put it quite that way, but in any event I have been talking with people who knew or," he nodded toward Bryce, "were connected to Maggie in some way."

"Like a husband and brother?"

"Right. No point in beating around the bush, since you don't. I know that you and Maggie had some trouble over your father's will, and to be blunt, some people are saying that her death was rather timely for you. I'm sure you know this and know why the conjecture is out there."

Hanson closed the windows and turned off the motor. He took his time lighting a cigarette, filling the car with smoke. "You are a busy body, aren't you?" he said. "Sure, I'm aware of the conjecture. Is that why you wanted to see me? To tell me something again that I already know?"

Sam tried to ignore the smoke, not wanting to give Hanson the satisfaction of seeing it bother him. "I understand that your sister was working on having your appeal of the will overturned, in which case you would have lost the piece of land on which your resort is to be built. And I also know that she and others were fighting your efforts to build your fancy resort."

Hanson started to reply, but it was Sam's turn to interrupt. "Nice car you have, by the way."

Bryce gave him a puzzled look.

"The police found tire tracks at Maggie's house, the kind found on SUV's." He glanced down at Hanson's shoes. "They also found size ten shoe prints. Your size."

Bryce looked down at his shoes. "What do you do, go around measuring people's feet?"

"No, I don't have to." He didn't know Hanson's shoe size, but they looked about right. Anyway, it was worth taking a shot, and Hanson didn't deny it.

Bryce pulled his head back and studied Sam, as if trying to figure him out.

Sam noticed it and burrowed in.

"Mr. Hanson, nobody had a stronger motive to see your sister dead than you. That valuable piece of property is about as potent a motive for murder there is. Couple that with the fact that it's common knowledge you disliked your sister and vice-versa, I'd say the police have good reason to have you in their sights."

Whatever Sam had hoped to provoke from Hanson didn't work. The only reaction Bryce gave him was a smirk.

"If you're going to play good cop–bad cop, you forgot to bring the good one. Oh, but you're not a cop, you're just a two-bit private detective." He snickered. "Big fucking deal."

"Why did you agree to see me?"

Hanson took a final deep puff on the cigarette and blew the smoke straight at Sam. He dropped the butt in the ashtray, where it continued to burn. Sam eyed the smoke trailing from the ashtray, which smelled even more toxic. That's why the son-of-a-bitch wanted to talk in his car.

"I was curious. I've been hearing about you, and I've wondered about your taking on Sarah Hastings as a client. You really don't have to look beyond your client to find my sister's killer. You know, I'm sure, that Hastings is bisexual, and had an affair with my sister."

Sam hoped Hanson hadn't noticed the look of surprise on his face. Stunned, though he was, he chose to ignore the comment. He would deal with it later. "I suppose you have a good alibi as to where you were the night your sister was killed." He paused and gave Hanson a Jack Nicholson smile. "Because if you don't, I'm going to make you my pet project—you know the old expression, be all over you like a bad smell."

Hanson's smirk faded. Something about the expression that crossed his face, his eyes cold and remote, told Sam the man sitting next to him was capable of murder. It wasn't anything he could put into words, but it was there.

"I don't have to tell you a fucking thing about my alibi." Hanson said in a hoarse whisper. "I'm an important man in this town, and if I were you I wouldn't tangle with me. Now get out of my car."

It was Sam's turn to snicker, as Hanson's cool façade collapsed. "Gee, I thought we were just starting to have fun. How about a ride back to my car and we can talk about your friend, Frank Baumert."

Hanson's expression changed. In that moment it changed several times, starting with surprise and ending with confusion. "What the hell are you talking about?"

"I'm talking about the Frank Baumert who threatened your sister after he was sentenced years ago, the Frank Baumert who worked for you on your ill-fated nightclub deal. Have you seen Mr. Baumert lately?"

Hanson's eyes burned with rage. "Get out!" he roared.

Sam watched the veins in Hanson's neck throbbing, his face contorted. He'd seen enough. He reached for the door, and turned. "Oh, by the way, you ought to give up smoking. It's bad for your health. Also, nice car like this, you should keep your ashtrays clean. Here, I'll empty it for you." He reached over, took out the ashtray, and dropped it out the window. "See you, Bryce. I'll keep in touch."

Walking back to his car, Sam thought about what he'd accomplished with Bryce Hanson. Funny, how Hanson made no effort to ask what he was talking about when he mentioned Baumert. Just got mad. The business about Sarah's affair with Maggie was a bombshell. Hastings forgot to mention that to him. What else hasn't she told him? All in all, he did feel like he'd managed his primary goal, which was to get to know something—anything—about Hanson. In that, he felt he succeeded. He also knew he had made what could be, a dangerous enemy.

But at the moment, more than anything else, he needed to talk to Sarah Hastings.

29

"Sam, it's good to hear from you," Sarah Hastings said. "What have you got for me?"

Sam bit his upper lip, trying to control his anger. "Sarah, I'm across the street in the park at Marina Jack's and I would like to come over and talk with you."

He waited through a brief silence before she replied. "Sure, Sam. Come on over."

Five minutes later Sarah opened the door to greet him. Her appearance hadn't improved much since he last saw her. She was dressed in a pastel warm-up suit and had alcohol on her breath. "Come on in, Sam. I've been waiting to hear from you."

Sam walked past her into the living room without saying hello and turned to face her. "Why didn't you tell me you were having an affair with Maggie Robbins. What else haven't you told me?" He opened his wallet and took out the retainer check she had given him. "You tell me the truth and all the truth now or you can have this check back. I must not have cashed it yet for a reason."

Sarah's face fell, and her eyes clouded. She walked over to the portable bar and poured herself a drink of whiskey. She stood with her back to him for a moment, straightened, and turned. "Who have you been talking with, Sam?"

"Never mind who I've been talking with. I've talked with a lot of people. Now I'm talking with you, Sarah, and I want the truth."

Sarah downed the whiskey, set the glass on the bar, and beckoned Sam to the sofa. "Sit down, Sam."

Sam eyed her as he might a cobra slithering along the rug. "I'll sit when you're ready to talk the truth."

"Please. Sit down Sam" she repeated. "I came to you for help, and I abused your trust. Let me redeem myself."

Sam, still glowering, sat on the sofa. "I'm listening."

Sarah looked him in the eye and began. "Maggie and I had a romantic relationship," she said. "It had been going on for six months. Paul found out about it and was furious."

"Was that the reason why Paul's company is no longer your client?"

She lowered her eyes. "Yes."

"When did you and Maggie . . . break up?"

"Just a week ago. Our relationship became strained, and eventually we ended it."

"Who broke it off? Was it mutual?"

Sarah's head drooped toward the floor and she fell silent again.

"Sarah, look. You came to me obviously believing I can help you. I can and I will, but you have to stop these evasive answers and lies, and truthfully tell me everything exactly as it happened. Otherwise, you're just wasting both our time."

She lifted her head and looked straight at him again. "Maggie broke it off. Paul was getting nasty. I don't think she loved him, but she wanted to keep the marriage together."

"What made you think she didn't love him?"

Sarah hesitated and shrugged. "I . . . I just didn't think she did."

"Did she love you?"

Sarah hesitated again. "I don't know." She closed her eyes and began to sob.

"Did you love her?"

She walked to the window looked across the water for a long time before answering. "I liked being with her, being intimate with her." Her voice trailed off, and she closed her eyes.

When she opened her eyes some of the tension seemed to have drained and her body relaxed. Sam felt she'd gotten through the most difficult part. Having got that off her chest, he hoped she would feel more comfortable with him. "OK, now how does all this tie in with CAPPS and your and Maggie's involvement in it?"

"When Maggie and I broke up it was not easy for either of us. We both said some things we shouldn't have, and Maggie said she couldn't work with me any longer in our CAPPS activities."

Sam waited but she appeared to be finished. "Sarah, you told me that your group had raised lots of money for you to buy properties and outbid the developers. And Maggie was a significant source of your money, right?"

Sarah nodded. "Yes."

Sam decided to take a wild stab. "And because of that, given her nature, she was trying to take over leadership of CAPPS."

Sarah's face crumbled. Sam watched her reaction and knew he'd hit a mother lode. "So you two were having a power struggle, and that's what you were overheard arguing about?" he said softly.

Sarah looked up sharply. "Who—"

Sam held up his hand, signaling her that he didn't want to pursue her question.

Sarah began to sob. She walked to a chair across from Sam and sat. Sam waited while she dabbed at her eyes and nose, stopped crying, and sat up. "Let's just say we had disagreements, Sam. But for God's sake, I did not kill Maggie." And then she burst into tears again and whispered, "I loved her!"

Silence filled the room as neither said a word. Sam watched her sobbing, shoulders heaving, waiting for her to let it all out. She pulled herself together and he walked over and took her hand. "Is there anything else you want to tell me, Sarah?"

She looked at him, studying his face, trying to read him. "Yes," she whispered. "There is one more thing."

He waited. "Yes?"

"I did drive over to Maggie's house the night she was killed."

30

"Good God, Sarah. What else haven't you told me?"

She dropped her eyes and he took her by the shoulders and gently raised her to her feet. They stood eye to eye. "Sarah, did you have anything to do with Maggie's death?"

She blinked and replied in a calm, measured voice. "Sam, as God is my judge, I had absolutely nothing whatsoever to do with Maggie's death."

Sam wanted to believe her. "And?"

She began pacing and speaking in a clear voice. "I hadn't seen nor heard from Maggie in a week. When she didn't return my calls, I swallowed my pride and drove over to her house. The house was dark when I got there, so I turned around and left."

"The police say there was a light on in the kitchen."

"That's in the back of the house. From where I sat, the house was in darkness."

"What time was this, Sarah?"

She nodded like she knew the question was coming. "Somewhere around 9:30 or so."

"That's roughly the time frame the police say Maggie was killed, give or take an hour or two."

She spun around and glared at Sam. "Goddamn it! Whose side are you on?"

Sam stood facing Sarah fighting off the sadness he felt, seeing that beautiful face contorted in anguish. He had to remind himself that Sarah Hastings might well be guilty of murder. He motioned her to sit. "Sarah, since I have agreed to work for you, I'm on your side—until and unless I find reason to believe I shouldn't be. Does that answer your question?"

Her breathing returned to normal and her face softened. "Yes, it does, Sam. And I'm sorry I blew up. I'm just under terrible pressure, not only from the police, but with the vote coming up at the planning commission soon and the negative PR I'll be getting from the press."

Sam felt very tired all of a sudden. Maybe he was tired of Sarah Hastings. All he wanted now was to leave and go home. It had been a long couple of days. "Sarah, if you have nothing else to tell me, I'm going to leave. Do we have it all out in the open now?"

She smiled, walked over to him and put out her hand. "Yes, we do, Sam, and thanks."

All the way home Sam replayed his conversations with Bryce and Sarah. Bryce was a heinous person, and he didn't know what to make of Sarah anymore. She was a spurned lover, on top of which she was involved in a power struggle with her former lover. He thought about Sarah's expression when she blew up at him. She's a volatile lady. No telling what she was capable of if she was angry enough. Still, it's all circumstantial. So far.

* * *

When Sam arrived home he checked his messages. Still nothing from Jennifer.

He was about to strip and take a shower when a car's horn tooted a musical jingle. It could only be one person. He went outside to greet Jimbo, who was having difficulty trying to climb out of what looked like an early sixties Jaguar XKE convertible.

"Jimbo, what's a big fella like you doing in that little tiny car?"

Jimbo had one leg out and a hand on the side of the car for leverage to drag out the other leg. He was stuck.

"Gimmee a hand, Sam and don't give me any cheap shit."

Sam grabbed Jimbo's hand and tugged. The big guy lurched forward and he was out.

Sam smiled at his friend. "Jimbo, why don't you hire someone to ride with you and haul you out when you need it?"

"Naw, I just got a little stuck there. No big deal." He grabbed Sam and gave him a bear hug. "How ya doin', buddy?"

Sam massaged his ribs. "I think I'm OK. Come on in."

Jimbo joined him on the porch and surprised Sam by not asking for a beer. "So, what's up with you, Sam?"

Sam smiled. "I've got my first client."

"Hey, you devil, you. Anybody I know?"

Sam hesitated. "I think I'd better pass on that, Jimbo, for now."

"Oh, I get it, private eye–client confidentiality, right?"

"Couldn't have said it better, myself. Jimbo, did you ever know a guy named Frank Baumert?"

Jimbo thought for a moment and shook his head. "Doesn't ring a bell."

"He's the guy who got sent up ten years ago for second degree murder. Maggie Robbins was his lawyer and people say Baumert threatened her when he got convicted."

Jimbo nodded. "Yeah, sure, I remember him now. I didn't know him though."

"You remember the night club project Bryce Hanson was working on eleven years ago?"

Jimbo nodded and laughed. "I sure do. The poor bastard got bushwhacked by his sister and his old man. Mostly blamed her, 'cause he didn't want to tangle with old Billy Hanson. Don't blame him. Neither would I."

"Well, I was shown microfiche of newspaper coverage back

then and there's a picture of some workers at the site. One of them is Frank Baumert."

"How'd you know it was him?"

Sam told him about the coral snake tattoo. "It was clearly him."

Jimbo shrugged. "Yeah, well I don't see why that's any big deal. Now that I think of it, he was one of them day laborers who would sign on for a job for a while. He probably worked on one of my jobs. So, he worked for Bryce. So what?"

"Nothing, I guess, but I find it a little curious that the guy who threatened to kill Maggie once worked for her brother."

"Yeah, I see what you mean."

"Jimbo, you're a developer," Sam said. "What's your take on all this CAPPS' business?"

"Haw," Jimbo erupted, like Sam had hit a nerve. "They can be a royal pain in the ass, but to be fair, they also do a lot of good."

"Yes, I gather that." Sam said.

"But you also have to look at it from both sides of the coin," Jimbo said, shifting in his chair. "Everybody likes open space and parks. But if there's too much, a city can lose its tax base, retailers can go under—lots of bad things can happen. Taxes can go up for people already living in the area. You know what I mean, Sam. Everything in city planning has to have balance."

"So you don't approve of CAPPS."

Jimbo raised both hands. "Nooo, I didn't say that. Like I just said, they do a lot of good, especially against some of our more thoughtless—or should I say greedy developers. But, you know, like any strong advocacy group, they attract some fanatics, and that's not so good. Anyway, I gotta get goin'. Just wanted to check in on you, make sure you're still alive and kickin'. How's Jennifer?"

"I don't know. I haven't seen her in a few days. She's been off on the Galt research boat tracking red tide."

"Well, you better keep trackin' her. She's a keeper. I gotta go see some doctors in Venice who want me to build a new medical complex for 'em. Gotta run."

Sam walked him to the XKE. "You want me to help you into your little car?"

"Hey Sam, nobody likes a wise ass. See ya." With a toot of his horn and a wave, he drove away.

Jimbo's comments about Jennifer came back to him. "She's a keeper." A little male chauvinism there. Not exactly how he would put it, but he agreed and dialed her number.

"Sam, I was just about to call you," she said. "What's the latest? Fill me in."

"Hey, slow down. First tell me about your trip."

"Oh, it was interesting. And tiring. We spent four days on the boat tracking red tide. You'll be pleased to know that the strain we've been following is moving westerly and won't be going anywhere near the Gulf Coast." She lowered her voice. "Missed you."

He liked the way she said it and toyed with the idea of hopping in his car. He could be at her house in twenty minutes.

She read his mind. "I'm totally exhausted, Sam. I'm already in my nightgown and going right to bed."

He pictured her in her nightgown. "Come on, Jennifer. It's not even dark out yet."

"I'm too tired, Sam. I wouldn't be very good company. But I'm taking tomorrow off. How about if I come to your place and we go to the beach? Have a picnic."

"Terrific idea. I can use a break myself. See you around ten, eleven?"

"Between ten and eleven. I've got some stuff in the fridge. I'll make the lunch."

Sam hung up, thinking about his conversation with Jimbo, not surprised that Jimbo would take a balanced view. And his comment about fanatics. Interesting. And tomorrow, a day off with Jennifer.

31

Larry Gump looked out the window of his double-wide at his fishing skiff sitting on its trailer. He'd had that little baby for going on ten years now. And he bought it used then. It had been a good boat at one time, but it was a piece of shit now. The 25-horse engine was on its last legs. No sense trying to fix it up anymore. It's shot. He was lucky to get back home last couple times he used it. But Larry wasn't gonna have to worry about beat up pieces of shit no more. No sir.

His ma always talked about when her ship comes in. But her ship never came in, and she died without two nickels to rub together.

Larry smiled and flicked open another Bud. Larry's ship was about to come in. He always knew it would. Just a matter of time, finding the right deal. Yes sir. No more lining up for day jobs at that fucking Labor Ready. No more fishing out of beat up boats with worn out motors.

Larry had made his contact and it was only a matter of time now. Cool as a cucumber he picked up that phone and made his call. Just put it right to the person driving that night. No beating around the bush. No bullshit.

"I saw you pull up in the yard, get out, go around back, come out twenty minutes later, and drive away," Larry said. "Since I was smart enough to get your license number, wasn't hard from there to get your name and everything else I needed. Just so's you know who you're dealin' with here." He sure would have liked to have seen the look on the killer's face about then.

Larry laid out nice and clear just what it was he wanted to keep quiet. Papers say there was jewelry stolen and some money. Larry wasn't going to be piggish. Twenty grand is all he wanted. Might even take some jewelry. Hell, Larry wasn't a hard man to deal with, but he could be tough if he had to—anybody tries to fuck with him.

Then came the stalling, which Larry expected. Need some time. Give me a few days. Call back in a week and we'll work it out.

"Bullshit," Larry says. "I'll call you tomorrow at six o'clock. And that's when we set up a spot to make the deal. That'll be the last call I make. We take care of arrangements then, or I go to the cops."

Larry had it all figured out. They would meet at a public place so there wouldn't be no monkey business. He knew how to cover his ass. If it didn't work out, he'd turn in that killer real quick. Cops ask why he waited so long, he'd say he was afraid. Then, just decided he couldn't be a coward no more. It was the right thing to come forward.

32

At 10:30, Jennifer's Jeep, with the top rolled back, pulled up to Sam's cottage. He watched her climb out looking freshly scrubbed with her hair back in a ponytail, wearing a white Galt T-shirt and khaki Bermudas. Her long legs covered the distance from the car to the house in four strides. He was on the porch waiting for her with his arms out. She took the cue and leaned into him.

"Hmm, you smell good," he said and kissed her. When she responded his first impulse was to bag the beach and spend the day making love to her.

"Sam, I've been looking forward to this for days—just sprawling on the beach with you, reading, relaxing, munching. Come on. You ready?"

He shrugged. "Yeah. Come in while I get my stuff. Henry wants to say hello."

Henry circled Jennifer's legs and barked. She picked him up and hugged him. "Henry, give me a kiss."

Henry obliged, she hugged him again and put him down. He remained at her feet, looking up at her.

"He's not going to be happy," Sam said. "We're going to Siesta Beach. No dogs allowed there, Henry. Guard the fort. See you later."

Henry sulked off to a corner, flattened his face, and watched them leave.

The beach was crowded, giving it the festive atmosphere Sam liked. He still marveled at the quality of the sand, which nearly every year was rated best in the country a fact he liked to brag about to his friends up North. He had been to many beaches, but none could compare with the flour-like sands of Siesta Beach.

They found a spot to settle in, and when Jennifer peeled off her shorts and T-shirt down to her bikini, Sam noticed three guys in their twenties, ogling her. All three sat up with their eyes riveted on her, while she stood applying sun block.

He wondered if she was aware of them watching her. Women seem to have eyes in the back of their heads when it comes to that sort of thing. Some like it, some don't, but his bet was that most of them dread the day they stop looking. When Jennifer sat down, Sam said, "Those three guys over there watched your every move."

She grinned and winked. "I know."

He stretched out on a chaise and watched her rummage through her beach bag, hauling out her ever present water bottle, coffee thermos, a bag of bagels, two newspapers, her cell phone, a copy of Sam's current book, and a small radio with head phones. And the bag still bulged.

"Jennifer, guess what?"

She stopped rummaging and turned. "What?"

"I have a client."

"Sam! Congratulations, Tracy." She hugged him and began firing questions at him.

He filled her in on everything.

"The thing about Sarah and Maggie is a shocker. Do you think she could have killed Maggie?"

"I dunno, but let's enjoy the beach for now."

They shared the coffee and bagels and settled into a comfortable quiet zone. Sam worked his way through the local newspaper while Jennifer read his current book.

The paper gushed with reports of all the local "celebs" on the party circuit. He turned to the Sports section filled with the latest in stock car racing, with the rest of it devoted to Florida's beloved Gators and Noles, though far less than during football season. The headlines of football games totally confused him. The writers never referred to the name of the college or high school. It was always "Bulldogs crush Razorbacks" or "Hogs defeat Bulls." His favorite, "Rattlers bite Dawgs." Happily, football season was over, and the headlines were a little less strident.

Later, he glanced at Jennifer. The novel lay on her chest, and she was asleep. He hoped it was the sun, not the book that put her out.

She rolled over and opened her eyes. "I fell asleep. What time is it?"

"Twelve-thirty." He pointed to his book. "Better than sleeping pills."

She struggled to sit up and hauled her beach bag to her side. "You want some lunch?"

"Sure."

They ate, keeping a wary eye on the predatory gulls surrounding them. Sam got up and shooed the gulls away. On his way back to the blanket a gull swooped down and grabbed what was left of Sam's sandwich and flew away. Sam stood, dumbfounded while Jennifer fell on her back, convulsed with laughter.

"Very funny," he said, rejoining her. "Hey, what else can you tell me about the turtles?" he asked, figuring that would stop her laughing jag if anything would.

She sat up. "Well, they're wonderfully interesting, and it's a shame they're on their way toward facing possible extinction. Four of the five species, the Green Turtles, Leatherbacks—which, by the way, grow to between 650 and 1300 pounds—Hawksbills, and the Flatbacks are federally listed as endangered, while the fifth, the Loggerheads are on the threatened list."

"Are they the little tiny ones?"

"No, not at all. They can grow up to 350 pounds. Florida is the most productive nesting ground for Loggerheads in the world. Twenty to 25,000 nest on our beaches every year. That's the good news. The bad news is that 1800 sea turtles, mostly Loggerheads and Green Turtles, were stranded in Florida last year."

"That doesn't seem like a high number when you consider that 25,000 nest here every year."

Jennifer stopped and shook her head. "Sam, only one in a thousand hatchlings survive to adulthood. I think I told you the other day that humans are the greatest cause of their high mortality rate. And anyway, the figure of 1800 stranded represent only the ones reported. Scientists believe the true total could be ten times that many."

Sam went quiet for a moment, admiring Jennifer's intensity.

"If you really care, you could join the Sea Turtles Protection League. They have a variety of ways that people can help," Jennifer said. She turned to him and smiled. "I realize that's not for everyone. Sea turtle survival is not high on the average person's list of priorities. But anyway, FYI."

Sam nodded, but said nothing.

Jennifer squeezed his hand, tickled the palm of his hand, and giggled. He recognized the move as one the boys would make with girls in high school—a not too subtle sexual overture. He turned to Jennifer who winked and nodded. It was enough for Sam.

"Hmm, what do you say we head back?"

She grinned. "Sounds good to me. Let's go."

A stiff breeze had come up and the sky clouded over. The once crowded beach was rapidly emptying as people scrambled to pick up their things and head for the parking lot.

Although he hated to see their day spoiled by rain, Sam was intrigued by the many shades of gray Florida clouds displayed. He had always thought gray is gray, period. Not so in Florida, where the endless textures of gray and black intermingle to create an ominous pall over everything—a phenomenon he found surprisingly appealing. They stowed their gear and left, driving home in the open Jeep, laughing all the way in the rain.

When they pulled up to the cottage, Henry was sitting in the window keeping vigil. He spotted Sam and Jennifer, leaped up, and disappeared.

"Oh, oh," Sam said. "I think he fell off his chair."

After a quick reunion with Henry, Sam put his arms around Jennifer. She grinned and moved into him. He took her in his arms and kissed her. She responded. "Hmm, you are ready, aren't you?" Sam whispered.

Her hand slid under his bathing suit and she grinned. "So are you."

They staggered into the bedroom. Henry sat on the bed, staring at them, but quickly sensed he was not wanted and scurried out of the room. Sam closed the door.

33

In the morning Sam woke to the smell of coffee. He pulled on a pair of shorts and found Jennifer on the porch eating a bagel and drinking coffee.

She turned with a smile that promised another day like yesterday. "Hello sleepy-head. Get some coffee and come on out."

He stood in the doorway scratching himself, peering at her through eyes still clouded with sleep. "Look at you," he said shaking his head. "Nobody has a right to look that good so early in the morning."

"First of all, it takes work—lots of it. Secondly, it's not that early in the morning. It's eight o'clock, and I have to go to work. So get your coffee and come on out."

He'd forgotten that somewhere during the night she told him she had to go to work today. He went outside and sat on the railing. "You can't go to work today, Jen. It's a gorgeous day."

"Sam—"

He held up his hand and broke in. "And I have great plans for us. First, we're going to have more coffee, then I'm going to make us a spectacular breakfast, then we're going to make love all day. So, you can't go to work."

She got up and slid her arms around his neck. "Sam, that sounds wonderful. And yesterday and last night were wonderful. But I told you last night I have to go in today. I've been gone for four days, and then yesterday I just said the hell with it, and took the day off because I've missed you and wanted to spend the day with you. Now I've got to pay the piper. I'm way behind, and I promised the director I would come in and go over the results of our research with him for his presentation to the board next week." She held his face in her hands and kissed him. "It's a done deal, Sam."

He nodded and smiled. "I understand. Go ahead. I'll take a cold shower and watch *Mr. Rogers* re-runs."

They kissed again, this time a real one, and he responded with an urgent passion. She felt it and backed off.

"Uh, uh. This girl's gotta go to work." She nodded toward his crotch. "That's trouble."

"That's desire," he said. "But anyway, you want to go to a movie tonight?"

She lowered her eyes and took a deep breath the way people do when they're about to say something they wish they didn't have to. Sam spotted it and braced himself.

"I can't, Sam. Today is a colleague's birthday, and I promised him I'd have dinner with him tonight after work."

Sam started to say something, but she talked over him. "Sam, my colleague—his name is Patrick Connolly—asked me a month ago and I said yes. I didn't realize it would be right after I got back."

Sam shrugged. "Hey, it's OK. No big deal. I know he works in the same field as you and—"

"Yes, Sam, he does. And yes, he was on the boat along with eleven other scientists and crew. He's a colleague and an old friend. And you're right, it's no big deal."

He suppressed a smile and walked her to her Jeep. She was getting a little aggressive about it, reaffirming the cliché about redheads. But hey, it was her feistiness and independence that were among the things he liked about her.

At the same time as he stood thinking all of this, watching her green eyes sparkling in the sunlight, he felt a twinge of resentment for the prick and his birthday. He grinned and said, "Save me some birthday cake."

They kissed again and she drove away.

* * *

After Jennifer left, Henry stayed close to Sam. He seemed to have a sixth sense about Sam's moods, and if he sensed something troubling Sam, he stayed near him, doling out extra dollops of affection, licking his hand, nuzzling next to him, and hopping onto his lap.

Sam decided to enjoy the gorgeous weather by taking a drive in the convertible before settling into any serious work. He and Henry hopped into the car, drove through the village and headed for the South Key. Sam was decked out in his new Panama hat replacing the one floating in the bay, and Henry was perched erect in the passenger seat, head swiveling about, surveying the landscape like he owned it.

They drove past the string of condos on either side of the road. The high rent district was on the right facing the Gulf, while those on the left faced the bay. Most of them were soulless piles of concrete with little to commend them but their proximity to the water. Built in the sixties, seventies, and eighties, they showed their age.

They reached the Stickney Point Bridge, which would take them off the Key onto the Tamiami Trail, a euphemism for crowded Route 41, and Sam decided to keep going straight and stay on the Key.

The ambiance abruptly changed. Elegant, newly built mansions looming behind gated walls, manicured shrubbery and stately palms, sat at the bay's edge. Sam had entered a different world with none of the bustling traffic, typical of this time of year in Sarasota—a world of tropical serenity.

He realized he was only a mile or so from the Robbins' place and decided to drop in and see if Paul was home, maybe have some coffee with him. Turning into the Robbins' long curving drive, he wound his way toward the house. As he was about to round the corner and head into the yard, he hit the brakes hard and stopped.

34

Through a large mass of schefflera, which hid his car from view, Sam saw an attractive blonde emerge from the house and walk to a red sports car. Paul walked along with her, holding her hand, and when they reached the car, they embraced and kissed, Paul's hands moving up and down her body.

Feeling like the Peeping Tom that he was, Sam watched while they engaged in some more heavy petting before she got into the car. Sam turned his car around and left.

Heading back toward the village, he felt a combination of disillusionment and anger. The grieving husband seems to have recovered nicely. He knew who the woman was, having seen her several times at the tennis club. Hard to miss her. She was a knockout. Paul has good taste in his choice of playmates. Suddenly he saw Paul in a different light. Hard to take a positive view of a guy kissing a beautiful woman who probably just spent the night with him in his home, with the body of his murdered wife still warm.

He reached the cottage, went inside and checked his messages. There were none. He thought of Jimbo's comment about Paul being a ladies' man. But what he saw this morning was more than a harmless flirtation. He doubted the woman was just an idle pick-up. He had seen him talking with her a couple of times at the tennis club but thought nothing of it. They'd probably had something going for a while.

"How many others are there?" He said aloud. Henry's head swiveled around as if looking to see who Sam was talking to.

He took Henry for a walk to think about it. Henry growled and barked at a strange dog wandering the street. The dog barked back and Henry scurried behind Sam, where he remained until the other dog disappeared around the corner. They reached Dog Beach where Sam sat under his new Panama hat, while Henry streaked across the sand, chasing nothing.

Sam continued to focus on Robbins. He's obviously a jerk, and not the nice guy Sam thought. But that doesn't make him a murderer. He would have to get Diane's take on him.

And what was it Sarah Hastings said? "Maggie didn't love him, but she wanted to keep him in the marriage." Could Paul have been angry enough with his wife's affair with Sarah to kill her? And depending on what her will revealed, money might very well be a major factor.

Just as he didn't want to believe Sarah was a killer, he hated to think that Paul could be. And anyway, he was in Miami when Maggie was killed. Doesn't seem to be any doubt about that. But he could have hired somebody to kill her.

And Baumert. No alibi and not much effort at trying to create one. If he did it, you'd think he would have made it his business to know exactly what was playing on TV that night and be certain of what he was watching, even if he couldn't tell the cops much about it. He said he'd been drinking. Then again, maybe he's just that dumb. He's a nasty guy. And the shells in his tires. No shells in either his yard or the bar's parking lot. Did the cops pick up on the shells?

Henry nudged Sam's hat off his face, letting him know he was ready to go. Sam got up. "OK, Henry. Let's go home."

* * *

Sam reviewed his notes on the Robbins' case and worked on his book for the rest of the day. He was beginning to feel the strain of balancing his writing with the private eye thing. Maybe he had taken on too much. Hell, he came down here to relax and write.

But he knew himself well and knew that he thrived on pressure. It's just the way he was built.

The day flew by and it was six o'clock when he finally shut down the computer. After a shower and shave he hopped in his car and headed toward downtown past Fred's restaurant in the upscale Southside Village neighborhood. The restaurant's outside tables were filled with Sarasota's young professionals, all decked out in the latest *GQ* and *Vogue* fashions, the men wearing their brightly colored suspenders over the obligatory striped shirts, the women in their tight body hugging lycra dresses, all looking nicely homogenous.

His mind circled back to Maggie's murder, and he wondered where the cops stood on it. He was dying to talk with Diane about Bryce and Frank Baumert, but she would have left the office by now, and no way was he going to call her at home.

Downtown, he swung by Burns Court, the small art movie theatre, located on a narrow side street lined with cottages not unlike his own. The distinctive purple building nestled under a large tree next to a Victorian styled café. He was shocked to see a portion of this charming, quaint neighborhood leveled. A sign stood on the ground announcing a new mid-rise condominium project, "Starting in the Low $800's."

After discovering he was out of sync with the movies' starting times he drove a couple of blocks to Florida Studio Theatre, whose stage productions he'd heard were uniformly good. FST, as the locals called it, was housed in an historic old building that the community had preserved.

He got lucky, spotted a parking space and went into the lobby to pick up a brochure listing the theater's schedule. Still feeling at loose ends, he walked the one block to Sarasota News and Books where he ordered a cappuccino and sat down to read the brochure.

He glanced outside in time to see Jennifer and the birthday boy stroll by. Her arm was locked into his. And they were both laughing.

When they passed out of sight he sauntered to the front of the store, and watched them turn into the restaurant next door, the one he'd planned to take her to. But hey, like they said, no big deal.

He headed back to his car and decided to take a little spin since it was such a beautiful evening. After cruising by the Hollywood Twenty theater he thought about taking in a movie, but passed the parking garage before making up his mind. Still looking for a place to park, he spotted Diane Lewis coming out of her building. Seven o'clock. This is one dedicated cop. He pulled over to the curb just as she was about to cross. "Hello there."

35

Lewis stepped back and glared at him, not recognizing him at first. At least that's what he hoped caused the nasty look.

And then the glimmer of recognition. Her cop's eye swept across the car. "Well, you do travel in style, Sam. What are you doing here?"

It was his turn to appraise her. She wore a tan sweater that looked a half-size too small, and tan pants that rolled with her hips when she moved. She had that tired look he'd seen before, which gave her a sultry earthiness—an observation best kept to himself.

"I was just driving by debating whether to get a bite to eat or go to a movie. What are you doing working so late?"

She rolled her eyes, like what do you think I'm doing? "It's been a long day, Sam. I'm going home and get some sleep."

"Have you had anything to eat?"

She shot him a sideways look, knowing where he was coming from. "No."

"Well, I just made up my mind. I'm going down the street to the Thai restaurant and have some pad thai." He winked. "Are you hungry?"

She ignored his question and turned, ready to leave.

"Hey, I remember you telling me once how much you love Thai food. How about joining me?"

She started to protest, but he interrupted her. "Come on, Diane. If I know you, you haven't eaten all day. You can't go to bed hungry and you're going to be too tired to prepare anything. Makes good sense to me." He gestured toward the front seat and nodded.

She hesitated.

Mulling over his offer? He thought he'd made a pretty persuasive case.

"Where's your biologist friend?" she asked, uncoplike.

"My biologist friend has a date tonight," he said, trying to sound cavalier.

She hovered at the curb, a half smile on her face. Sam wondered if the expression meant tough shit for you, Sam.

Before he could say anything she opened the door. "OK, I am hungry, and the Thai food did it. Let's go."

The restaurant was dimly lit inside, rather than sitting at a table in the middle of the dining room, they settled into a booth and ordered Thai beers. While waiting for the drinks, Diane excused herself and went to the ladies room. When she returned, she wore a light coat of lipstick and smelled of something fragrant and sexy.

They drank their beer in silence, each waiting for the other to open the conversation. Sam wanted to talk about the Robbins' case, but knowing Lewis, thought it best to be cool for a while. "Where do you live, Diane?"

She sipped her beer before answering. "I live in the Hyde Park Condominiums."

"Yes, I know it. Nice place."

She nodded and drank more beer.

"It's funny, Diane, but you know a lot about me. Being the good cop that you are you made it your business to check up on me when I started butting into your last murder case and I told you I was once a cop in Boston. Right?"

She nodded.

"But I know nothing about you. How long have you been in Sarasota?"

She took another hit on her beer. "I was born here, Sam. Grew up in Newtown." She paused. "That's the black section of town."

"I know."

"Anyway, I went to Florida State, got a degree in Criminal Justice, and started with the County Sheriff's Department as a patrol officer. I worked my way up because I was smart, tough, and had a large pair of balls."

Sam smiled. "Why do you women have to use our anatomy to describe your toughness?"

She laughed, a hearty, relaxed sound. "Touché," she said, hoisting her beer.

"Ever been married?"

"Once. Divorced after five years. I've been single now for eight."

The waiter arrived and asked if they were ready to order. "I'm in no hurry," Sam said. "You want another beer?"

Diane checked her watch and hesitated. She looked at Sam and shrugged. "Sure, why not?"

They were well into the second beer when they ordered, both going for the shrimp pad thai. When their entrees arrived they ordered two more beers.

Sam got a kick out of watching her eat and drink. She charged into both with a gusto, wolfing down the food, licking her fingers, and quaffing the beer in long, satisfying gulps. Very sensuous, like in the old movie *Tom Jones* where they managed to make the great eating scene into the sexiest one in the movie.

The more Diane ate and drank, the more she loosened up and their conversation flowed. They had been chatting easily for half an hour when Sam decided to take a shot at the Robbins' case. "Anything new on Maggie Robbins?"

Diane stopped chewing and set her fork down. She patted her mouth with her napkin, taking her time, studying Sam.

He squirmed and gave her a little half smile.

She replaced the napkin on her lap and shook her head. "Sam, you are so transparent. You ply me with food and alcohol, soften me up with small talk, and then zero in on the real purpose of inviting me here."

"That's not true, Diane. I invited you here, because I thought it would be an opportunity to get to know you a little better." He grinned. "And anyway, I hate to eat alone."

She started to say something but he continued.

"I tried to call you, but they said you were out of town. I think I have something for you." He told her what he knew about Bryce and the nightclub deal and the animosity between him and Maggie.

She rolled her eyes. "We know about that, Sam. And by the way, since we're now talking about the Robbins' case, I hear that Sarah Hastings has hired you."

Sam took a quick pull on his beer. "Uh, yes, she has."

"Well, since Hastings is on our suspect list, I don't think I should be discussing this case with you anymore."

"Come on, Diane. She didn't hire me as her lawyer. Since she strongly denies that she had anything to do with Robbins' murder, she hired me to help find the real killer. Said she was very impressed with my role in solving the murders several months ago. Now I have even more incentive to help you, right?"

Lewis lowered her eyes and slowly shook her head.

Sam plowed ahead. "Anyway, here's something I bet you didn't know about the nightclub deal. There was a picture in the paper back then, which included some of the laborers, and guess who's standing next to Bryce Hanson?"

She gave him a bored look and shrugged, like she wasn't interested, but would suffer through him telling her.

"Our friend Frank Baumert."

Her expression changed, and he knew he had finally told her something she didn't know. "Interesting connection, isn't it?"

"Maybe. Anything else?"

Sam grimaced and shook his head. "What's it take to excite you?" He couldn't resist a smile at the look she gave him. "Anyway, that's my news item for the day, but I think it bears looking into, don't you?"

Lewis took another hit on her beer. "Sam, I do appreciate your help, and I respect your insights, but it's been a long day, and I would like to simply enjoy my dinner." She paused. "And your company."

Oh, oh, Sam thought. That one came out of left field. "OK, no more shop talk. You enjoy my company and I'll enjoy yours." He waited, wondering what was going on in her head. He never knew what to expect.

She finished her beer and turned, studying him. "I'm going to tell you something now that I probably shouldn't, and tomorrow I'll deny having said it."

Sam waited.

"I feel a grudging kind of attraction to you."

Sam waited for more. But that was it. He grinned. "Forgive me, Diane, but you have a rather odd way of displaying this feeling."

"I said it was grudging," she snapped. "But it's there, and we'll just let it go at that. Now, having got that out of the way, what else do you want to discuss about the Robbins' case?"

36

Sam slowly exhaled, hoping she wouldn't notice. He was tempted to tell her how often he's looked at her as a woman, not as a cop, but decided for the moment not to go there. "I thought you didn't want to talk about the case."

"I changed my mind."

He hesitated again, trying to keep up with her ever shifting moods. "OK, let me share some things that might be of interest."

He told her of his conversations with Sarah Hastings, Paul Robbins, and Bryce, but decided it best not to mention his visit to Baumert nor the affair between Sarah and Maggie. She must know about it by now, anyway. He told her about Paul's negative comments regarding Hastings and Maggie's brother, Bryce, and Hastings' disparaging remarks about Bryce.

"I'm sure you'll charge me with jumping to conclusions, but my observations of that man tell me he is capable of murder." She frowned and started to say something, but he cut it off. "Hey, I'm just giving you my impressions of him."

"There is nothing in what you've told me, Sam, that we don't already know. But thank you for sharing it."

"Is there anything you can tell me, Diane?" He watched her rolling the empty beer bottle around in her hand and wondered if she was contemplating ordering another or using it as a prop while thinking.

"Well, first of all, don't ask me anything about your client. That topic is now off limits. The only thing I will tell you is something I'm sure you already know. We have some compelling evidence against her."

"Yes, she's told me."

"What I will tell you is that Maggie Robbins' will has been read, and she left some large sums of money."

"How did it break down?"

"That's the interesting part. She left a total of fifty million dollars, most of it the inheritance from her father."

"Of which Bryce got some valuable land," Sam said.

Lewis nodded. "That's right."

"Yes, and I understand that Maggie was in the process of getting that overturned when she was killed. Convenient for Bryce, wouldn't you say?"

Lewis ignored the question. "Do you want to hear the breakdown of Maggie's will or don't you?"

"Sure I do."

Diane folded her hands on the table and cleared her throat. "Listen to this. She left fourteen million to various environmental charities, including three million to that CAPPS group, thirty-five million to Paul, and one million to Sarah Hastings."

"Nice little windfall for Hastings and Paul, especially since from what I've heard, Maggie and Paul may not have been all that lovey-dovey, and she had kissed off Sarah," Sam said.

"Yes, and what makes it even more interesting is that Maggie had called her lawyer three days before she was killed. Said she wanted to see him about some changes. They had an appointment for Thursday, but she was killed on Monday."

Sam struggled to keep his cool on hearing this blockbuster. "I assume your implication is that she planned to cut Hastings out of the will."

Lewis shrugged and arched her eyebrows. That and her tight little smile gave him his answer. "Who's her lawyer?"

She screwed up her face and shook her head. "Sam, Sam." After a brief silence she said, "Knowing you, you'll find out anyway. His name is Walter Gerrity."

"Do you think she might have wanted to cut Paul's share?" Sam asked.

"Possibly. Or Sarah's. She didn't tell her lawyer what changes she wanted to make."

She's being cozy again, he thought. "Now, let me tell you something else." He proceeded to tell her what he had seen at Paul's house yesterday when he drove by. "I remember telling you he's also got a bit of a rep as a ladies' man around the Bath and Racquet." He felt like a shit adding the last part, which was strictly innuendo, but in a way, it did have a bit more relevance now.

Lewis acknowledged his little bombshell with nothing more than arched eyebrows.

"From what I hear, Maggie Robbins was a pretty savvy lady. Don't you think it's possible that she knew what was going on and confronted him?"

Lewis looked at her watch. "Sam, anything's possible and we're not overlooking anything."

"OK, but don't you think that Maggie closing in on cutting Bryce out completely from their father's will ought to move him up in the suspect pecking order—maybe over my client?"

"Sam, I think I've told you enough. You know I have appreciated your help in solving the murders last year, and I think I have now fully repaid my debt." She moved the beer bottle aside and looked him in the eye. "And that's the only reason." Her hair, which had been pinned back, came loosened on one side. Sam waited as she shook her head and let it all hang out. The effect was not lost on him.

They sat in silence for a moment. Diane threw her head back, flicking the hair from her eyes and watched Sam watching her.

Sam said nothing. Damn! This woman was complicated. The situation was complicated.

They eyed each other, both feeling the undercurrent of sexual energy charging the air. Sam watched her chest heaving up and down, her eyes challenging him. He leaned toward her, not sure where this was going.

The waiter arrived, and the moment passed. "Can I get you something else?" he asked.

They declined. Diane looked at her watch. "I have to go, Sam," she said in a half whisper.

"OK." He paid the check and they left.

Inside the car, even with the top down, he found her perfume intoxicating. When they reached her car she shook his hand and thanked him for dinner. He gave her hand a gentle squeeze and she squeezed back. They held the position, Diane making no effort to leave.

Sam decided to share her honesty and flat out tell her what must have been obvious. "Diane, even though tomorrow you'll deny what you told me in the restaurant, I have to tell you that I also have been attracted to you. FYI. Just in case you haven't picked up on it."

She smiled back and released his hand. His little joke seemed to have softened the tension. "I think we'd better leave it at that, Sam, and just go about our business, don't you agree?"

Yes, he thought and nodded. What she just said made sense.

Her presence so close to him had become overpowering, and he realized their faces were almost touching. When she took his face in her two hands and gently kissed him, the combination of the alcohol and her sensuous smells sent him into vertigo. She released him and slid out of the car. Before leaving, she turned back and leaned into the convertible. "For now."

She got into her car and drove away.

On the way home, Sam almost went through two red lights and a stop sign, thinking about the evening. There were a couple of moments there when they could have said the hell with it, and been in the sack in the time it took to get to her place.

Jesus! He was tempted. The woman exudes sex. Is that it? Pure physical attraction satisfying basic biological needs? Two people fulfilling each other's sexual desires with no strings attached, each giving the other something. No takers, no deceit, no bullshit. Simple gratification. No complications.

He smiled, but there was no mirth in it. In a perfect world, how sweet it would be. But since they were not in a perfect world, they had to look at the broader picture. Sex does have a way of changing things. Could they continue to cooperate with each other professionally, where, to be selfish about it, he needs her more than she needs him?

Would he feel guilty because of his relationship with Jennifer? Until this morning the answer was a resounding yes, and he would not have let the evening go as far as it did. But now? Their relationship was suddenly unclear. This is go-slow time. Maybe a time to test the waters before shutting doors.

He wasn't sure where Diane was coming from. Could she just enjoy the sex and let it go at that? Some women can. Some can't. He didn't know her that well, but his gut told him she was too complex a woman to simply have a roll in the hay on a whim. It could get complicated.

He could let things take their natural course. See how it plays out and hope he'd be smart enough to figure it all out. Or he could forget it happened and cut out the games. He decided on the latter.

Diane's parting words, however, still rattled around his head as he arrived home. "I think we'd better leave it at that . . . for now."

He arrived at his cottage to find his door unlocked. Odd. But as he thought back, he didn't remember locking it. Dumb! He suddenly realized that Henry was not at the door to greet him when he walked in.

37

Larry Gump was satisfied with his first meeting with Maggie Robbins' killer. Larry played it smart. He arranged for them to meet in the last two parking spaces away from Saks Fifth Avenue in the Southgate Mall.

Larry had never been in Saks, but he had often driven by and thought the place he selected was perfect, enough out in the open to be safe, but secluded enough so nobody would pay any attention to two people sitting in their vehicles talking. Larry was no dummy. He was taking no chances with a killer.

He drove up to the left of the killer's car and moved over to the passenger's side of his own car, and slid his window open. The other did the same, and they were practically cheek to cheek. Larry lowered his head a tad as a car drove by.

Larry didn't beat around the bush. Just got right to it. "You bring the money?"

Then come the excuses. "Not yet. I wanted to meet you first, and I need a little time."

Larry broke in. Cut right through the bullshit. "You tellin' me you ain't got the money?"

"I don't have it all right now, but give me a week and I'll have it. If you go to the cops now, you don't get anything. Give me a week and you'll have the whole 20,000."

Made sense to Larry, but he was not about to let this pigeon fuck with him. "Look, I'm tellin' you just this once. We meet here again in three days. That's all I'm givin' you. You bring the money then. I don't care how you get it. That's your problem, but you have it with you. Same time, same place. You don't have it, then I drive straight to the cops, and spill my guts. And you're dead meat. You got that?"

"I'll have it, and I'll be here. Same time."

Larry waited until the other car left, watching the driver back out, trying to see Larry's number plate. Old Larry didn't just get off the turnip truck. No sir, no way anybody's gonna see Larry's plate, not with all the goo plastered across them numbers.

Larry snickered. All this bullshit about having to wait and raise it. Larry knew better than that. Stallin' for time, that's all. Think maybe Larry's going to forget about it. No way.

Larry didn't give a shit how or where the money came from. Just so's it lands in his pocket.

Three more days and Larry's got a cool twenty grand. Maybe more later.

38

Sam hurried into Henry's bedroom and found him curled up in a corner, staring at Sam without moving. He knew his dog, and knew when he was spooked. He also knew that after a few barks of bravado Henry was a little coward. "Come here, fella. What's the matter?"

Henry pulled himself up and slowly made his way over to Sam. He stood in the way he did when he wanted to be picked up. Sam did so and carried him out to the kitchen, where he gently set him down and put some kibble in his dish. Henry ignored the food and curled into a ball again, never taking his eyes off Sam.

Something had troubled his dog, frightened him, more likely. Sam searched through the house, looking for any sign that someone had been there. He found none, until he opened a drawer in the kitchen. It was the drawer where he kept a notebook containing the extensive notes he'd been taking since he began investigating Maggie's death.

He kept the notebook under two magazines and a blank yellow pad with a small piece of tissue paper on top. He always carefully arranged the items for the very reason that he could tell if they had been disturbed. They had. The notebook was under the two magazines but on top of the yellow pad instead of under. Someone had taken it out.

A creepiness passed over him and he shivered. Some son-of-a-bitch had been in his house. He felt the sense of violation that comes with realizing your house has been broken into. Was it the same person who broke into Sarah's place? He thought about his needling Bryce. Could he have pushed Bryce over the edge? And then an ugly thought crossed his mind. Was it Sarah?

Since there was nothing he could do at the moment, he took Henry out for a walk and some reassurance before returning to the house and checking his messages. There was one from Circle Books, reminding him of his book signing there tomorrow night.

* * *

Circle Books was located on the main street leading to St. Armand's Circle, a trendy area filled with shops and restaurants. In the center of it all was a small park with perfectly groomed gardens, statues and symmetrical walkways. John Ringling, the wealthy circus owner, created St. Armand's in an effort to duplicate the posh ambiance of Worth Avenue in Palm Beach. He missed the mark, but the Circle did have some style and an upbeat atmosphere.

The small bookstore, one of those cozy independents that holds its own with the big chains, attracted some of the biggest names in publishing for book signings. Sam had been asked to do a signing and considered it a privilege to be included in such company.

After his somewhat perplexing dinner with Diane Lewis last night, he was glad to be involved in an event relating to the marketing of his book.

At seven o'clock he settled into a chair at a table filled with stacks of his book. He liked the poster with the little squib from *USA Today.* He chatted for a few minutes with the personable owners of the store, and began gearing himself for the possibility of no one showing up.

It was one of his recurring nightmares: sitting in a bookstore, waiting for the crowd, and no one comes. It hadn't happened yet, but he still couldn't shake the fear, still considered himself a rookie, pretending to be a real writer.

He kept glancing at the *USA Today* quote for reassurance. "Sam Wallace is a bright new star on the mystery horizon."

At 7:15, when he'd decided that his worst fears were about to be realized, people began trickling in. A short, scholarly looking man approached him with a friendly grin and a book in hand. Sam recognized him as Jerry Loevner, a Siesta Key resident he'd met at a cocktail party. He remembered being charmed by Jerry's sense of humor and tales of his travels many times around the world—an interesting man with an intriguing background, not unlike many people now living quietly in Sarasota. Sam hoped to meet more nice people like Jerry and his wife, Sandy, whom he understood had basically founded the Sarasota WineFest, contributing tons of money to children's charities over the years.

He had signed about four books, when he looked up and recognized several people from the Key, led by Brenda Green, his buddy from Donegan's Deck, chatting with Shelly Gordon, the Siesta Key Village masseuse, wearing an earring in her lip.

For nearly an hour he had a fairly steady stream, including Jimbo, who bought an even two dozen for presents "to help my friends with insomnia fall asleep." At 7:45, he looked up to greet the next visitor. Jennifer stood there, a tentative smile on her face as she handed him a book to sign.

"How about an autograph from my favorite author for my mother?"

His stomach flipped over, and that shaky nervous feeling that hits without warning swept across it. She looked tired and her face was sunburned. "Hi," he said, unable to think of anything more.

He wrote what he thought was a suitable inscription, signed it, and handed the book back to her. "Thanks for coming," he said. "What a nice surprise."

"Well, I happened to be in the neighborhood and my mom likes mysteries. Then I remembered your book signing." She grinned. "And thought maybe I could talk you into buying me an ice cream."

"Good idea. Give me another fifteen minutes to see if anyone else is coming."

At a little after 8:30 they were seated on a bench in the small park in the middle of the Circle licking ice cream cones. "Been having a good week?" Sam asked, trying to sound casual.

Jennifer fidgeted, still arranging herself on the bench, getting comfortable, watching the crowd on the street, absorbing herself in the ice cream. She turned to Sam and grinned, knowing what he really meant by his question. "Well, my 'date' with Patrick was fun and platonic, the kind of evening you spend with a buddy."

"As opposed to. . . ?"

She winked and flashed him another grin. "As opposed to an evening with you, Sam."

All doubts vanished.

They made small talk for a while: Sam's signing, progress on his new book, and Jennifer's work.

"As you probably know, Sam, red tide is fickle. It had started to move toward the west away from us, but it's shifted direction again. I've been on the boat today again tracking it."

"That's where you got the sunburn."

Her hand went up to her face. "Yes. The red tide, by the way is one of the biggest culprits with the sea turtles' problems."

"Really?"

"Yes, particularly here on the West Coast, where the red tide blooms linger for much of the year. The microscopic algae releases a toxin that kills turtles as well as other sea life. Anyway, that's why I couldn't call you either day. Then, when I got home and saw the notice about your signing, I thought I'd come over and surprise you."

"Nice surprise."

"I'll be on the boat again for the next few days, but I'll give you a call when I get back in. We're going way up the Gulf coast. What are you going to be doing?"

Sam ran his hand through his hair. "I've been poking around the Robbins' murder—talking with several people connected in one way or another. I think I'm going to drive to Miami in a couple of days to talk with Paul Robbins' partner. Want to come?"

She groaned. "I can't, Sam. I can't make any plans for the next few days while we're involved in this tracking project. Anyway, if you're going in a couple of days I won't be back by then."

"That's OK. I do want to get over there soon, and I understand you can't get away. If it turns out that I don't go, I'll let you know."

She nodded and they both fell silent.

Sam had a nagging sense that the usual, easy banter between them just wasn't there. He couldn't put his finger on it, but as the saying goes, you know it when you see it. He wasn't sure if it was because of him or Jennifer, or both.

"It's a beautiful night," Sam said. "Want to take a little stroll around the Circle?"

She looked at her watch. "It's getting late for me Sam, and I've got to be on the boat at seven. I really should go home."

"OK, I'll walk you to your Jeep. Where are you parked?"

When they reached her Jeep, she hesitated before getting in. Sam put his arms around her, and they kissed. Nothing passionate, just your basic good night kiss. She was the first to disengage.

"Are you OK," Sam blurted out.

"Yes, I'm fine," she said without looking at him.

He held the door open as she slid into the Jeep. "I'll call you when we get back," she said and drove away.

Sam stood for several moments in the nearly empty parking lot, watching her Jeep disappear.

39

Sarah Hastings sat at her desk typing a proposal due to a client in the morning. Her head swirled with a confusing array of emotions while her body ached with fatigue.

The emotions had been cutting a swath that could easily result in a nervous breakdown if she wasn't careful. She had always considered herself tough—a tough broad as some referred to her. But who could deal with depression, elation, fear, sorrow—to name only a few, without feeling the toll?

Her life was spiraling out of control and she seemed helpless to stop the spiral. She tried to focus on the positive.

Just two nights ago she had delivered an impassioned and persuasive presentation to a large crowd gathered at the Sarasota County Commissioners' meeting to discuss the proposed resort to be built on land owned by Bryce Hanson.

That scum, Sparky Waters had first presented his group's plans along with a convincing rationale to the commissioners. When he finished he turned and smirked at Sarah.

She then went on to her finest moment, with a combination of slides depicting the negative physical impact such a resort would have on the ambiance of Siesta Key, and a masterful presentation of the major problems such a resort would cause with turtle nesting. She received a standing ovation from the hundreds of people jammed into the large room.

The sense of the tide turning against the developers was palpable. But there was still work to be done. Tired and depressed as she was over other events in her life, she was up to the task.

* * *

The man stood in the darkness, invisible behind one of the large palm trees lining the street. He checked his watch again: 9:45.

It had been a long several hours and he'd grown tired of tracking Sarah Hastings. His vigil had begun at seven P.M. when he spotted her and two other women entering the Two Senoritas Restaurant one block from her small office building. Yes, he knew a great deal about Sarah Hastings.

He had waited patiently in the small park across the street from the restaurant until the three women emerged and turned down Palm Avenue. When they reached Hastings' office building she said good night, unlocked the door, and went in. The others continued down the street toward a parking garage.

Forty minutes after he'd seen the light go on in the building's second floor the man was still waiting, watching. Except for the dim light coming from the second floor of the building the street was dark, deserted. Sarasota was not a late town.

He was tired and beginning to find the vigil annoying. He would wait no longer. What he had to do could be accomplished just as readily now. He stepped from out of the shadows, looked both ways, and crossed toward the building.

* * *

Sarah's eyes began to close but she fought off the crushing fatigue and the overwhelming desire to lay her head down on the desk and sleep. One more page, and she could turn off her computer and go home.

She had thought that the dinner with her friends and colleagues would relax her. The two margaritas had helped, but now the nice little buzz they'd given her had turned into a downer, making her not only sleepy, but worsening her depression.

* * *

The man checked the lock on the door and smiled. She'd neglected to lock it. He opened the door, slipped into the building, and stood for a moment in the semi-darkness, adjusting his eyes and other senses to the surroundings.

A small night light near the floor allowed him to make out a half dozen small cubicles and an enclosed office at the end of the building. He had made it his business to know that the first floor of the building where he now stood housed a real estate company, while Hastings' public relations firm shared the top floor with a small ad agency.

The man instinctively flattened his body against the wall as the air conditioning clicked on, breaking the stillness. He wiped his brow and took several deep breaths before moving toward the narrow strip of light coming from the open stairway. He reached into his jacket pocket, withdrew two items and carefully moved across the room toward the stairs.

* * *

Sarah keyed in the final sentence of her proposal and sat back to read it. In spite of her frame of mind she was impressed. She made a few adjustments, printed the proposal, snapped off the desk light, and sat back and rubbed her eyes with the palms of her hands. The exhaustion she'd felt earlier was now a good tired, the satisfaction of a job well done.

* * *

The man reached the top of the stairs and paused. The light he'd seen coming from the room to the right of the stairs had suddenly gone out. He flattened his body against the wall and moved toward the doorway, and peered into the room, now in darkness. At the far end he could make out the silhouette of a woman, framed against the moonlight outside her window. He soundlessly made his way across the carpet toward her.

* * *

Sarah slipped the proposal into her briefcase, snapped it closed, and was about to leave when she felt a presence behind her, and in one horrifying moment knew she was not alone. She turned to see a figure standing behind her wearing a hideous halloween mask, holding a garrote over her head.

As the figure lowered the garrote she screamed, rolled off her chair and crawled along the floor behind another desk. Away from the window and on the floor, she was now in total darkness. She heard a man's voice curse as he stumbled on something, and fell to the floor a few feet from where she huddled. She inched her way toward a water cooler and crouched behind it.

She heard the man scramble to his feet and outlined against the window at his back she saw the terrifying silhouette of her pursuer. He stood for a moment before his heavy footsteps began moving toward her. As she slid further behind the cooler her gold bracelet jangled. The steps quickened and as he rushed toward her, she pushed the large water cooler, hitting the man head on with it. He fell to the floor and the cooler toppled and smashed.

Sarah dashed toward the door and flew down the stairs, his footsteps sloshing behind her. She reached the door and managed to get it open when an arm slid around her throat and she felt herself being dragged back into the building. She managed to scream before she felt her windpipe closing.

Outside, two men were about to get into their car when they heard Sarah scream. Just before she passed out, she saw the men running toward the building, felt the arm release her, and saw her assailant bolt out the door and down the street. It was the last thing she remembered.

40

The incessant ringing of his phone brought Sam to a sitting position. He shook the cobwebs out, turned on the light, and looked at his watch. Twelve-thirty in the morning. Who the hell could that be? "Hello," he said, more a question than an answer.

"Sam, somebody tried to kill me tonight."

Sam bolted from the bed. "Sarah, is that you?"

He listened to her sniffling, followed by a whispered, "Yes."

"I'm at home now, Sam. The police drove me here a little while ago."

"What happened?"

Between sobbing and pauses she told him everything that had happened, starting with her dinner at the restaurant. And then she suddenly seemed to run out of steam. "Sam, I'm totally exhausted and I'm afraid. I've already called my sister, and tomorrow morning she and her husband are coming to drive me to Naples to stay with them for a few days. The cops say it's OK, but were kind enough to remind me that I am still a suspect in Maggie's murder."

"So, you say the guy got away?"

"Yes."

"Do they have any clues, any idea who might have done this? Do you?"

"It's got to be those developers and . . ." Her voice trailed off and she started sobbing again. "Sam, I don't want to talk anymore. I'll call you from Naples. I'm sorry I woke you up. Go back to sleep."

She hung up and Sam pondered her call for a while before climbing back under the sheets. He was still thinking about the attempted murder on Sarah when he fell asleep.

In the morning he called Diane Lewis, but was told she was not in. He left a message, saying he was calling about the murder attempt on Sarah Hastings.

Next he called Walter Gerrity's law office. A woman answered in a brisk, officious voice.

"Gerrity and Johnson. How may I help you?"

"Uh, yes, I'd like to speak with Mr. Gerrity."

"Who shall I say is calling?" the woman asked, sounding irritated that a caller would be so naïve as to think he would immediately be put through to someone as important as Mr. Gerrity.

"My name is Sam Wallace, and I am a private investigator. It's important that I speak with Mr. Gerrity about Maggie Robbins."

The pause came as no surprise to Sam. He waited until the woman finally replied. "Please hold."

After a few moments, a polished, confident, voice boomed through the phone. "This is Walter Gerrity."

"Mr. Gerrity, my name is Sam Wallace, and as your assistant may have told you, I'm a private investigator. I wonder if I might see you for a few moments. It won't take long. I just have a couple of questions I'd like to ask that might help with the investigation of Maggie Robbins' murder that I'm conducting along with that of the police." Better, Sam thought, "conducting along with that of the police." Definitely better.

Gerrity's sigh was audible and Sam suspected it was meant to be. "Mr. Wallace, I'm a very busy man and I have to be in court in fifteen minutes. I have no time to see you. Perhaps I can answer your questions on the phone. But please be brief."

Good enough, Sam thought. "Well, sir, I understand that you were working on having the reversal of Maggie and Bryce's father's will turned back to its original intent. Were you optimistic about that happening?"

Gerrity chuckled. "Well, you don't waste any time, do you?"

"You said to be brief."

"Let me say this, Mr. Wallace. Maggie Robbins was very well connected as, if I may say, am I. I might further add that reversing a will that has already been contested and changed is a very difficult endeavor. I don't have time to go into all the reasons, but I can tell you this. I had every confidence that we were very close to prevailing. Now what else can I do for you?"

Sam was both delighted and surprised at the man's candor. "Thank you, Mr Gerrity. Just one other question. I know that Maggie had an appointment to meet with you three days after she was murdered. Can you tell me what was the purpose of that meeting?"

The lawyer responded in a voice no longer connected with a chuckle. "Mr. Wallace, that's not a question I should be answering. You are aware of client privilege. Aren't you."

"Yes, sir, I am," Sam said, not backing down.

"Good. However, I will answer your question. I was very fond of Maggie, and if there is anything I can do or say that would assist in any way to bring her killer to justice, I am more than happy to cooperate. I'm not suggesting that I know anything that would be of any material relevance, but again, I am happy to cooperate. Maggie said she wanted to meet with me about some changes she wished to make in her own will."

"Did she say what those changes might be?"

"No, she didn't. Now, I believe you said you had a 'couple' of questions, to which I have responded. I'm afraid I do have to go. Goodbye, sir."

Sam sat on the porch, wiped out, physically and emotionally. His life was getting out of control. He liked it when it was much simpler. Jennifer was his girlfriend and he wrote books. Period. Now his ex-wife surfaces, and all of a sudden his relationship with Jennifer doesn't seem quite as simple and comfortable as it had been.

Since getting involved with Maggie's murder, his focus on his writing was getting blurred. He could see it in the quality of what he'd turned out in the last few sessions. It was supposed to get better. "One hand washes the other," as Sarah said. And speaking of Sarah he assumed she was safe at least for a while with her sister and her husband in Naples. She never did give him the sister's phone number, but he knew she would be calling him soon. He would phone Lewis again and see what she has on the murder attempt.

41

Thirty minutes later Sam got the call he'd been expecting. "Sarah, I'm glad you called. Are you doing OK down there?"

"I'm not in Naples. The cops called and told me they wanted me back here."

"Why? Why did they order you back so fast?"

"Because . . ." Her voice cracked and she paused before continuing. "Because they want to lean on me some more about Maggie's murder. Because they are increasingly interested in me as a suspect. Because they want me here in Sarasota where they can have immediate access to me in case they want to charge me." She said it all slowly, enunciating each syllable and word, as if working at remaining calm.

"What about the attempt on your life? Are they working on that?"

"Yes, I guess—in a half-hearted way. Sam, can you come over? Can we talk?"

"Sure, but it sounds to me like you need to talk with your lawyer more than me."

"I've been with him for the last three hours. He tells me he still doesn't think they have enough to charge me. Can you come over?"

An hour later Sam rang her doorbell.

When she opened the door, she peered up and down the hall, as if expecting someone to be lurking behind him, reminding him of his first visit to her. The woman has been through a lot, he thought. "Come in, come in," she said, sounding like she was inviting him in from a storm.

Sam hoped she hadn't noticed his expression when he saw her. He was surprised at her appearance when she came to his place and hired him, but he was now stunned. Her face, devoid of make-up was ashen. Her usual perfectly coiffured hair looked in need of washing, and the jeans she wore hung loosely under a shapeless sweater.

He stepped inside and gaped at her apartment. The place was a mess. Half-filled coffee cups sat on every flat surface, and shoes lay wherever Sarah might have taken them off. He thought back to the first time he had visited her here, when both she and her condo looked so terrific. A twinge of sadness crept over him. He stepped into the living room and stood in front of the glass doors. At least the view hadn't changed.

"Thank you for coming, Sam. Sit down." She cleared some newspapers off a couch, and he sat.

"Sarah, it pains me to see you like this," Sam said softly. "Try and pull yourself together."

She managed a wan smile. "Well, my place has been broken into, my clothes cut up, somebody tried to kill me, and the cops think I'm a murderer. Other than that I have no reason to be upset."

Sam stood and steered her onto the couch next to him. "I can't even begin to comprehend what you must have gone through the other night. And I am so sorry," he said. "But you have got to take care of yourself to get through this."

She nodded and her hands went up to her hair in a futile effort to primp it. "The police have been relentless, asking me the same questions over and over. My lawyer and I are both cooperating, but they're wearing me down."

"Have they charged you with anything?"

"No, not yet, but clearly, I'm their number one suspect.

They're making a big thing out of the fingernail they found. They've matched it to others I have."

"But," Sam hesitated. "You have been in her bed, right?"

She nodded and looked away.

"So, it's not by any means conclusive evidence. What else?"

"The perfume thing. The stuff has been around for a long time, but it's expensive and not used by everybody." She bit at a cuticle and looked around the room. "Would you like something, some coffee?"

Sam shook his head.

Sarah got up and poured herself some coffee before turning back to Sam. "And those damned tire tracks. They refuse to believe that I went over to see her, saw the house dark, and left."

"You say your lawyer still feels they don't have enough to arrest you?"

She held the cup with both hands and sipped the hot coffee. "He says they want to indict me but are afraid they don't have enough to get a conviction, yet. And that's why they're trying to wear me down." She turned and spread her hands out. "Look at this place, Sam. Look at me. Which do you think looks worse, the condo or me?"

Sam smiled. "Definitely the condo. It would take more than an attempted murder and police harassment to make you look bad."

He bought a smile from her. "Thanks, Sam. You're sweet. Even though I don't believe you."

"But you have to pull yourself together, Sarah. You're playing into their hands, acting like this. Your lawyer's right. Everything they have is circumstantial. The nail thing is tough."

"Sam, I've slept with her," she said. "I told them that. This whole thing is not only nerve-wracking, it's humiliating." She pulled a pack of cigarettes from a drawer, studied it briefly and put it back.

"You never struck me as the smoking type, Sarah."

Again she smiled. "I'm not. I bought these yesterday. Don't ask me why. Have you made any progress?" she asked.

"A little. I'm going to drive to Miami tomorrow and talk with Paul's business partner. Both he and Bryce have gained a great deal from Maggie's death." He hesitated, and then added, "Of course, you didn't do too badly yourself."

He braced himself, expecting an outburst at that one. She surprised him by calmly replying, "Yes, the police have reminded me of that."

"Well, it does seem like a lot of money for the relatively short time you and she were involved." He waited but she didn't respond. "Did you have any idea she was going to leave you that much money—or anything for that matter?"

"Sam, I did not know she was going to leave me anything. I was flabbergasted, if you want to know the truth. Even though she dumped me, the time we were together was good—very good. She said I made her happy during that time."

Sam locked eyes with her for a long moment until she looked away. "I don't suppose you knew about the appointment she had with her lawyer."

Sarah wheeled around. "No, Sam, I didn't!"

Sam held up his hands in surrender. "Just asking. The more I know the better I can help you. Anyway, hang in there. From what I know, no one but Paul has much of an alibi, and I'll be digging into that. This Baumert is a rough customer, and I'm sure the police are far from finished with him.

"And I know that Bryce says he was home alone that night,

supposedly working on a proposal to a prospective client. The guy has a very short fuse, by the way."

"Bryce is a nasty man, Sam."

"Yes. Some people give you a gut feeling that they simply are not capable of murder—right or wrong. I would not say that about Mr. Hanson. Anyway I'll fill you in when I get back from Miami. By the way, Maggie was killed just a few days before she had an appointment to see her lawyer. Any thoughts on why she wanted to see him?"

She finished her coffee and shook her head. "No, but I'm not surprised."

"What do you mean?"

"If she had an appointment with her lawyer, you can bet your fanny, she was planning on cutting Paul out of her will."

"Why?"

"Why? Because she was fed up with his playing around."

"How do you know that?"

"Because she told me so. Why do you think she hooked up with me? I knew she wasn't a lesbian, and I asked her why she was attracted to me. She said she liked to try different things. But later over a few drinks she told me that if Paul kept screwing around the way he did, then why shouldn't she? And then she slammed her drink down and said, 'Well, he's going to damn well pay for it.'"

"Any idea what she meant by that? Did she elaborate?"

"No, but, I have a pretty good idea what she meant, don't you?"

"Maybe. Anyway, don't let them wear you down. That's their strategy. All cops do it. They get onto one person they consider the most likely perpetrator and never let up until they break 'em down. And very often it works."

Sam walked over to the window and watched a boat cruising toward Marina Jack's. He turned to Sarah. "Do you still believe the developers had something to do with the break-in?"

Sarah threw her head back and looked to the ceiling. "Sam, I can't believe you. Of course, I do." She beckoned him to the sofa to sit. He did and she joined him.

"Listen to me, Sam. In one week the meeting for changes in downtown and Siesta Key zoning will be held. If we get the zoning changed the fancy Siesta Key resort is dead meat, but at the very least I'm sure we can succeed in gaining another delay.

"My name is identified with all of this and these guys are running scared. Somebody broke in here to frighten me and then they tried to kill me so I'll back off."

Sam waited until she resumed normal breathing and the flush in her face faded. "You think Bryce is behind this?"

"You're damn right I do, and I wouldn't put it past him to try and set me up for Maggie's murder. He wants to discredit me in every sleazy way he can."

Sam got up and reached out his hand to her and helped her to her feet. "I have to go now Sarah. I'll keep in close touch with you, and please try not to worry. The police have plenty of reasons to be looking at other people for Maggie's murder. You are not the only suspect. They only want you to think you are."

Sarah closed her eyes and barely nodded.

As Sam was about to leave she called his name.

"Yes?"

"Sam, I am not a murderer."

He smiled and left, exhausted.

42

Sam walked to Dog Beach and stood, absorbing the serenity of the Gulf of Mexico. Florida was really all about the water: the bays, the inlets, the Gulf of Mexico, the Atlantic, the rivers, the Straits of Florida. Yes, all about the water—and the weather. He thought of a line he once read in a biography of Frank Sinatra, quoting a woman who disliked him, referring to his singing. "How can such beauty come from such ugliness?" Working the Maggie Robbins' case had him thinking the reverse. How can such ugliness come from such beauty?

Anyway, tomorrow morning bright and early he would drive to Miami and talk with Mark Folven, Paul's business partner. Folven, who had been very affable, agreed to meet Sam at his home.

Sam reviewed where he stood on the Robbins' case. Four people with motive. Some of it money, but there is also anger, revenge, maybe jealousy, and money. Bryce, Sarah, Baumert, Paul? Who else?

* * *

Early the next morning Maggie Robbins' killer drove aimlessly about with no destination, seeking only solace for a troubled mind—a place to think, to be alone. After driving for over two hours, through all of Longboat Key, along the bay front, and the entire length of Siesta Key, the killer wound up at secluded Turtle Beach at the far southern tip of Siesta Key—a perfect spot to wind down—and reflect.

The beach was deserted except for two vehicles in the parking lot near the boat ramp, both with empty boat trailers attached. Boaters off for a day of fishing or cruising.

One of them looked vaguely familiar. The pickup truck. What was it? Yes, that ugly tannish color, the dent on the passenger door. Jesus Christ! It's that guy's truck—the blackmailer.

The truck was unlocked. He probably couldn't lock this piece of shit if he tried. And the glove compartment—unlocked also. How convenient. And there was the registration. Lawrence Gump. Sarasota address. "Nice to meet you, Lawrence," the killer said and headed off the Key onto Route 41, and into the traffic.

43

In the morning, Sam called his dogsitting neighbor, Brewster, who was delighted to have Henry for the day, put up the top on the car, and left for the three and a half hour drive to Miami. He enjoyed the stretch of I–75 between Naples and Miami called Alligator Alley. Traffic wasn't as bad as he expected and the canals running parallel to the highway justified the road's nickname.

He had trouble keeping his eyes on his driving, watching the gators gliding along the narrow waters or sunning themselves on the banks. He had heard that the efforts in Florida to protect alligators had succeeded to a fault. They were overpopulated now and beginning to cause problems.

It was not uncommon for residents near a canal or pond to spot an alligator in their back yards. In the short time that Sam had been in Florida there had been two incidents of alligator attacks. A week after he arrived, a three-year-old boy had been grabbed and dragged into the water. His partially eaten body was found several hours later. In the other incident a woman saw a gator grab her dog and disappear into the water. In both cases the offending creatures had been tracked down and killed. Little solace for the victims.

Sam had also learned that the Florida Everglades had a crocodile population of some 500. But the Florida crocodile was nowhere near as large and fierce as those in places like Africa or India. Nor were they as dangerous as the Florida alligators. Still, to Sam there was something about the word crocodile that generated a visceral fear inside him. Alligators didn't do much for him either.

He reached the end of I–75, where there had been nothing but canals on one side and thick foliage and underbrush on the other and abruptly entered another world. Wall-to-wall housing developments appeared out of nowhere extending their tentacles toward the remoteness of Alligator Alley and the Everglades. Without warning, traffic appeared from every direction. He was on the outskirts of bustling Miami.

He reached Mark Folven's house, a bungalow in the Coconut Grove section at a little after noon. The house, painted in pastel blues with bright yellow shutters, was pure Florida. The colors reminded Sam of his own cottage on the Key, but Folven's was much larger. Paul had mentioned once that his partner was a bachelor. The house seemed big for one person.

Mark Folven greeted him at the door with a friendly smile. "Come in, Mr. Wallace," he said, leading the way. "You don't look like a private investigator. But then, I don't know what they're supposed to look like. Would you like some coffee, a soft drink, a beer?"

Sam declined and Folven led them through a living room of wicker furniture and colorful throw rugs and hardwood floors. Floor to ceiling bookcases lined one wall, the books ranging from thick business and economics tomes to Fitzgerald and Hemingway. The room was not only stylish, but it had a friendly look—the home of a man comfortable with himself.

"We can sit out here on the lanai. There's a nice breeze today." Folven beckoned Sam to a rattan chair, while he settled into a love seat.

For a guy living in Miami, Sam thought, Folven looked like anything but a Floridian. His complexion had the pallid appearance of a man who hadn't seen a beach in years. His face was long and angular, the kind that projected a seriousness of purpose, that made him look older than he probably was.

He wore a white shirt, open at the collar, dark slacks, and black oxford shoes. He looked like he could play Richard Nixon in a movie. If opposites attract, he could see why Folven and Paul Robbins worked well together. After some perfunctory chit-chat, Mark asked, "What can I do for you, Mr. Wallace?"

Sam nodded, acknowledging that when someone says, "What can I do for you," they want to drop the small talk.

"Well, first of all, please call me Sam. As I mentioned when I called, I've been hired by Sarah Hastings to look into the death of your partner's wife. I believe you know Sarah, don't you?" He glanced at a table next to where Mark sat, spotted a pipe sitting on it and prayed that Folven didn't light up.

"Yes, I know Sarah Hastings—met her a couple of times when I was with Paul and Maggie. She also did some PR work for us for a while, as you may know. I'm curious about her hiring you," Mark said.

Sam wondered how much Folven knew about the murder investigation, given his relationship with Paul. "Ms. Hastings has become a suspect in the case. She insists that she had nothing to do with Maggie's murder and hired me to help find the real killer."

Folven lowered his eyes and said nothing.

"By the way, did you tell Paul I was coming to visit you?" Sam asked.

"No, I haven't talked with him in a couple of days." He smiled. "Did you tell him?"

Sam returned his smile. "No, as a matter of fact, I didn't."

Folven nodded as if to say, I thought not.

Sam debated whether to leave it at that, but thought it best not to. "Paul and I are friends. We play tennis together, and to be honest with you, I'm not sure how he would feel about my coming over here, 'poking around,' as people like to refer to what I do."

"I understand," Mark said. "Are you suggesting I not tell him?"

Sam grinned. "I guess I'd have to leave that up to you."

Folven crossed his legs and sat back, waiting for Sam to continue.

"Mark, people in my line of work do roughly the same kinds of things the police do," he said. "We talk with anyone who was in any way connected with the victim, no matter how far removed."

Folven broke in. "Then you must know the police have already questioned me. They wanted all the details about Paul on the night of the murder. Is that what you want?"

Sam glanced outside and watched a large heron tiptoe across the yard, pausing to stare at him and Mark. He poked his bill into the grass, extracted something and continued on his way. "Yes, if you don't mind, Mark."

Folven smiled. "Sure, Sam. I'll be glad to." He proceeded to describe how he and Paul had spent the day working on a big account. "By the end of the day we'd had a handshake on a sale of kayaks and canoes. The buyer had a couple of concerns he wanted to think through before signing the sales agreement, and we made a date to meet that night for dinner, and hopefully, finalize the deal.

"Paul had been feeling queasy and weak all day. He was coughing and sneezing and seemed to be coming down with something. In any case, he and I ended the day over drinks at the Sheraton Key Biscayne. I drove Paul to his apartment and was to pick him up for dinner at seven o'clock."

"Was he feeling any better when you dropped him off?"

Mark shook his head. "Uh, uh. He was worse. I wasn't surprised when he called and said he wasn't going to be able to make it for dinner."

"So you went on without him and closed the deal."

"Yes. Paul is the salesman, not me. I think he was a little unsure that I would be able close it without him. He told me to be sure to call him."

"And?"

"I was all pumped up after dinner and called him."

"How did he sound?"

"Terrible. When he first answered he was hoarse, no energy in his voice. But when I told him, he kind of came alive."

"What did he say?"

"He said something like, 'Hey Mark, that's fabulous. I knew you'd do it.'"

"And you said?"

"I said it was easy. He was ready. We had already pre-sold him."

"And Paul said?"

"He said OK and that he had to get some sleep now and try to shake this thing off and for me to call him in the morning. And he hung up."

"How was Paul the next morning?"

"He still looked a little shaky, but said he felt better. Said he took three aspirin and slept the night through. We had an important appointment that morning, and he said he felt good enough to go with me. If the deal the night before hadn't been pretty much settled, he would have joined us for dinner if he had to crawl."

"So you headed for that meeting, and that's when Paul got the call."

"Yes. He was almost catatonic. I drove him back to his apartment where he got into his car and drove to Sarasota."

"Did he say anything on the way to the apartment?"

Mark shook his head. "No, not really. He sobbed a lot and kept saying, 'I can't believe this. I can't believe this.' He was in tough shape. I asked him if I could drive him to Sarasota. He just shook his head. The only thing he said when he left was, 'I'll call you.'"

"Mark, did you ever feel at any time that there was anything unusual about his behavior? I mean the day he got sick or the next morning?"

"What kind of question is that? No, not at all."

"I'm sorry. The question wasn't meant to imply anything sinister. It's just that you seem like a perceptive guy and sometimes the smallest things you might notice can be important." Sam could tell from the expression on Mark's face that he'd best drop it. "Anyway, thanks Mark for taking the time to see me. Been a pleasure meeting you. Oh, by the way, how long was Sarah doing PR for you?"

"Hmm, I'd say it was just a little over a year, maybe a year and a half."

"How was she? I mean did she do a good job?"

Mark sucked in a breath and let it out before replying. "Yes, I'd say so. She was very big city if you know what I mean. She was smart, smooth, and knew how to get things done."

"Do you remember why the arrangement was terminated?"

Folven thought for a moment. "I'm, uh, not sure. Paul handled most of the outside vendors and freelancer details."

"Was the termination amicable?"

Folven smiled. "I'm afraid I don't recall that either, Sam."

Sam nodded and smiled back before getting up. "OK, thanks again Mark for the time and courtesy. I've enjoyed meeting you."

Folven rose and extended his hand. "Same here, Sam."

They shook hands and walked toward the door. Mark stopped and turned to look at Sam. "Have you been a private investigator long, Sam? You just don't strike me as a P.I. type."

"Why not?"

"I don't know. You seem more like a professional man, I mean like a lawyer, business exec, or—"

"College professor?"

"Yeah," Mark said, like a light bulb had gone off in his head.

"That's what I was. I didn't think it showed. Mark, let me ask you one more question."

"Sure."

"Did you and Paul socialize much when he would come to Miami?"

Mark shot him a quizzical look and resumed walking. "Uh, no, not really. We have a good business relationship, but we're different types and . . ." He stopped and changed the subject. "Are you heading right back or are you going to see a little of Miami?"

"I'm going right back. Uh, you were starting to tell me something about you and Paul, then stopped. What were you going to say?"

Mark looked uncomfortable for the first time, and Sam expected him to blow off the question. But Folven surprised him.

"Let's just leave it that Paul has his own life here. He does his thing, and I do mine." He opened the door and gestured toward it. "Look me up any time you're in Miami, Sam."

Sam said he would, thanked him, and left. He drove away pondering Mark Folven's last comment about Paul. "Paul has his own life here." Sam knew that Paul's apartment was here in the Coconut Grove area. Paul had given him the address and told him to come by if he was ever in the area.

"I belong to a great tennis club there," he said. "We'll play some tennis and go out to dinner. You'd love Coconut Grove."

He also knew that Paul was in Sarasota as they had a date to play tennis at eight tomorrow morning. And then he had a startling thought.

44

He had put his lock picking expertise from his cop training to good use on the murder case in Sarasota several months ago. Since then he had kept his tools in his glove compartment. Still— it's risky, and if he got caught, he could be in serious trouble. The cops would fry his ass with Lewis leading the charge.

He asked a man on the street for directions to Paul's address, which turned out to be only a few blocks away. He still wasn't sure what he was going to do there.

The building, a modest, five-story condominium, looked like it had been built in the seventies, little more than a beige box with no style. He parked on the street and reached the front entrance as an elderly man came out carrying a stack of books.

"Here, let me hold the door for you," Sam said as the man emerged.

"Thank you," he said. "Gotta hustle these books back to the library. They're already a day overdue. Can't afford to be paying any damn fines."

Still holding the door, Sam watched the man struggling down the street and hoped the library wasn't too far away. He stepped inside, checked the directory and found "Robbins 422."

As he walked toward the elevator, the front door opened, and a young woman carrying a bag of groceries entered the building. Sam checked her out from the corner of his eye. Late 20's, maybe early 30's, long black hair, gorgeous complexion about five-seven, most of it legs.

The elevator creaked open, he waited for her to step in and he followed. She pushed four and looked toward Sam. He smiled and said, "I'm going to four also." Her scent filled the elevator. She shifted the bag of groceries, threw out one of her hips, and rested the bag on it. Nice move, he thought.

The elevator reached the fourth floor and again he waited for her to get off. He noticed the door facing the elevator was number 418, the one to the left of it, 420.

The woman turned left and Sam went to the right. After a few steps, he half turned. His hunch was correct. She stopped at 422, unlocked the door, and entered.

"I'll be goddamned," Sam muttered and left.

* * *

Sam arrived home at eight o'clock. He was glad he'd stopped for a bite to eat along the way, as he was too tired to fix anything.

Henry greeted him at the door, did a few pirouettes around Sam, and settled into his favorite corner, keeping a sharp eye on Sam, who listened to three messages, one from Paul reminding him of their tennis date in the morning, one from Diane Lewis, and one from Brewster.

Neither Paul's nor Diane's were welcome. He no more felt like playing tennis at eight o'clock than running a marathon.

And Diane's message could only be trouble. "Please call me, Sam. If you get in after I've left the station, call me at home." She left the number. Call her at home. He didn't like the sound of that.

The next message was pure Brewster.

"Sam, Brewster here. Henry has been fed, pooped, and had a nice long nap. He should be a happy camper. I dropped him off at 7:30 and left for the theatre. Henry is a splendid little fellow, well-behaved as always, and I am happy to report, our relationship continues to blossom. Thank you for placing him in my charge."

Next, the one he wasn't looking forward to. He picked up the phone and called Lewis. "This is Sam, Diane."

"Frank Baumert has disappeared." No 'Hi Sam,' no nothing, just a flat, 'Frank Baumert has disappeared.'

He wasn't sure what to say, but he didn't have to say anything. She got into it right away.

"Frank Baumert is gone. We went to see him this morning and he's disappeared. The last time we talked with him he was not co-operative. Said we were after him, and that you had been out there bugging him and harassing him, too. He said he just wanted to be left alone."

"Look Diane, I—"

"No, I don't want to hear any of your Diane shit. You listen to me. Baumert has moved out of his place and hasn't shown up for work at the bar. He's vanished. And I blame you."

Maybe he was tired of taking crap from her. Maybe he began to wonder if the whole P.I. thing was worth it. Maybe he just wished he were back being a professor when nobody ever talked to him like this. Whatever, he lost it.

"Go to hell, Diane. Who do you think you are, talking to me like I'm some criminal? Yes, I went out to see Frank Baumert, but if my talking with him caused him to run away, then you now know something you didn't know before. Maybe you should have been spending more time on him instead of beating on Sarah Hastings. Why don't you get off my case?" And he hung up.

"Damn, that felt good," he said aloud and cracked open a beer.

He sat in the semi-darkness of the house, sipping his beer, the only sounds, Henry's squeaks and moans. He thought of his outburst with Diane and hoped he hadn't gone too far. The woman was so unpredictable. One minute she's friendly, even coming onto him, the next she's yammering at him like he's a schoolboy.

Actually, as he thought about it, he could see her point. If Baumert said what she said he did, he could understand why Lewis would blame him. But why does she have to be such a tight ass with him? He wasn't going to worry about it. It'll work out. He did what he had to do—stand his ground with her.

Anyway, at the moment he preferred to think about his personal life. Still no word from Jennifer.

He got up and stretched. After opening another beer, he went out to the porch and sat. Henry waddled along behind him and sprawled across Sam's feet.

It was nine o'clock and the only sound was the gentle lapping of the water against the rocks. No mosquitoes, no bugs, nothing but a soft breeze bringing with it the smells of the sea mingling with the intoxicating scent of his tree's oranges. His house was a full block from the Gulf, but the air was so clear and still, the surf could be in his front yard.

He relaxed and began to unwind. The contentment he felt in this simple little cottage was hard to measure.

The phone roused him. "Hello."

"Hello, Sam."

"Lisa? Is everything all right?"

"Yes, everything is fine—thanks to you."

His first reaction was to ask, "Then why are you calling?" Instead he said he was glad he could help and that she could now get her life back on track.

"I am, Sam. In fact, I decided to treat myself to a little vacation—just get away from Boston for a while."

"Good idea. Where are you going?"

"I'm already here."

"Where?"

"Sarasota."

Something rolled inside his stomach and knotted. "Sarasota? You mean this Sarasota?"

She laughed the lusty, infectious sound he'd heard so often. "Is there another?"

"Uh, no, I . . . maybe I thought you said Saratoga," he said, making no sense.

"No, Sam. I'm here at The Colony on Longboat Key. I'm sure you of all people would know it—the number one tennis resort in the country?"

"Yes, Lisa. I know it, but what are you doing here? Why here?"

He listened to her silence. His reaction was obviously not what she had expected.

"Made sense to me. I've always wanted to see it. I needed to get away, relax, play some tennis, swim, just totally unwind, and wash all the bile of Walt Piro out of me. "And . . ." she hesitated. "I thought it would be nice to see you."

She said the last line so softly he barely heard her. Her laughter of a moment ago still resonated. He'd carried it with him for months after their breakup, unable to shake the line from an old song he loved, "I heard the laughter of her heart in every street café."

He held the phone against his chest for a moment, gathering his thoughts, fighting the temptation to drift back into the easy banter they had once enjoyed, the seductive way she could turn ordinary conversation into verbal love making. He had long ago gotten over all that, and he was not about to get sucked back into it. "Gee, I don't know, Lisa. I'm . . ."

"Come on, Sam. I won't bite. Come over tomorrow and hit some tennis balls, and sit on the beach with me for a little while. Just for . . . yes, I'll say it: old times sake."

"How long are you going to be here?"

"I've got three glorious days. I love The Colony, by the way. Coming over?"

"Um, I'm not sure that's a good idea, but let me sleep on it, and I'll give you a call tomorrow." She gave him her number and they hung up.

He sat in silence, replaying their conversation until his eyes grew heavy and began to close. He forced them open and switched his thoughts to the new deadline for his book. Tired as he was, he pulled his manuscript up on the computer screen and started to work. An hour and a half later he shut down the computer and went to bed. Two minutes after his head hit the pillow he was sound asleep.

45

Larry Gump sat in his garage repairing his crab pots. They were still usable, so even though he was about to come into some real money, why throw 'em away? The rest of the pots weren't worth a shit, and he would replace them with brand new ones. Old Larry goes first class from now on.

Larry liked nice things—like his new garage that he built himself. None of this carport shit for Larry. No sir, he got himself a full-blown, first class garage. How many trailer owners around here can say that? Got the double-wide sitting on a nice piece of land out here, plenty of privacy. No more livin' next to all that trailer park trash. Now with this baby tucked in alongside the double-wide, old Larry's got some style.

Already got the new skiff picked out, brand new thirty-five horse on it. Got himself a good price that'll leave some left over for some new fishin' gear.

He took a beer out of his compact refrigerator and turned on the TV. Larry liked hanging out in his new garage. Maybe get himself a new Barcalounger, put it in front of the TV. Got room.

* * *

Paul Robbins was waiting at the tennis court when Sam arrived at 8:10.

"Sorry, Paul. I got in late last night, and I overslept."

"It's OK. Let's get started. We only have the court for an hour and a half."

Only? The way Sam felt at the moment, an hour and a half sounded like an eternity. Paul seemed a little abrupt. Guess he doesn't like people being late.

They got in two and a half sets before their time ran out. The tennis had rejuvenated Sam, and he was sorry to quit.

"Good tennis, Paul, a set apiece and three all in the third. Can't get any closer than that."

On the walk back to the clubhouse Paul was unusually quiet. "Sam, how 'bout some coffee at Manhattan Bagel?" he asked.

They drove their cars the hundred yards to the restaurant's parking lot and settled down to coffee and bagels. The place was a hangout for the morning tennis players.

Sam had to work at being warm and friendly given what he'd learned about Paul during the past several days. He sipped his coffee and spread cream cheese on his bagel. When he looked up, Paul's eyes bore into him. "I understand you took a little trip to Coconut Grove."

Sam stopped chewing for a mini-second and quickly resumed. He nodded, but waited until he swallowed the piece of bagel before responding.

"Yes, nice place. I hope to see more of it." If his reply irked Paul, it didn't show, except for the hard stare, which was beginning to make Sam uncomfortable.

"Why did you think it necessary to go to Miami and question my partner, Sam?" Paul's tone was more of concern than anger.

Sam finished his bagel and used his napkin. "You want some more coffee?"

Paul shook his head.

"I'm going to get some. Be right back."

Sam returned and stirred his fresh cup of coffee. Paul waited.

"Paul, as you know, Sarah Hastings hired me to look into Maggie's murder."

Paul started to speak, but Sam held out his hand and continued. "I know, I know, she's the chief suspect right now, but I have to give her an honest effort. As such, I've been talking with everybody who had any connection with Maggie no matter how remote or distant. Mark's connection is you." He wanted the last to be abrupt and to the point.

"What the hell does that mean, Sam? Mark's connection is me. What did you expect to find out about me by going to Mark and asking him all kinds of questions? Asking about Sarah Hastings and why we let her go. You want to know why we fired Sarah Hastings. Ask me. She was insolent, and besides that she was not very effective. That's why we let her go.

"It's embarrassing, Sam, you going to see my partner. I'm puzzled why you would do that. I thought you and I were friends. It clearly implies that you think I have something to hide." He shook his head and looked away. "I can't believe you would do that."

It was Sam's turn to study Paul. He actually said the last like he was hurt. Christ! He half expected a tear to fall.

"Paul, I wanted to start from the beginning—when she was found, when the police contacted you, when you got back here—the whole scenario. It helps to put everything in perspective to get it from every vantage point possible." He paused. "I know you don't have anything to hide, which is why I'm surprised at your reaction."

Paul said nothing for a moment, and just stared at Sam. And then he grinned, "Sorry, I keep forgetting you're now a private investigator doing what P.I.'s do, like your character Dirk Flanders, right?" His grin broadened into a smile, and he gave Sam a friendly punch.

Slick, Sam thought. It looked like Paul was losing it for a minute, but made a quick recovery. "Yeah, in a way, I guess. But Dirk is much smoother than I'll ever be. What's up for the rest of the week?"

"Nothing special. I'm going over to Miami the day after tomorrow to spend a few days working with Mark. It'll be good to get away from here for a while, get out of that house. I've been holed up there like a hermit ever since this thing happened." He looked away and said softly, "I miss her."

Sam nodded. Holed up, but not exactly like a hermit.

"By the way," Paul said. "I'm not leaving until noon or so on Monday, so do you want to hit some balls again tomorrow early, like eight o'clock?"

Sam thought for a moment. "Yeah, OK. I'll see you at eight."

"Set your alarm," Paul said with a grin.

46

Sam replayed their conversation all the way home. It was about what he expected. As affable and friendly Mark Folven was, Sam was not surprised that he told Paul. Why shouldn't he? They were friends and business partners. Of course he would tell him.

Paul did get huffy about it, maybe a little too much so. He was the one who brought up the business about having nothing to hide. Does he? Because a guy has women all over the place doesn't make him a murderer. How about the possibility of being cut out of thirty-five million?

And he says Sarah did a bad job. That's not what Mark said.

Sam parked his car in the garage, relieved not to see Peter since he had missed the Sea Turtle meeting. He started across the street in time to see a red Chrysler Sebring convertible pull up in front of the cottage with a woman at the wheel. When she turned her head he recognized her. It was Lisa.

She spotted him at the same time. "Hi, Sam," she said.

"Lisa, what . . . what are you doing here?"

"Nice to see you, too, Sam," she said, feigning a pout.

"I'm surprised, that's all. Give me a minute to recover."

She was still sitting in the car looking terrific. If he had seen this woman sitting in this car drive by and didn't know who it was, he would have damned sure wanted to find out.

Her hair was more blonde than he remembered, either from some time in the sun or a little touch up. The slight tan highlighted her hair, and she looked cool in her large oval sunglasses.

"You like my car?"

"Yeah, I figured you were a tourist. That's what they all rent down here."

"I am a tourist. Are you going to invite me in?"

He looked up and down the street as if inviting her in would be an illicit act. "Uh yeah, sure. It's not much." He shrugged. "But it's home."

She got out and smoothed her shorts. The halter-top she wore left little to the imagination, although he didn't need imagination to know what lurked underneath.

She leaned over and pecked him on the cheek, and he wished she didn't look so great. "You look good, Sam. I see you're still playing tennis," she said, eyeing his tennis outfit. "It's been a long time."

"Yeah, it has," he said and led her into the house.

Henry went berserk. His tail wagged in circles. He leaped to her waist, slid down, and hopped up again.

"Henry," Lisa squealed. She picked him up and hugged him. Henry wrapped his paws around her neck and lapped her nose.

Lisa put the dog down and looked around. "Cute place. Got any coffee?"

Sam shifted his feet. "Yeah, sure. Sit down and I'll make a fresh pot."

She sat with Henry on her lap for a few more licks before snuggling into her and closing his eyes. Lisa took his head in her hands and with her fingertips, massaged the backs of his ears. Henry moaned.

"I think he remembers you," Sam said.

"Yes, I'd say so."

Neither of them spoke for several moments before Sam finally broke the ice. "What brought you here? How'd you find it?"

"Well, when you didn't call this morning, I decided it was too nice out to sit around and wait, so I figured I would go for a drive and see the town."

Sam brought her coffee. "Black, one Equal, right?"

She nodded. "Anyway, I'd heard so much about the famous Siesta Key Beach, I wanted to see it. And then I knew you lived on the Key, so I looked up your address, checked my map, and here I am."

"Did you see the beach?" he asked, unable to think of anything else to say.

"Yes, I stopped by to check it out, but I didn't stay. It's gorgeous." She looked up from her coffee and arched her eyebrows. "Want to go?"

He hesitated, groping for something to say. "Lisa, I—"

"Come on, Sam, it won't hurt you to take a couple of hours to enjoy the beach." She smiled the smile that once did strange and wonderful things to him.

"I came down here to see the Colony and enjoy the beach . . . but I also wanted to see you."

Aw shit, he thought. Why couldn't she have shown up here looking hard and tired? And used? But no, she has to arrive on my doorstep looking as feminine and lovely as I've ever seen her. The hell with it. A couple of hours on the beach can't do any harm. "OK, let me put on my suit. How about you?"

"Mine's already on," she said.

He started for the bedroom when she got up with her cup and squeezed by him. "I'll help myself to more coffee while I wait."

They nearly touched in the small space. She was so close he could smell the coffee on her breath, along with the familiar shampoo, which kindled old memories. He eased by her and into the bedroom.

Sam emerged from the bedroom wearing a Red Sox baseball cap and a Bath and Racquet T-shirt hanging over his bathing suit. Henry stood expectantly by the front door. "Sorry, buddy," Sam said. "You have to stay here and guard the fort."

As they stepped off the porch, Lisa looked back at Henry, who was on his chair, peering at them from the window. "Oh, Sam, look at him. He looks so sad. Can't we take him with us?"

"Can't do it, Lisa. No dogs on Siesta Beach."

47

They found a quiet spot on the beach and spread their blanket. Sam lay back and partly closed his eyes, leaving them open enough to watch Lisa walk toward the water. She wore a bikini that looked better on her than most of the twenty-year-olds.

Being here with her suddenly seemed natural, evoking other times at other places. He thought of the time when they made love on a deserted beach they had discovered in Bermuda, after which they both fell asleep. They awoke to a gentle shower and made love in the rain.

When Lisa returned, he feigned sleep. She lay down next to him, the fresh, moist scent of her body, blending with her sun lotion. He tried to block it out, and focus on other things, but distant memories kept returning, brought to him by the feel of her body touching his.

"Sam, are you awake?"

Best to fake it, play it safe, don't answer. "Yes."

"Please just lie there with your eyes closed and let me talk, OK?"

He took a deep breath and slowly let it out. "OK."

"I want to tell you some things I never had a chance to when the trouble began. It may not make a difference, but I want to at least tell you." She waited, but when he said nothing, she continued.

"You remember, Sam, that when you left for the conference in St. Louis, things were a little testy with us. I had told you that I was feeling . . . neglected, I believe was the word. I felt that you had gotten so wrapped up with your teaching, your students, your writing, tennis, your buddies, that I, well, I missed you. I know that sounds melodramatic, even now, but it's true. I tried to talk with you, but as was often the case back then, you were in a hurry, and said we would talk later. Well, I waited, but we never did. Are you still with me?"

"Yes."

"Two days after you left, I went shopping. I finished at about 5:30 and decided to treat myself to an early dinner at the Excelsior. About ten minutes after I sat down, Walt Piro walked in and was shown a table. He looked up and spotted me and came over. We chatted for a minute, and he said that since we were both there for dinner, he asked if he could join me rather than both of us eating alone. It was an awkward situation. I didn't know how to gracefully say no, so I said OK.

"Later, after he joined me, he said it was his birthday and asked if I would celebrate it with him over a bottle of champagne. I felt sorry for him, eating alone on his birthday, so I said yes. I was feeling a little down myself, and I thought maybe the champagne would cheer me up."

Sam remained still with his eyes closed. "All very agreeable of you," he said.

"Please, Sam," she said and touched his shoulder. "We had dinner and to tell the truth, it was fun. You know that I've never been much of a drinker, so it probably was the champagne, but I found him to be good company.

"Anyway, after dinner we walked out to the street where I said goodbye and started to hail a cab. His car was valet parked in front, and he offered me a ride home. I declined and said again that I would take a cab."

"I'm not sure I need to hear this, Lisa," Sam said.

"Please, Sam, it's important to me that I tell you exactly how the awful thing happened. Maybe I'm being selfish, but I have to tell you. It's been driving me crazy, never having had the chance to talk it through with you."

Sam nodded and braced himself.

"While we were standing there discussing him driving me home, with me juggling several boxes, a man and woman came out of the restaurant and hopped in the cab. Walt took my packages, put them in his car, and we left.

"When we got to our apartment, instead of dropping me off, he grabbed the boxes and said he would carry them up for me. I was tired, so I said OK."

Sam was tempted to interrupt her at this point, but said nothing.

"Inside the apartment, I suddenly felt woozy from the champagne and sort of staggered to the couch. Walt went to the kitchen and brought me some water. My head was resting on the back of the couch. He cradled it so I could drink the water, and the next thing I knew . . . he kissed me."

Sam tensed his body and rolled on his side, away from her.

"Sam, as God is my judge, I don't know why, but I suddenly responded. And I just . . . just let it happen." She began sobbing. "And that's when you walked in."

She leaned over and touched his arm. "I am so, so sorry. I will live with that horrible mistake forever."

Sam sat up, not sure what he would say or do. He studied her face, now wet with tears, and took her face in his hands. "It's OK, Lisa," he whispered. She started to slide her arms around him, but he moved away.

"Thank you for telling me, Lisa. I'm sure it made you feel better, getting it all off your chest." He couldn't think of anything else to say, and wasn't sure he wanted to.

"I don't know if that's true, Sam. But there was so much emotion and anger, we never did take the time to talk about it and see if there was a way we could salvage our marriage . . . and our love.

"I understood your hurt and when your anger took over, I got my back up, feeling guilty and defensive, projecting the blame onto you, convincing myself it was your fault for making me so vulnerable. Crazy, selfish, and stupid, I know, but I wasn't reacting rationally. I was ashamed and at the same time terrified at losing you. And then everything happened so fast. We didn't talk. We didn't discuss anything. We simply got a quick divorce leaving nothing but the terrible image of you seeing me and Piro like that." She closed her eyes and shook her head for several moments, as if trying to shake loose all the welled-up emotion.

She finally looked up and managed a wan smile. "Anyway, thanks for listening."

Sam looked at his ex-wife and neither of them said anything for a long time. She looked so sad, and he regretted her losing the chipper, upbeat attitude she had when she arrived. He wished he could take her back to it, but he couldn't. There were many things he wished now. He wished they had talked through their problems before she reached the point of being vulnerable to the attention of even a jerk like Piro. He wished he had tried harder to understand. But it was all too late now. He had moved on. The sounds of the song *My Way* drifted over from a radio next to a nearby couple. *Regrets, I've had a few, but then again, too few to mention.*

Sam smiled and nodded, "Let's head back," he said softly.

They walked together, leaving perfect sets of footprints in the sand.

Lisa pulled the car up to Sam's house, and they both sat in silence. Neither had spoken during the four-minute drive from the beach.

Sam broke the ice. "Lisa, I thought I had forgotten you and resumed my life. But I can see I haven't, completely. There's a part of me that will always love you. But right now, there's just too much baggage. As tempting as it is, I can't let myself drift back and expect that we can go on together and live happily ever after. And I'm sorry about that."

His hand was on the car door, but when her eyes filled with tears, his own watered and his lips quivered. He leaned over and kissed her. They whispered goodbye and he left.

48

Inside the cottage Sam homed in on his umbilical cord: the message machine. There was one message from Jennifer. He thought about how his encounter with Lisa made him realize how important Jennifer had become in his life. He missed her. You don't have to see a person every day to feel the comfort and security of a good relationship. That's how he'd been feeling about Jennifer, but things seemed different lately.

He felt like a kid, nervously dialing her number. He had dialed it a hundred times or more, without giving it a second thought, like calling to order pizza. She answered on the second ring.

"Hi Jen, it's me. Welcome home."

"Hi Sam," the familiar upbeat musical sound. "Thanks, it's good to be back. How are you?"

"I'm fine. When did you get back?"

"About an hour ago. I'm exhausted. I just took a long shower, and I'm going to bed."

She talked about the trip, tracking red tide, and writing up her research reports. And then her voice took on a different tone. "Sam I need to talk with you. Are you free tomorrow night?"

"Uh, yeah, free as a bird."

"You want to have dinner?"

"Sure. Where would you like to go?"

"Do you know The Columbia on St. Armand's Circle?"

"Yes, I know it. Shall I pick you up?"

There was a long pause—a pause he didn't like.

"Sure. See you at seven."

"OK, I'll make the reservation."

After calling the restaurant, he played over their conversation. "Sam, I need to talk with you," he said aloud. What the hell does that mean?

No answer at Sarah Hastings', nor her cell phone. He left a message and turned on his computer. It was after nine when he turned it off. He'd been working for nearly four hours, but would have to review what he had written tomorrow to see if any of it made sense. Right now he was exhausted.

He set the alarm for seven, taking no chances this time. Actually, he looked forward to some good, hard tennis, and to talking with Paul Robbins again.

In the morning, after making coffee, he discovered he was out of milk. Rather than deal with black coffee, which he hated, he would drive to Siesta Market and be back in five minutes.

Inside the garage he noticed that he'd forgotten to close the trunk after checking for tennis balls last night, and the light was out. Oh, oh.

He tried to start the car. Nothing. The battery was dead. He went back to the house and called Paul. "Paul, my battery's dead. Can you pick me up?"

"Sure. Pick you up at quarter of."

After feeding Henry, he sat on the porch, waiting for Paul, longing for a cup of coffee, and thinking about his car. He hadn't had the oil and filter changed since he first arrived in town. He was overdue.

Paul was right on time. "Hop in, Sam, I have to swing by Siesta Market and get some Gatorade. It'll just be a minute."

Sam pulled out a bill and held it toward Paul. "Can you grab a quart of milk for me?"

Paul waved Sam's money away. "Sure. Be right back."

Paul left the motor running while Sam waited. He idly glanced around the car and noticed something that puzzled him.

49

Paul returned with a bag full of Gatorade. "I got six bottles. You want one?"

"Uh, no thanks." Sam said little else on the way to the tennis club.

Sam lost badly in two sets, 6–2, 6–1. "You were too good for me today, Paul."

"Well, I have to say this was not the best tennis I've seen you play. You just weren't with it today. Want to try one more set?"

"Naw, getting the shit beat out of me twice is enough. Let's go in the lounge and have some coffee."

Sam watched Paul over coffee, not sure what he was looking for. He couldn't help noticing how neat and perfectly pressed his tennis outfit still looked after two sets. Paul always wore the latest in tennis fashion, everything color coordinated, and not a hair out of place. Sam glanced at his own image in the plate glass window—hair sticking up in two directions, his shirt covered with sweat and Har-Tru clay where he had fallen.

"You making any headway toward getting your life back to normal?" Sam asked.

Paul frowned and looked off at nothing. "It's been tough, but each day gets a little better." He sighed and turned back to Sam.

"Yeah. How about the business? Have you been able to keep up with it? It must be hard staying on top of things through all this. But I'm sure Mark is running things well. You're lucky to have him."

"I'm the brains of that company," Paul snapped. "I'm the one who 'runs things well'."

"I'm sorry, Paul. I didn't mean to imply otherwise," Sam said, stunned by the ferocity of Paul's comment.

Paul grinned. "It's OK, Sam. Sorry I overreacted. It's just that I founded the company and I'm very paternalistic about it. Mark, is a good man, but we work best together. He tends to feed off my enthusiasm and . . . I don't want to sound like I'm bragging, but I've been the idea guy and the brains behind the company. I guess it's important to me that you know that. Mark needs me to be down there with him."

"And you haven't been able to get down at all since Maggie's death?"

"Shit, no. There've been too many things to do here, just a million and one details: the memorial service, the funeral and burial, settlement of her estate. And I'm having work done on the house to spruce it up for sale. I haven't had time to go anywhere"

"You're going to sell the house?"

Paul heaved another sigh. "Yes, too many memories, and it's too big for me to rattle around in there alone. I'll probably move to Miami where the business is, and we can run it the way it should be."

Sam eyed him for a moment. "Well, I don't mean to sound crass, but you're not exactly going to have to rely on your business for survival."

Paul's look told Sam he didn't appreciate the comment. "I take pride in my business, Sam, and my work is important to me."

Sam nodded. "Yes, I know it is, Paul. Anyway, I've got to get back. Are you ready?"

Paul finished off his coffee. "Yep, let's go."

Sam was lost in thought on the way back and said little, still thinking of Paul's overreaction—a fragile ego he had not picked up on before. "Thanks for the ride, Paul. When do you want to play again?"

"I'll call you when I get back from Miami."

Sam watched him drive away and went inside, his heart pounding with excitement. Henry acknowledged his presence with a few pokes with his nose on Sam's leg and padded back to his perch by the window.

"Goddamn!" Sam said aloud. He poured himself some coffee and some of the milk Paul bought him, and thought about the last couple of hours while peeling off his sweaty tennis clothes. Henry came over, nudged the damp shorts and socks, took a few whiffs and wandered away. Sam paced around the cottage in his underwear, sipping his coffee, unable to take his mind off what was troubling him, and then a thought occurred to him.

Paul's going to Miami tomorrow to be with his little chickee. Sam thought of his conversation with Mark and Mark's evasive remark about Paul's personal life in Miami. Woman buys groceries for him and stocks his apartment, she's got to be more than a one night stand.

I'd love to know more about that personal life in Miami, Sam thought. His apartment would have to yield something. He looked at his watch: ten o'clock. He could jump start his car with his battery cables and be on the road by 10:30. Get to Miami by two o'clock and hopefully be back on the road by three or 3:30. That wouldn't get him home until seven or later.

He called Jennifer and asked if they could change their date to tomorrow night. She agreed.

After a quick shower, Sam dressed in a pair of jeans, an old T-shirt, and a plain black baseball cap. He and his neighbor, George Zerendow, rolled Sam's car out to the street, where they attached jumper cables to the batteries between their two cars. George was a painter who spent most of his time in his home studio, and seemed happy for the break. They both winced when Peter came bouncing out the door.

"Hey guys, what's up?" He looked at the cable hooked up to the two cars. "Trouble, huh Sam? I saw you pushing the car out."

"Uh, yeah, Peter and I'm in a real hurry to get going to Miami," Sam said, knowing that Peter would not let that deter him.

"Be right back," Peter said. "I want to get you a brochure and a statement of purpose for our program on the speed bumps." He disappeared into the house.

Sam's car started on the first try. He looked toward Peter's house and back to George.

George read his mind. "Get going, Sam. I'll deal with Peter."

Sam thanked George and took off.

The drive to Miami took a little longer than last time. He ran into a construction delay around Naples and arrived in Coconut Grove at 2:30. He parked his car in a covered pay garage, and attached the thick mustache he had brought with him, not wanting to take any chances of someone in the building seeing him and later describing him. He then walked the six blocks to Paul Robbins' apartment.

Standing outside Robbins' building, Sam reflected on the wisdom of why he was there. First of all, even coming to Miami was a spontaneous, impetuous thing to do. For all he knew Robbins' girlfriend could be in Paul's apartment right now, getting the place spruced up for his arrival tomorrow. He would take that chance.

He sat in the park across the street, waiting for someone to enter. Fifteen minutes later, a man about his age approached the building. Sam hurried across the street and arrived at the same time. He pulled out a set of keys and dropped them just as the guy opened the door. Sam scrambled for his key, while the man smiled and held the door for him.

"Oh, thanks," Sam said. "Appreciate it."

He got off at Robbins' floor while his benefactor remained on the elevator. The corridor was empty and quiet. He stopped at 422, rang the bell, and hoped he wouldn't have to use his phony story about being the new superintendent, making the rounds, introducing himself.

No answer after three tries. He looked around, checked the door lock, and was relieved to find that it was a simple Kwickset lock. No problem. He easily picked the lock and opened the door. He felt an odd sense of pride that he still remembered a skill he had learned so long ago. But he was no longer a cop, and what he just did was blatant breaking and entering. Christ! He could go to jail. He held his hand on the doorknob, debating whether to open the door or go back to his car and go home. Screw it. He had come this far. He opened the door and entered.

Although it was mid-afternoon, with the blinds closed the apartment was dark, and cool as a cave. The place was immaculate, and there was a vase of fresh flowers on the kitchen table. Looks like she's already been here, Sam thought. But she'll most likely be back.

He moved through the living room and turned down a corridor toward the bedroom. The smaller of the two was an office, which he decided to check out first. Paul's desk would be the logical place to begin.

50

Gia Fuentes left her hairdressers and walked the two blocks to her car. She checked herself in the car mirror, satisfied that Michelle had styled it exactly the way Paul liked it full and blown out, hanging to her shoulders—the wild look as Paul called it. Gia was tired, but the thought of seeing Paul tomorrow energized her. She wanted everything to be just right when he arrived, especially her hair, which he said was a turn-on for him. She felt a tingle thinking about him.

When she arrived at his building she had barely remembered the drive there, her mind was so focused on seeing Paul and fantasizing about the glorious sex they would have the moment he walked in the door of her apartment, and she had him on the bed.

But he liked her to stock his apartment also, since he would be staying in Coral Gables for a while. She wished he would stay with her the whole time, but he preferred having his own place, and she had given up arguing the point. She pulled her car into the building's garage, parked, and headed for the elevator.

* * *

Twenty minutes after Sam entered the apartment he began putting things back the way he'd found them. He made sure that everything was left exactly as he'd found it and headed toward the door.

As he was about to turn the doorknob, he heard footsteps approaching. He started to peer through the peephole but before he could focus, he froze at the sound of a key being inserted in the lock. He slipped into the hall closet and pressed himself against the wall. Huddling in the darkness, he listened to the footsteps clatter across the tiled entry. A strong perfume fragrance told him the new arrival was a woman.

Sam remained motionless inside the dark, stifling closet, afraid to move. He heard the woman's footsteps enter the kitchen just down the hall from where he stood, and he listened to what sounded like keys being dropped on the counter and items being removed from a bag and put into cupboards.

The temperature in the tiny closet seemed to rise by the minute. Sam flattened his body against the wall, wiped his forehead with a handkerchief, and pulled the baseball cap tight over his eyes, hoping the woman would simply put away the items and leave. He wasn't sure how much longer he could take the heat in the stifling closet.

The noise from the kitchen stopped, but she was still there. He heard her humming and muttering to herself. And then to his relief he heard her keys jangle. She's picked them up, he thought, and is going to leave.

At that moment a wave of nausea swept over him and a soft cough slipped out before he could stifle it. He doubted she heard it.

The sounds from the kitchen stopped. Sam placed a hand over his mouth and struggled to contain his heavy breathing.

The apartment was deathly silent. He reviewed the possible scenarios, none of them good. Would the woman step outside and call the police on her cell phone? Would she call for security?

Still no sound. He knew he couldn't hold out much longer in the hellacious heat of the closet. And then he heard the unmistakable sounds of the woman's footsteps leave the kitchen and stop outside the closet door.

He held his breath and slowly exhaled, pondering his options, when the door flung open. The woman, holding a kitchen knife, stood just outside, staring at Sam. He stared back from underneath his cap. Neither of them moved for what seemed to Sam like an eternity, when she screamed and lunged with the knife.

Sam dodged to his right as the knife plunged into a suit hanging just behind him. He bolted out of the closet as she retrieved the knife and struck at him again, still screaming. He caught her hand and shoved her into the closet, opened the apartment door and scrambled down the stairs, the keening wail of her scream following him as he reached the bottom and burst out into the sunshine.

Once outside, he removed the baseball cap and mustache, put on his sunglasses, and still trembling, made it to his car without incident.

He arrived home at 8:15 and immediately called Lewis at her home, got her machine, and left a message. Should he call the sheriff's department? Not a good idea. This is Lewis' case, and she's the one to talk with. She would go ballistic if he called someone else.

He called Jennifer and got no answer and no machine. She probably went to bed early and shut off everything.

In the morning Sam tried calling Lewis at home again, and again, no answer. He called her office and learned she'd gone to Orlando where her mother had been in a car accident and suffered a broken arm, but was doing fine. Lewis hoped to be back in the office tomorrow or the next day. Frustrating, but he could wait a day or two.

He called Sarah Hastings, who sounded more upbeat. "They appear to be cooling it on me, Sam, at least for the time being. So, it sounds like I finally have a little breathing space. How about you? Making any progress?"

"A little. I'm working on something that could be important. Too early to say now. Any progress on the attempt on your life or the break-in?"

"No, nothing new. I've installed a bolt lock on my apartment door, and I watch my back wherever I go. But tell me what it is you're working on."

"I can't say, Sarah. I haven't had a chance yet to discuss it with the police, and in any event, it may lead nowhere. Trust me, and bear with me for a while."

* * *

Gia Fuentes arranged the casa blanca lilies and added a ginger bloom, before stepping back to admire her work. She went to the mirror, splayed out her hair and watched it gently fall over her shoulders.

The anticipation of soon seeing Paul had put yesterday's incident with the intruder in the background. Paul's building superintendent told her that thieves had occasionally gotten into the building, but this was the first in a while. Because of her shock on opening the closet door and the darkness inside it, she wasn't much help in describing the person other than he was a man wearing a baseball cap and had a thick brown mustache.

She had called Paul and told him of the incident. His primary concern was for her safety and whether anything had been taken. When she told him she was fine and as far as she could see nothing was missing, he told her to forget it. He wanted no publicity.

Now, waiting in her apartment for Paul, she felt the same sexual craving which occurred whenever she thought of him, which was almost always. Gia had been with many men. And God knows she'd been with enough wrong ones, too many jerks, like the one before Paul, that loser Rick. She grimaced, thinking of the ugly scene when she told Rick she didn't want to see him anymore. Men can be such assholes.

Her thoughts returned to Paul. She knew she loved him, but there were things that bothered her, mainly whether he was willing to make a commitment to her, whether he truly did love her. But he was free now, and she would expect a commitment.

She was glad Paul was coming here to her apartment. She liked her place much better. It had some style and class. But she hoped that soon she and Paul could move into their own place together. She went into the bedroom, removed her clothes, and stepped into the shower. Her body began to vibrate in tune with the warm sensuous water, while her hands gently massaged those parts of her body that brought her pleasure.

51

Sam spent the rest of the day writing up his notes on all his activities, with special attention to his second trip to Miami. And he was still trying to figure out a way to discuss it all with Lewis without getting his nuts cut off.

He eased his mind onto the dinner with Jennifer tonight. He had been so wrapped up in the Robbins' murder and his book that he'd had little time to think of much else. His mind drifted back to Lisa.

It was a very emotional thing, saying goodbye. He wasn't sure what he was going to say or do, until it all flowed out of him. Even now he wasn't sure if he would regret kissing off everything the way he did. She was genuinely suffering and looking for forgiveness. He gave her that, but it was clear that she wanted more. What would he have done if Jen were not in the picture?

Which brought him to Jennifer. Is she still in the picture? She sounded strange on the phone. "Sam, I need to talk with you." A statement like that is never a prelude to a casual conversation.

* * *

Larry Gump stayed close to home all day. Tomorrow would be his big payday, and he wanted to be rested and sharp. He didn't expect any problems, but still he had to be on his toes, watch out for any flimflam, any bullshit to con him out of his money.

Larry also had to keep reminding himself that he was dealing with a killer who wasn't too happy about being blackmailed. He snickered and finished off the last of his sardines. Ain't no way Larry was going to put himself in any danger. He was too smart and the killer knew it. Sittin' right there in front of that fancy Saks Fifth Avenue, that's where they would conduct their business.

Larry would watch his pigeon leave and then he would drive off in the other direction in his rental car. Smart move there. He'd return the car tomorrow after the transaction and turn it in for another. Leave the truck in the garage for a while and then trade it in. Take no chances. Smart.

He went out to the garage, pulled a beer out of his mini-refrigerator, cracked it open, and sat back in his new Barcalounger. One beer ain't gonna hurt nothin'. He'd shut himself off after that. Be nice and fresh in the morning for his transaction.

* * *

Sam checked himself in the mirror: new polo shirt, chinos, loafers, and a blue blazer. Formal wear for him these days.

At 6:50, he pulled into Jennifer's driveway. Her bungalow, about the size of his place, sat behind a white picket fence, and if it were not for the tropical foliage, he would have thought he was looking at a summer house on Cape Cod.

Bougainvillea clung to the fence and trailed over the top. Impatiens neatly lined the shell path leading to the front porch. Everything was pure Jennifer.

He walked onto the porch and approached her doorbell, an old fashioned key-like turner in the middle of the door. He turned it, chuckling at the thick sounding *brring*.

Jennifer popped out at the first ring wearing a simple black dress, its brevity accentuating her long legs. Her hair glistening under the porch light curled softly around her shoulders, emitting a clean scent like it had just been washed. Did she look better than he'd ever seen her, or was it because he hadn't seen her in a while? Whatever, she stood for a moment, a broad smile on her face that reminded him how much he had missed her.

"Hi Sam." She gave him a quick peck on the lips, not quite what he expected, but it would do for now.

"Hi there." He stood for a moment, looking her up and down. "You look fabulous."

"Thanks, Sam." She pulled her head back and studied him with mock seriousness. "You look pretty dapper yourself." She opened his blazer and touched his shirt. "New shirt, huh?"

He looked down at the shirt. "Uh, yeah."

Neither said much during the short drive. Jennifer took several sips from her water bottle. Sam watched her from the corner of his eye, wondering if it was his imagination or did she seem fidgety tonight?

The restaurant had a warm, friendly atmosphere, with the smell of Cuban cooking in the air. But something just didn't feel right to Sam. Jennifer remained quiet as they settled in, while Sam fumbled with small talk. What the hell was it? "Sam, I need to talk with you" came back to him.

After ordering a bottle of wine, they leaned forward and touched hands. "Missed you," Sam said.

Jennifer slid her hands away and picked up her glass. "I missed you, too. Cheers."

Sam studied her for a couple of beats before lifting his glass. "Cheers."

"How's the investigation going?" she asked.

"It's not much different from when we last talked. Tell me about your trip."

She sipped her wine, started to put the glass down, and brought it back for another quick sip. She set it down, and focused her eyes on the glass rather than on Sam. She looked around the restaurant as if studying it or expecting someone. Sam felt like he was on one of his early high school dates. When at a loss for conversation, he and his date would intently examine matchbook covers, like each was making a major discovery in the words.

Sam watched her, wondering what she was thinking. "How's the wine?" he asked, groping for conversation.

"Hmm," she nodded. "It's very good."

"What is going on here?" He was about to ask, when Jennifer put down her glass and looked straight at him.

"Sam, I have to tell you something."

52

Paul Robbins paced around Gia's apartment. She tried to mellow him with kisses and maneuver him toward the bedroom. He was on edge in a way that made her nervous as well. But she soon had him on the bed, where she began taking off his clothes. She knew all the things he liked, knew how to please him.

Paul went at their love making with a frenzy, all pent-up lust with none of the tenderness she found so satisfactory when they had sex. He reached a climax and rolled over before she ever got into it. She tried to bring him back, fondling him, kissing him everywhere. "Hmm, this is what you can look forward to every night, sweetheart, when we are married."

He slid away from her. "I'm sorry, Gia. I guess I'm just not into it at the moment." He sat up and reached for his clothes.

She forced a smile and nodded. "I understand." She was disappointed, but she knew they had a lifetime of quality sex and love ahead of them. She had become accustomed to his shifting moods and she needed to be patient and supportive.

"I know you must be tired, Paul. Let's go into the living room and relax over a drink. Have you had anything to eat?"

He shook his head. "No, I haven't really thought about food."

"For God's sake, it's five o'clock, and you've had nothing to eat all day?" She led him into the kitchen, opened the oven and set a plate of food on the table. "I fixed you your favorite lasagna and I made a salad just before you got here. What do you want to drink?"

"I'll have a cold beer."

"All right, cut the lasagna and get the salad out of the refrigerator while I clean up the sink."

Paul watched her put on her rubber gloves to clean the pans, bowls and around the sink. She was a fanatic over her perfect nails as she was about everything. She was protective and possessive over anything that was a part of her, including him, which sometimes seemed to Paul to be a little creepy. It was also a part of her that he found very sexy—the creepy part.

The lasagna and salad looked good, and his appetite was back. He pulled a knife from the drawer, and did as he was told.

Gia returned and joined him at the table. Paul ate some of the lasagna and salad, put the rest in the refrigerator, cleaned off the utensils and the plate and left them on the sink to dry. He sat at the table, closed his eyes and let his mind wander.

His life had changed enormously and he wasn't sure he could handle it all. He did like Gia and God knows the sex was fantastic. But her pressing him for total commitment, even marriage, was getting on his nerves.

"Hey, are you there?"

He snapped out of the zone into which he had drifted and looked at Gia, her face inches from his. "Oh, sorry, Gia. I guess I got lost in thought for a minute."

She leaned in and kissed him. "It's OK, but I think we need to talk." She grabbed and held his chin firmly. "I want you to listen to me."

"Goddamn it, Gia. Don't do that," he said and pushed her hand away. He saw the fire flash in her eyes and sensed trouble coming.

"Paul, I've done a lot for you, and I love you. But sometimes you treat me like shit. How can you tell me you love me and then act like this? I'm sick of it."

Maybe it was because he was tired. Maybe he was beginning to feel hemmed in by her. Whatever the reason, he blurted, "Fuck you."

Gia's eyes widened and her face flushed. "You son-of-a-bitch," she shouted and punched him in the face.

Paul, reacting instinctively, grabbed her arm and flung her to the floor. She screamed and began yelling in Spanish. Before he could react she was on her feet and in his face, clawing, tearing at his cheeks and shirt, still screaming. Again, Paul pushed and slapped her hard on the cheek.

Someone pounded on the door. Paul stood in front of it for a moment. Gia, on her feet, froze against the wall. Paul opened the door and faced an elderly man and woman.

"What the hell is going on in there?" the man demanded. The woman, a tattered robe wrapped around her, glared at Paul.

"I'm very sorry," Paul said.

"Well, you damn well should be," the man snapped. "Bothering decent people with your screaming and swearing. What kind of animals are you?" The man poked his head around Paul, looked at Gia and shook his head. He drew his head back, looked Paul up and down, and shook his head again, letting them know the disgust he felt.

"I'm sorry, sir," Paul repeated. "Just a little squabble. It's over now, and we promise to be quiet." He held his hands out in a peace gesture, backed away and slowly began closing the door.

The old man, who appeared to be enjoying intimidating Paul, pointed his finger. "One more time and I call the cops," he said as Paul closed the door.

Inside Gia's apartment he walked over to her, hugged her and they kissed. "Sorry for being so rough," he said.

"Me too," she replied.

They stood for a moment and embraced. Paul took her by the hand and led her into the bedroom.

53

Jennifer's hand rested on Sam's, and the look in her eyes told him that he probably wasn't going to like what she had to tell him. In any event, it should at least liven up the conversation.

"What is it you need to tell me, Jen?" he asked and waited while it seemed all conversation in the room had stopped and there was nothing but a silence that roared and buzzed in his ears.

Her hands remained over his. "Sam, I wasn't totally truthful with you about the date I had with Patrick."

Hmm. Not a surprise.

"I told you it was an old friend and colleague who had asked me some time ago if I would celebrate his birthday with him."

Sam nodded.

"That part was true. He is an old friend, and I did promise to celebrate his birthday with him. What I didn't tell you was that he and I once had a very close relationship. We weren't engaged, but we did talk about marriage. It was that kind of relationship."

Sam felt the wine curdle in his stomach. He raised his brow in a silent invitation for her to continue.

"Patrick worked at the Galt, which is where we met. Two years ago he received a very attractive offer to be a senior biologist at a very prestigious marine laboratory in Australia, where he would study shark behavior, which is his primary interest. And the money was nearly double what he'd been making here. And . . ." she waved her hand. "Anyway, he accepted the job and asked me to go with him."

"To work at the same place?"

"No. There would be no job for me. I would have to give up

my work at the Galt, essentially give up my career. I couldn't do it, and didn't."

Sam grinned. "I'm glad."

She gave him a little half smile and continued. "Three weeks ago he returned to Sarasota. He didn't like Australia and was homesick. He had kept in touch with the Galt while he was in Australia and had kind of an open invitation to return if ever he wanted to."

"Did you and he keep in touch as well?"

"We did for a while, but it just sort of petered out." She paused, sipped her wine, and looked away for a moment. "And then I met you and . . . well, I didn't really think about him any longer."

"I like that part, too."

The waiter arrived with their dinner, which brought a hiatus to her narrative. They ate in silence for a while, intermingled with updates on their work and other chitchat. Sam poured them each the rest of the wine and waited for her to continue.

"Anyway, Patrick returned to work at the Galt, and we resumed a collegial relationship—nothing more. I told him about you, and he didn't press anything except to ask me if I would share his birthday. I hesitated at first, but then I relented. I didn't think it would do any harm."

"Did it?"

Her hesitation gave him the answer he didn't want—the answer he knew was coming from the time she started talking.

"Not at first. We had a nice time, had a few laughs. All in all, it was a pleasant evening. We arranged to meet downtown, had dinner and after dinner, we went our separate ways."

Sam thought back to peering out the window of the bookstore, being privy to some of those laughs. He decided not to mention that, and finished the last of his pork, which he suddenly realized, was splendid. Too bad he missed most of it.

"Then Patrick got assigned to the research boat, and he was on both of the trips I was on."

Getting to the bottom line now, Sam thought.

"The boat is not that big, and with nine scientists on it, you do see a lot of each other."

"Of course."

"Come on, Sam. This isn't easy."

He finished off his wine and wished there were more. "I know it isn't, Jennifer. I'm sorry you're not having as much fun as I am." He managed a grin. "I'm ready for the punch line."

"OK. Patrick and I saw a lot of each other on the boat, and some embers were rekindled. I know it sounds melodramatic, Sam, but it's true. He says he's still in love with me, and that's why he came back here."

"He has good taste. And you?"

"That's my problem, Sam. And that's why I'm telling you all this. I would be less than honest if I said there wasn't still a strong attraction. I thought it was long gone. But it's not."

Sam shrugged. "I'm a quick study. I think I've just been kissed off."

54

Larry Gump took a hefty slug of the last beer in his mini-fridge. He was only going to have one but he was wired about his big day tomorrow and the beers helped calm him down. Anyway, four beers wasn't nothin'.

And shit, who wouldn't be worked up over pickin' up a cool twenty grand with no heavy lifting involved. Larry smiled as he finished off the last of the beer. He liked the way he'd worked this deal—playing cool, but tough. Let the pigeon know that Larry Gump was not a man to be fucked with.

Larry took a pull on his empty beer bottle and frowned. He was wide awake and still had some heavy thinking to do about tomorrow's deal.

He got up and headed into the double-wide. Maybe pour himself a little of the real stuff, keep the juices runnin'.

* * *

Frank Baumert drove quietly through the night. No radio on, little traffic, only Frank and his thoughts. He'd spent the last few days in Everglades City with an old prison buddy until he could clear up some final bits of business before leaving Florida.

Heading north on I-75 he felt reasonably safe having switched number plates with the pickup his pal, Chuck, hardly used anymore, mostly just to haul trash. Kind of a dirty trick to pull on Chuck, but fuck him. He couldn't afford to get picked up now.

He kept his speed at a nice safe seventy, right about at the speed limit. Last thing he needed was to get pulled over by some fucking cop. He looked at his watch which said 10:15 as he passed into Sarasota County.

Tomorrow night he would do the coke deal and be on his way with twenty-five grand. Fuck Norm, too. He needed the money more than Norm did.

* * *

Sam watched and waited as Jennifer shook her head after he said he'd just been kissed off. What's that supposed to mean? He wondered. Was he missing something?

Jennifer reached across the table and touched his hand. "Here's what I'm trying to say, Sam, and I'm not sure how well I'm going to say it. But here goes. Yes, I do feel a very strong attraction to Patrick, but the other side of that coin is . . . well, damn it, I feel a very strong attraction to you which shouldn't come as any surprise."

"Hmm, we each get a very."

"Come on, Sam, be serious. I told you this is not easy. What I'm trying to tell you is that I don't think I have ever been happier than I have been since you and I met. I think you're smart, funny, sensitive, and . . . adorable."

Sam nodded. No problem so far. But he bit his lip and kept his mouth shut, waiting for the 'but.'

"Anyway, I guess what I'm saying is that." She paused, groping for the right words. "Now you have competition."

Does that mean I'm going to have to work harder? He was tempted to ask, but continued to show the restraint for which he wasn't noted. He rested his face on his hand and continued to listen.

"I know that sounds pompous, Sam, and I didn't mean it to come out like that. It was the wrong thing to say. Knowing you, I'm risking you saying adios." She paused and touched his hand again. "Please don't." She arched her eyebrows, asking him to respond.

"I'm listening," was all he said.

Her expression told him she would have liked to hear more,

but she continued. "The bottom line, Sam is that I'm feeling very," she turned her face away, looked back, and gave him a sheepish grin. "Screwed up."

Sam lowered his eyes as a mirthless smile crossed his face. He was smart, funny, charming, and adorable, all admirable qualities. But she was feeling very screwed up—the classic dilemma which has plagued men and women since time began. Except Adam. He didn't have any competition.

"I think I understand what you're trying to say, Jennifer. Your attraction to Patrick has come back strong, and my adorable charm is making it difficult for you." It was the wise-ass defense mechanism remark he'd been restraining himself against, and out it popped. He held up his hand, "Sorry, I didn't mean to be flip."

She shook her head and laughed. "See, that's what I mean. It's part of your charm."

He nodded, accepting his due. "Well, anyway, where does that leave us?"

"It leaves me asking for your . . . understanding?" She managed to barely squeak out the last word. "And your patience. I don't want to lose you, Sam, and—"

"You don't want to lose Patrick." He shrugged with a nonchalance he didn't feel. "It's a problem."

"I'm not sure what else to say at this point, Sam. I'm in a terrible quandary, and it's tearing me up inside."

"Hey, I'm cool about it," Sam said. "You can see me on Monday, Wednesday and Friday and Patrick on Tuesday, Thursday and Saturday. On the seventh day you can rest."

She slammed her napkin down and started to get up. He took her arm and gently eased her back down.

"I'm sorry. That was uncalled for. I guess that was my less than sensitive way of trying to inject a little levity—not that I'm feeling any. Jen, I think you're a fabulous lady in every way, and you know how much I care for you. But like I said, you've got a problem now. I think that's something you need to work out.

"In the meantime I'm going on with my life, and to be honest with you Jen, I'm not going to wait around for you to tell me that Patrick is your guy and it's been nice knowing me. Sorry, but I'm just not built that way. You do what you have to do and I will do the same."

Jennifer said nothing, just kept nodding her head as if trying to think of what to say next. Sam watched the moisture gather in her eyes and resisted the urge to reach over and hug her.

"I know you're not built that way, Sam." She smiled and touched him again. "You're also a very sweet guy." She went quiet for a moment. Sam said nothing, letting her think through whatever it was she might be wrestling with.

Sam motioned for the check. "I think we'd better go, Jen. I don't know if there is anything more that can be said. Call me if and when you want to talk."

Jennifer puckered again, said, "OK," and they left.

They were both quiet during the drive to her house. Sam felt like all that could be said was said, and he was sure Jennifer felt the same.

After dropping her off, he took his time driving home, trying to process their conversation. He often found that he did his best thinking *after* a serious discussion, and like most people, thought of things he should have or wished he'd said. But not this time.

This was her deal and something she had to work through. As far as he was concerned, he's been down this road before and as much as he cares for her and loves their relationship, he would move on. Life was too short to worry about things over which you had no control. Maybe the most ominous part though, was her telling him he's sweet. When a woman calls a guy sweet, it's a brotherly thing—like let's be friends.

When he arrived home he decided to call Sarah, check in and see how she's doing and have her fill him in on any new developments. It was 10:30. A little late but she had told him he could always call her anytime up to about midnight. When her machine answered he left a message and went to bed.

* * *

Bryce Hanson was annoyed when he got the call. His partners wanted to meet with him at the Ritz at ten o'clock. Tonight, especially, was not a good night for Bryce and he thought they were being inconsiderate, expecting him to come on such short notice.

"It's important," Sparky Waters said in a tone that told Bryce he had best be there. But what the hell could be so important that couldn't wait until tomorrow?

At ten sharp Bryce walked into the bar. Pete, the head bartender, waved and called, "Hi Bryce!" Now that he was here, Bryce was no longer annoyed. The Ritz was his kind of place, and he liked the way people turned when Steve called him by name—Bryce Hanson, one of the town's movers and shakers. He swaggered across the room, smoothing his new Saks necktie, smiling at his admirers.

Sparky and the others greeted him and asked if he wanted a drink. He said yes and ordered a round for everyone. "Put it on my tab," he told the waitress.

The four men exchanged some small talk while waiting for the drinks. When they arrived, Sparky said, "Bryce, I'm going to come right to the point." He looked toward the other two men, who nodded, but avoided eye contact with Bryce.

"Sure, Spark. What's up?" Bryce sipped his scotch, peering over the glass at his partners.

"Our deal doesn't seem to be going anywhere Bryce, and we're going to have to dissolve it." Sparky said. The others nodded again.

Bryce had just taken a sip of his drink and it stuck in his throat. He coughed to release it and stared at the three men for a moment. They met his stare.

"I don't understand, Sparky." He turned to the others. "Frank, Howard? Is this true?"

They nodded. "I'm afraid so, Bryce," Howard said.

"But why?"

Sparky sat back and folded his arms. "We can't wait any longer, Bryce. There have been too many hang-ups. First we had to wait nearly a year for you to get your father's will squared away. Now, these goddamned turtle people are causing more delays. We know we can eventually prevail, but it's going to drag on for longer than we can afford to wait. They're appealing to every agency that will listen to them about how our resort is going to destroy the ecology of turtle nesting. And we're being hit on all sides by those CAPPS assholes. It's going to get ugly before we can move ahead."

"But—"

Sparky talked over him. "The bottom line Bryce, is we've found another piece of land up in Bradenton. The land is on the Gulf, but unlike your piece, it's not in an area where turtles come to nest. And we're not going to have to put up with any CAPPS bullshit. Those people up there welcome a new resort. It's good for their economy. Vacationers in a resort like ours spend money. In fact there is nothing controversial about it."

"And the owner is willing to come in for a smaller piece of the action than you had demanded," George added, the friendliness now gone from his voice.

"But you can't do this," Bryce wailed. "We're partners, Spark," a desperate whine in his voice. He waited, but when there was no response, he sat up and squared his shoulders. "I'll call my lawyer."

"You do that, Bryce, but I assure you we are perfectly within our rights. Your lawyer will tell you that," Sparky said.

Bryce began to protest but his ex-partners got up and walked out leaving him in a blind rage—with the check. He was glad they had left, as there was no telling what he might have done. He checked his watch: 10:30. Time to go. He downed the rest of his scotch and left.

55

Larry Gump lay slumped at his kitchen table. A half-empty bottle of Seagrams whiskey sat next to him. The only sounds in the room were Larry's muffled snoring and the soft, steady breathing of the person standing over him.

He never heard the vehicle pull up next to his trailer and stop. Nor did he see the person peering at him through the window or hear the footsteps approach his front door.

Larry's visitor winced at the stench of stale beer and whiskey, cigarette smoke, and body odor. The intruder looked down at Larry, enjoying the feeling of power over the little fool who thought he was the one in control.

Putting on the handcuffs was easy, first clamping one over Gump's wrist, then gently placing Gump's arm with the cuff on it in back of him, and clamping the second cuff over his other wrist. Gump's head jerked forward, and he opened his eyes. He blinked twice and struggled with the handcuffs. "What the fuck?"

"Hello, Mr. Gump."

"What the fuck?" Larry repeated. He blinked twice more, trying to focus and figure out what was going on.

"Remember me?"

Gump, now fully awake, strained at the cuffs holding his arms behind him. "You! What the hell are you doing here?"

"I've come to pay you, Gump. We made a deal, remember?" the intruder said.

Larry seemed to relax. "Yeah, that's right, we do have a deal. But hell, you don't need no gun or handcuffs. I'm harmless."

"Sorry Gump. We don't have a deal anymore. I changed my mind."

Gump shook his head, trying to clear it and absorb what he had just heard.

"Who did you think you were dealing with, some little mouse who was going to roll over and give in to your fucking greed?"

"Hey," Larry said with a smile. "I was just doin' a little negotiatin', that's all. Shit, everybody likes to negotiate. You know, a little give and take. Everybody does it. Ain't no need to get all worked up. I didn't mean no harm. I figured you'd come back with a counter offer and we split the difference, settle it nice and peaceful. You don't need no cuffs or gun to settle our business. I'm a reasonable man. Tell you what. Let's just go for five and call it square. Shit, you ain't gotta worry about Larry Gump. His word's his bond. Ask anybody."

"You stupid fool. A little give and take? Call it square? You little asshole. I'm not giving you anything. No, that's not true. I'm going to give you a drink of your whiskey."

Gump tugged to be free as he watched Maggie Robbins' murderer take a paper cup from the sink, fill it with whiskey, and empty the contents of a small packet into the liquor.

"What are you doin'?" Gump yelled. "Come on. Shit, you ain't got no cause to fuck with me. I ain't done nothin' to you. I just figured I'd take a shot at seein' if I could make a little money. I figured you had ways of gettin' it. I can see now I was wrong. Believe me, I ain't gonna mess with you no more. I learned my lesson. Now, let me go, and we'll forget the whole thing."

Tired of listening to this fool, the visitor grabbed Gump's face, forced his head back and mouth open, picked up the cup of whiskey, and fed it into Gump's mouth and held his mouth closed. Larry struggled and sputtered, trying to resist the whiskey flowing into his throat until the cup was empty, and he was released.

Gump coughed and tried to spit out the whiskey that was no longer in his mouth. "You're fuckin' nuts. What are you makin' me drink all this whiskey for? What's that stuff you put in it? Get outta my house."

"Relax, big shot. The chemical in the whiskey works fast. I won't have to hang around this shit hole much longer."

Gump continued to squirm and rant until the squirming slowed and the ranting turned to incoherent mumbles, and his eyes began to flicker. "What'd you do to me?" he managed to spit out before his head wobbled aimlessly, and his eyes closed. They popped open and he began struggling again.

"Relax, Gump. You're not going anywhere. You're just going to take a little nap, that's all. In a couple of minutes you'll be unconscious and in another fifteen minutes or so you'll go into a nice deep sleep for at least two hours."

Gump still wasn't fully asleep, but he would be no problem to handle. After stuffing the cup in a pocket, the intruder uncuffed him, and dragged him out to the garage, still muttering, but capable of little else.

Inside the garage Gump's tormentor placed him into the driver's seat of his pickup and went back into the house to make sure nothing incriminating had been left behind. After shaking and pinching Gump, and deciding he was truly out, the killer poured more whiskey into him before setting the bottle on the seat and closing the door.

The truck's gas gauge showed the tank three quarter's full. Gump would be long dead before the gas ran out. Satisfied with a good night's work, the visitor removed the handcuffs, started the engine, and left.

* * *

Gia Fuentes sat at the kitchen table tugging and playing with her long hair, thinking about her future with Paul. She did love him and especially liked the idea of all that money. But she worried about his commitment to her. He said all the right things but lately she had begun to wonder.

The doorbell rang, and she spun around as if an animal had growled. She checked her watch, which showed a little before midnight. "Yes?"

"Pizza man."

Gia checked the peephole, opened the door, and took the pizza. "You're right on time. How much do we owe you?"

"That'll be sixteen dollars, ma'am."

She fumbled in her pocket and stepped inside. "Paul, do you have a twenty dollar bill for the pizza?"

"Yeah, there's some money here on the bureau."

"Excuse me," she said. "I'll be right back." She went to the bedroom, picked up a twenty-dollar bill, and started for the front door.

"Twenty bucks for a small pizza! That's robbery," Paul yelled.

Gia responded. "It's only sixteen dollars. Don't worry, I'm not going to steal your change. You want the pizza in the kitchen or the bedroom?"

"The kitchen."

Gia paid the man and he left.

56

Edgar Pratt was fed up. This was the third month in a row that Gump was late with the rent. Three weeks now and all he gets is "the check is in the mail" crap. Edgar was going over there to get his money. And he was not leaving until he got it. Either that or Gump moves his trailer elsewhere. He would pay Gump a fair market price for the garage he'd built and then he wanted him gone.

Still, Edgar hated confrontations, and as he drove along the dirt road to Gump's trailer, he hoped Gump would have the rent, and they could avoid a scene. He wouldn't appreciate Edgar coming so early in the morning, but he had much to do today and wanted to get this out of the way. He pulled into the driveway and was startled to see and smell exhaust fumes coming from the garage.

He ran around to the side and looked in the small window. The entire garage was shrouded in smoke, and he could see nothing but the dim outline of Gump's pickup.

After trying the door to the garage and finding it locked, Edgar picked up a large rock and flung it through the window. Fumes poured out, but it was still too murky to see if anyone was inside, and the window wasn't big enough for him to climb through.

Edgar took out his cell phone and called 911.

* * *

That same morning Sam finally reached Diane Lewis. Not surprisingly, he received a cold reception. He told her he had critical information, and he needed to talk with her as soon as possible. Urgent, was the other power-charged word he used.

"All right, Sam. Come on over, but this better be good."

"Thanks. By the way, how is your mother?"

Her voice softened. "She's going to be fine. Thanks for asking."

Fifteen minutes later he knocked on her office door. "Yes?" the voice from inside called.

"It's me, Sam."

"Come in."

When he opened the door, she was sitting at her desk, writing. He stood, waiting to be acknowledged. Lewis remained absorbed in her writing. Sam shifted his feet and cleared his throat. She continued to ignore him.

"Helloo."

A moment later she put the pen down and looked up. "What can I do for you, Sam?"

He grabbed a chair and hauled it in front of her desk. Without being invited, he sat and said, "I have some information for you that I think you will find interesting."

"Why don't you let me be the judge of that, Sam?"

He plowed ahead. "A couple of days ago I went to Miami and—I, uh, dropped into Paul Robbins' apartment."

"You 'dropped into' Robbins' apartment? Was he there?"

Sam hesitated. This could get ugly. "Diane. I've had a very strong hunch about Robbins, ever since I noticed a mileage discrepancy on his car's odometer. I've been trying to reach you about this but haven't been able to.

"The other day I was riding in Paul's car to the Bath and Racquet Tennis Club when I glanced at the windshield and noticed a Jiffy Lube sticker in the corner. The date was May 8 exactly three months from the date Paul drove to Miami to meet with Mark and close the big deal. As a reminder to their customers for their next lube, Jiffy Lube puts the month and date exactly three months from the date the customer brings the car in for a lube. The mileage read

17,650. Now, that's the mileage on the car on the day they put on the sticker plus 3000 as a reminder that that's when you're supposed to have the car lubed again. So the actual mileage on that day was 14,650. Then I looked at the current mileage on the odometer, which read 15,576. Nine hundred and twenty-six miles.

"Round trip between Sarasota and Miami is 420 miles. I know because I recently drove it. Where did the other 506 miles come from?"

Sam knew from the expression on Lewis' face that his news had made an impression. But she said nothing.

"Jesus, Diane. Doesn't that make you just a little bit curious?"

She ignored his question. "And because of that you broke into his apartment?"

Typical Lewis, he thought, jumping to conclusions. He knew he would have to deal with a lecture from her, before he could go on. "Uh, yes, I guess you could say that, but—"

Lewis was on her feet moving toward him.

"Please, Diane, please listen before you throw me in jail. Will you do that?" He danced away from her, holding out his hands, waiting, watching her face, trying to see if she was going to have him cuffed and taken away or hear him out. The look in her eyes told him, at best she was about to give him a royal ass chewing.

"I cannot believe you!" She caught up to him, and jabbed a finger at his chest. "You just may have gone too far this time, but for the moment, I will reserve judgment and listen to what you have to say. And as I said on the phone, this better be good."

Sam had expected much worse and hurried with his story before she changed her mind. "Well, there was a pile of mail on Robbins' desk which included an American Express bill with a postmark of two days earlier. So it had just arrived. His girlfriend probably brought in his mail.

"As you know, a credit card bill tells a lot about a person's activities during the month it covers. So . . ." This was the part Sam was dreading. "I steamed it open and checked every entry."

Lewis' head snapped back like she'd been punched. "You what? You—"

Sam held up his hand. "Please Diane. Let me finish." He hurried on with his story before she could interrupt again.

"It was all pretty ordinary until I noticed a gas charge at a Texaco gas station in Sarasota for $34.86 on February 9—the day Maggie Robbins was killed. I made a copy of it on Robbins' copier." He handed it to her.

"It gets better. I called the Texaco station in Sarasota where Robbins apparently charged the gas. The manager told me that when a customer pays by swiping his card through the slot, the transaction is recorded on a master log in the station's computer. This master log records the time and date a purchase is made, the credit card number, and the amount charged. He says he keeps his log for six months before throwing it out. So, you can get that info from the station."

He paused before springing his coup de grâce. "Robbins filled his gas tank at 9:45 P.M., right around the time frame the coroner said Maggie Robbins was killed. He told you and me and everyone else that he had been in Miami since the eighth."

The silence hung in the air, punctuated only by the sound of a car's horn from outside. Sam waited while Lewis walked slowly across the room and back to her desk. "That is interesting, Sam. Very interesting."

"Diane, I know you can't use what I found as evidence, because of the way I found it. But you can sure as hell get a copy of his statement from American Express as well as the data on the Texaco station's log. Maybe it's something you've already done," he added.

She looked up sharply, but said nothing. He knew her well enough by now to see that she was connecting with what he told her. And she had not checked with American Express.

"Diane, Robbins told me he hasn't been anywhere since his wife's murder. And yet, he's got nearly 500 miles that he can't account for. You saw the gas receipt I just showed you. Robbins was here the night Maggie was killed—the night he was supposed to be in Miami, taking all of his telephone calls."

He paused, waiting for all of what he had just said to sink in. "Diane, Paul Robbins is our man. I know he is."

Lewis nodded, letting everything she'd just heard sink in. She pursed her lips and remained silent, while Sam held his hands out in a "well?" gesture.

Lewis slowly began to nod. "Robbins' wife placed a call to him at his Miami apartment at 9:03 P.M.," she said, pacing about the office, ticking off points with her finger. "The phone company records show that the call was answered and the conversation lasted for thirty-two seconds."

She ticked off another finger. "His partner, Mark Folven said he called Robbins at around 9:30 and told him he had just closed the deal he and Robbins had been working on. He said Robbins congratulated him, said he was feeling better, and would see him in the morning.

"As you know Robbins was supposed to join him and their prospect that evening at dinner, but he had been ill during the day and had to beg off. We talked with the man they were dealing with that day, and he confirmed that Robbins appeared to be quite ill. He said he wasn't surprised that he couldn't make it for dinner."

She held out a third finger. "Robbins' partner picked him up at eight A.M. on the morning after Maggie was killed. They drove to the prospect's building and arrived a little after 8:30. That's when Robbins got the call from us about his wife's murder."

Sam followed her around the room. "I know I told you about the woman I saw leaving Robbins' house the morning I drove over there, and the kiss they exchanged. When I was in Miami the second time I saw another beautiful young woman carry groceries into Robbins' apartment. The guy's got women all over the place, and his wife has been dead for less than two weeks."

"You saw a woman carry groceries into his apartment," she said in the kind of voice that implied this was no big deal. "Was that before or after you broke in? And will you stop following me?"

He bolted in front of her and stopped. "Jesus, Diane, would you give me a break and stop busting my balls? Paul Robbins was not in Miami the night his wife was killed. He was here in Sarasota, killing her." He backed up and stood, waiting for her reaction.

57

Several seconds went by before Diane began to nod and motioned Sam to sit. Was he finally breaking through? He remained standing, awaiting her response. When there was none he started to speak, but she talked over him.

"We talked at some length with the woman you saw coming out of his house. She admitted that she and Robbins had been having an affair. She also told us that she spent the night with Robbins at his apartment the night his wife was murdered.

"Paul Robbins has continued to be high on our list, but I've been leaning toward the possibility that he paid someone to do it, like your friend, Mr. Baumert, who has vanished as I believe you know.

"Further, we have had two lengthy discussions with Bryce Hanson and his possible connection with Baumert. We will continue to include Hanson among our suspect list, which of course, is all the more reason why Baumert's disappearance is so troublesome. And we have found no reason as of the moment to exclude your client as a strong suspect."

Sam shook his head, as if to clear it of everything he'd just heard, especially the part about the woman spending the murder night with Paul. That was a curve ball.

"Look, Diane, I'm sorry about Baumert. But I don't think Robbins would have hired somebody. He's not a rocket scientist, but I think he's too smart to take a big chance like that, especially hiring Baumert, a guy who once threatened to kill Maggie. Also, he has to know that if the cops got hold of Baumert, they would sweat him and talk him into a deal to turn over Robbins. No, I think he did it all by himself."

"Your observation about what 'the cops' would do with Baumert is right on, which is precisely why we are so anxious to find him. And if you think Paul Robbins is not dumb enough to hire Baumert, why are you making such a big deal about Bryce Hanson's connection with him? Or do you think he is dumb enough."

Sam squirmed in his chair. Lewis did have a point. He shook his head. "I guess I don't have an answer to that, Diane."

Lewis got up from her desk and walked around the office stroking her chin. "Robbins certainly had motive. You probably know that Maggie's lawyer told us Maggie had an appointment to meet him three days after she was killed. He said she wanted to discuss her will."

Sam nodded vigorously, excited to see her starting to come around. "Where do you go from here?" He was tempted to say "we," but decided against it.

"I'm not sure." She looked around the room, studying each wall before turning back to Sam. "How do you account for the fact that Robbins' girlfriend said she spent the night in his apartment with him? Do you think he can be in two places at the same time?"

"I can't account for that, Diane—unless she's lying."

Lewis nodded. "Yes, that's always a possibility." She walked back to her desk and sat. "We're going to get him in here and talk to him right away."

"He's in Miami, went over there yesterday. I'm not sure when he'll be back."

"We'll have the Miami police pick him up. By the way, on the American Express receipt?"

"Yes?"

"It's possible, Sam, that he could have lost the card, and somebody else used it."

Sam started to say something, but she talked over him. "Look, Sam, if Robbins did this, I want to nail him as quickly as you do. But you know as well as I we can't go off half-cocked. Wait here." She got up and left.

Fifteen minutes later Lewis returned. "Sorry to keep you waiting so long. We're waiting for AMEX to fax us the Robbins' statements. We should have them shortly." She frowned and slumped into her chair.

"What's the matter?" Sam asked.

"They informed me that Robbins called and told them he lost his American Express card and had it canceled. The date he called was the day after Maggie Robbins' murder."

"Shit."

"It gets worse."

"What do you mean?"

"They have a receipt where the card was used the next day to buy a laptop computer at Computer Buyers Warehouse in Venice. Doesn't look anything like Robbins' signature. Later that night, Robbins called and canceled the card. Said he'd just discovered it missing."

"So the computer was bought the day Maggie's body was found and you called Paul," Sam said.

"That's right."

"What time was the purchase made?"

"It was made at 1:10 P.M. I know what you're thinking. If Robbins bought it, it would have been just about the time he was getting close to Sarasota."

"Right. And Venice is on the way driving north, which is where he'd been driving. Jesus, do you think he was cool enough to stop on the way, buy the computer and even dump it before arriving at the house?"

"Could be," Lewis said. "We'll show his picture to the store and see if they recognize him. As for the gas station, if he got the gas at night, their camera won't likely have a clear photo. Maybe we'll recognize his car." She paused and gave him one of her looks. "Now, will you sit down in that chair and stop hovering over me?"

Sam sat. "He's smarter than I thought. Ten to one when he bought the computer, he used some kind of disguise—baseball cap, maybe a wig with long hair. If he's been smart enough to think everything else through, he's not going to let himself be tripped up by buying a computer. What do you think the chances are of finding the computer?"

Lewis got up and stretched, walked to the water cooler, drank a cup of water, and stood for a minute, looking out the window, before returning to her chair. "Not good. He probably buried it somewhere in the woods by now or dropped it in deep water out in the Gulf. He has a boat and he could have taken it out any time."

"How long was Robbins with you and the other officers when he returned from Miami?" Sam asked.

"Most of the day. We were in and around the house all day and he was there."

"What time did the investigative team finally leave?"

She thought for a moment. "Hmm, I'd say everybody was out of there by six or so."

"So Robbins was alone for the rest of the night?"

"Yes, I'd say so. What are you getting at? Are you suggesting he could have gone out that night and dumped it?"

Sam shrugged. "It's a thought." He slumped in the chair, collecting his thoughts. "Interesting, though, that he only lost his AMEX card. Convenient, huh?"

Lewis shook her head. "He didn't. Most people have more than one credit card. We called Visa and MasterCard, and guess what?

Both companies told us he reported them lost."

"Same time?"

"Same time."

"He is cute, isn't he? For some reason he found it necessary to use his card here that night. And then managed to cover his ass very nicely."

"Maybe he used his card to buy the gas that night. And maybe the person who found his card did," Lewis reminded him.

An officer came in with a sheath of papers. "Here's the stuff from American Express, Diane."

Sam got up and joined Diane looking through Paul Robbins' American Express statements, along with the receipt from the computer store. The odd ball signature on the computer store receipt stood out.

"This makes it tough," Diane said. She got up and poured herself some coffee. "You want some?"

Sam shook his head. "He's still going to have to explain all those extra miles on his car. What's your take on them? They fit in perfectly with another round trip between Sarasota and Miami."

"Yes, but all he has to do is make up some story about hopping in his car sometime after the murder and simply driving around to clear his head—you know, just get away. People do that in times of stress. Maybe he drove to the Everglades. Maybe he just drove."

"You're forgetting that he told me he didn't go anywhere after the murder. Stayed close to home. Hell, he had all those women to service."

She gave him a patronizing look. "Sam. He can simply say he didn't tell you that. You misunderstood him. Then it's just your word against his. And don't forget we're not finished with Hastings yet. She still hasn't been able to explain how her perfume was all over the bedclothes. And the fingernail. And the size ten footprints."

"Come on, Diane. Robbins has been around Hastings enough to know what perfume she wore. He must have also noticed her fake nails. He could have easily planted both. He's very clever . . . and I think he's a killer. And I believe you know that."

Lewis slammed the coffee mug on the table. "Goddamn it, Sam, you come up with these simplistic little theories of yours and then you make this sweeping assumption that I know that. Well, you want to know something?"

Sam braced himself.

"My gut tells me you're right. But we don't have near enough here to charge him. He can explain away everything, and we would be left with a case full of circumstantial evidence that a good defense attorney would tear to shreds. Which takes us back to the little matter of him being in Miami at the time his wife was murdered. The prosecutor's office wouldn't touch this with what we've got so far."

Sam felt validated. The always unpredictable Lewis was on the same note with him. "Maybe not, but you can bring him in and sweat him. Keep the pressure on him."

"Yes, we can do that, and we will. We'll start by calling Miami and have them pick him up."

58

Sam's mind was in overdrive as he headed home. His eyes strayed to another motorist who had pulled up next to him at a red light. He observed the man for a moment, and his eyes widened. "Oh my God!" he said aloud, and raced toward his cottage as the light changed.

* * *

Paul Robbins and his partner, Mark, sat in their small office going over the files of the several people they had interviewed for the sales rep position, and arranged to conduct follow up interviews with three of them. They discussed expanding their line of sporting goods, but decided it needed more study.

Paul wasn't feeling well again and knew he wasn't thinking all that clearly. He also realized he might be losing some of his incentive now that he would soon have the kind of money that precluded his having to work for a living. But he liked what he and Mark were doing, was proud of their little company, and the successes they were beginning to have. People are going to finally begin to see that he's every bit as smart as his wife was.

"Mark, I'm going to go over and follow up on that Marshall account, and then I've got some errands to run. I'll see you here in the morning."

* * *

Sam picked up what he needed in the cottage, jumped in his car and drove straight to the sheriff's department, took the elevator to Lewis' floor, and approached the receptionist. "Sally, is there an empty office I can use for a few minutes?" He flashed her his killer smile.

She returned his smile. "Sure, Sam. The conference room is open. Go ahead and use it."

He thanked her and went into the empty room. A few minutes later, Diane Lewis' phone rang.

"Lewis here."

"Diane, this is Sam. I'm coming over to see you again."

"Sam, what do you want now?"

"Let you know when I see you. Bye."

Thirty seconds later Sam walked into Lewis' office without knocking. "Hi!"

She looked up from her writing and dropped the pen. It clattered to the floor. "Sam! What the hell?"

"Diane, Paul Robbins finessed everything with a tape recorder while he was here killing Maggie." His voice was hoarse with excitement.

Lewis studied him for a long moment, absorbing what he had just said. After taking a deep breath, and slowly letting it out, she lowered her eyes, and asked, "And how do you know this may I ask?" She picked up her pen and resumed writing.

Sam went to her desk, leaned on it, until he made eye contact with her. "Listen to me, Diane. Driving home from your office, I noticed a guy stopped at a light next to me, talking into a tape recorder. That's when it hit me."

"You mean a cell phone?"

Sam shook his head. "No, it was clearly a hand-held tape recorder."

She put the pen down again. "Sam—"

He interrupted her. "Diane, listen to this." He took a small tape recorder from his pocket and turned it on.

Lewis listened to Sam's part of the conversation between him and her a few minutes ago. Her expression and demeanor changed.

"I simply taped my call to you," he said. "When you answered the phone I turned on the recorder and played my message, then turned it off when you talked and turned it back on when I wanted to speak again. I easily controlled the conversation."

Lewis put the pen down and sat back. "He would have had to have an accomplice to work the recorder when his wife and Folven called."

"Exactly. And I'll bet the farm it was his Miami girlfriend. She worked it for both phone calls. He knew Maggie was going to be calling. He told me, and I'm sure he must have told you that she always called him at the same time when he was in Miami. And Folven said Paul told him to be sure and call after his meeting with their client. He knew what Folven was going to say. He knew the deal was a slam dunk."

"So he could have anticipated the conversation from each and tape his comments accordingly," Lewis said.

"Sure, same as I did. You said the phone company records showed that both conversations were very short."

Lewis pursed her lips and sat quietly.

"Well?"

"You might very well be right, Sam. You just might. I look forward to talking more with Mr. Robbins."

59

Paul Robbins went straight to his apartment after he left Mark. He was tired but he also needed a good strong drink. He sat at the kitchen table and poured himself a double bourbon—with a little bonus added. It had been a difficult couple of weeks, a period in his life that he would never forget. The bourbon warmed his stomach and soothed his mind. His head began to clear. He finished his drink and climbed into bed for some much needed rest.

Within minutes he fell into a deep sleep and dreamed of a sleek sailboat with him at the helm. Gia stood next to him, her dark hair flying in the wind as he maneuvered the boat somewhere in the Caribbean.

They pulled into a cove and dropped anchor, and made love. After they made love they sailed further into the sea. Gia urged him to turn around, but he refused. She began shouting at him, and he slapped her. She slapped him back.

A storm came up and the winds blew harder, ripping the sails and breaking the mast. The boat foundered, and Paul watched in horror as the waves pulled it toward the rocks jutting from a small island.

The boat pounded against the reef and began to break apart. He called for Gia, but she was gone. And then he heard voices calling his name. He awoke, his body covered with sweat, and sat up in the darkness. "Thank God. It was only a nightmare," he whispered.

But the voices and the pounding continued. He heard his name. Someone was banging on his door, calling his name. He crawled out of bed and made his way toward the door.

"Who is it," he yelled.

"Police," a voice answered.

Paul peered through the peephole in his door and saw two men in business suits standing at the door. One of them held credentials with a badge prominently displayed. "Please open the door, sir," the voice said.

"What the hell?" Paul muttered as he slid the lock and opened the door.

Two men stood facing him. "Paul Robbins?" one of them asked.

"Yes, I'm Paul Robbins. What do you want?"

"Mr. Robbins, we'd like you to come down to the station with us," the spokesman replied.

"What for?"

"Suspicion of murder."

"What the hell are you talking about? Murder of whom?"

"The murder of Gia Fuentes."

60

Sam and Diane Lewis sat in her office. "Some turn of events, huh Diane?" Sam said. During the past several days, ever since he called her about Robbins' mileage and the AMEX receipt, Diane had been not only cooperative, but downright friendly.

"How was your trip to Miami?" he asked.

She rotated her hand back and forth. "Good and bad."

"Meaning?"

"Meaning Miami has him and they're not going to let go. A first year law student could get a conviction."

"Is that the good part?"

"Let me finish. He was with his girlfriend in the apartment all evening. Gia Fuentes is her name, by the way. They fought. Neighbors came over and complained. His shirt was torn, and there were scratches on his chest. They said she was disheveled and had a welt on the side of her face. He talked to his partner on the phone, and then at midnight the pizza delivery man said Robbins was there and paid him."

"He saw Robbins there at midnight?"

"No, but he heard Fuentes and him talking. She asked him for money, and he told her there was a twenty on the bureau. The guy said Robbins complained about the price and Fuentes gave him a sarcastic reply, something like, 'Don't worry, I'm not going to steal your change.' Then they talked about where Robbins wanted to eat the pizza."

"Where was he when he was saying all this?"

"In the bedroom."

"What else?"

"Here's the clincher. The knife that killed her had Robbins' fingerprints all over it."

"Jesus. How dumb could he be?"

"Hey, Sam, this is the same guy who used a credit card to buy gas in Sarasota the night his wife was killed."

"Yeah, but if he did, he's also the same guy who was smart enough to come up with a pretty good alibi for that."

She nodded. "True. In any event, Miami says they have an air tight case."

"Is all that the good part or the bad part?"

She smiled and shook her head, like you'll never change. "Probably a little of both because I still believe the son-of-a-bitch is our killer, and I want to nail him so badly I can taste it."

"So the bad part is that Miami gets him, and you want him. But maybe it's not air tight in Miami. With thirty-five million bucks he can afford the best lawyer in the country."

Lewis shook her head. "Given all that's happened that money will be tied up in litigation and probate for at least two years. The best lawyers will want a minimum of several hundred thousand up front and right now, from what we have gleaned, Robbins doesn't have a pot to piss in until he gets his money—if ever. It's too risky a situation for any top lawyer. Hell, they don't need to take that kind of risk. He's more likely to wind up with a public defender. He's going to be convicted, Sam.

"We're going to keep digging on this, Sam, but," her voice trailed off. "We ordered the videos from the gas station where Robbins' AMEX card was used to see if we could pick him up in it, but it was too grainy and dark."

"What about the car?"

"You can make out that it's an SUV, but it's not clear enough to determine the make or even the color. What's maddening to me is we're going to come up empty, because the real killer is now Miami's property. I don't have a good feeling about what we have left. I had a meeting earlier today with my boss, the sheriff and the State Attorney. We went over everything we have on Paul Robbins."

She got up and paced the room, nibbling on her cuticle. "They both agree that it's quite possible Robbins killed his wife. They are also in complete agreement that what we have would not be nearly enough to indict him, and if we did, the odds would be heavily against our getting a conviction. He would walk.

"I'll tell you something else, Sam, I'm beginning to think Robbins also might have had something to do with the death of a man named Larry Gump. You may have seen a small piece about it in the papers."

Sam nodded. "I did, but why do you think Robbins might have had something to do with that? What I read sounded like the guy was drunk and fell asleep in his car in the garage with the motor running."

"There are reasons to believe Robbins might have used his tape recorder again to establish his presence in Miami, while he was here killing Gump."

"And they are?"

Lewis glanced at her pad again and set it down. "We would have simply written Gump off as a drunk who fell asleep in his vehicle inside his garage and died of carbon monoxide poisoning." She extended her hand toward Sam. "As you said. It certainly has been known to happen. However, there were several things that caused us to take another look at him.

"We found a sheet of paper in his bureau drawer with a half dozen phone numbers on it. Apparently it was his telephone directory. Mr. Gump did not have a wide circle of communicants. One of the numbers belonged to Paul Robbins. We then checked

Gump's phone records and found three calls to Robbins, the first coming two days after his wife's murder."

"Have you talked with Robbins since Miami picked him up?"

"Yes, they let us talk with him—with two of their people in the room. He said Gump and he had talked about a small boat Robbins had for sale. Said they'd been negotiating on a price."

"Which you think is bullshit."

"Which we think is bullshit. And I'll tell you why in a minute."

Sam sat back and folded his arms. "OK."

Lewis continued. "We then also followed up on the other phone numbers Gump had on the sheet of paper. One of the numbers was a gentleman who fished with Gump. After some rather extensive questioning, we got an interesting piece of information from the man."

Extensive questioning. Uh, huh. Sam pictured the man sitting in a warm windowless room, being interrogated by two, maybe three, hard-nosed cops. "And?"

"The man works in the Department of Motor Vehicles and he told us that Gump had leaned on him to provide him with the name of the owner of a vehicle for which he had the registration number."

Sam bobbed his head up and down. "I can see this one coming."

Lewis, on a roll now, continued "Yep! The name he came up with—"

"Paul Robbins."

"You got it."

"Did Gump tell the guy anything else?"

"No, and that would be a problem for us in court. With Gump dead, there could be no way to conclusively prove why he wanted that number."

Sam got to his feet. "Wait a minute. You said the man fished with Gump. Did he say where they usually fished?"

Lewis grinned and beckoned him to sit. "We're on the same page, Sam. They often fished just off shore in the bay on the south Key."

"Right off the Robbins' house, among others," Sam said.

Lewis pointed a finger at him. "Bingo!"

Sam got up again and walked about the office. "So Gump was fishing in one of his favorite spots, just off Robbins' house, saw a car drive up, and someone sneak around the back of the house. He got curious, pulled his boat up, ran over to the car, and wrote down the license number." He returned to Lewis and stood next to her. "And then–"

Lewis joined in with him, "He started to blackmail Robbins."

Sam sat. "I'll be a sonofagun."

Lewis mouthed the words slowly. "For which Robbins killed him or had him killed."

Sam shook his head, letting it all sink in. "Nice work."

"Thanks, but not nice enough. No matter what our theories, my bosses are still looking at two unsolved murders—on my watch. Whatever we have, including what you've come up with and what we have between Robbins and Gump is all strictly circumstantial, if that." She got up, walked to her desk, and sat, which Sam took as a signal their visit was over.

Sam remained seated, studying Diane. Her shoulders hunched, and her face sagged. "So, he gets away with murder here, but—"

She finished his sentence. "He's going to be convicted in Miami."

Sam watched her walk to the door, another signal to him. The woman is definitely not subtle. He walked slowly toward her.

"What about Sarah Hastings and Baumert?"

Lewis frowned. "We're not totally finished with Hastings. But everything we have is circumstantial, and the DA's office is reluctant to indict her on what we have. The perfume she wears isn't commonplace, but still a lot of women in this town wear it. Lots of people wear size ten shoes.

"As for the fingernail, we don't know how long it was on the bed. She was on that bed with Maggie Robbins only six or seven days before the murder. A good lawyer would demolish that piece of evidence."

"What about Baumert?"

"He seems to have disappeared. He's obviously broken his parole and will be back in jail if he's ever found.

"Oh, and I have some news for you. The Sarasota police matched some prints they found in Hastings' apartment and picked up the guy. He had a locksmith business here, but went bankrupt. He also has a record for forgery and assault. He confessed to picking the locks on the building and on Hastings' apartment. And guess what?"

"What?"

"We offered him a deal if he would tell us if he had anything to do with the attempt on Hastings' life. He confessed to that and said he was only trying to scare her."

"What was the deal?"

"That he give us the name of the person who paid him to do it."

"And?"

"Bryce Hanson. They've already picked him up."

Sam smiled. "Justice triumphs. And I take it you have nothing further on Bryce."

"Not yet. Certainly Bryce had a strong motive, but we really have nothing else to connect him with Maggie's murder."

Sam said nothing. He felt her pain.

"That son-of-a-bitch, Robbins," she muttered.

Sam reached the door and stopped. "But, if Robbins was over here, killing Larry Gump, who killed his girlfriend?"

"Let sleeping dogs lie," Lewis said and opened the door.

Sam stood for a moment, moved by the look of despair on Lewis' face. She's a good cop and deserves better. He wanted to hug her and tell her it's all right. Instead, he shook her hand and left.

61

A few days later Diane called Sam to tell him that they were officially dropping their case against his client. Unable to convince the prosecutor's office that there was enough solid evidence to indict Hastings, they had no choice. Sam was not surprised. His discussions with Lewis had hinted in that direction. Anyway, Robbins was Miami's now.

There was a sadness in her voice and he wished he could think of the right words. But nothing came. He wished her well and they hung up.

After hearing the news he took Henry for a stroll and as they returned, Sarah Hastings pulled up. He invited her in for coffee.

"Sarah, you're back to your old self. You look great."

Looking at her, he realized his compliment was an understatement. The upside of her ordeal was that she now looked better than ever—which was saying a lot. Dressed in jeans and a striped shirt, her hair styled, and wearing new designer sunglasses, she looked years younger than when he had last seen her.

"Thanks, Sam. I closed on two contracts so I have some new business coming in. I even cleaned my condo. You'll have to come by and see it and have a drink. I'm still working with the Sea Turtles Protection League, developing more community awareness. You should join, Sam."

Sam smiled. "Maybe I will."

"Which, come by for a drink or join the League?"

"Both. And you're still with CAPPS?"

She nodded.

"Congratulations on prevailing over that resort. I hear they've moved on."

"Yes, I take a lot of pride in that." She took out her checkbook and began to write. "Time to settle up."

Sam shook his head. "No way. I didn't do anything to earn that. Put it away."

Sarah protested, but he was adamant. "You hired me to find the real killer, and I didn't do that. You're off the hook, because they know there wasn't enough evidence to indict you.

"I should tell you though, that these are good cops, and they will not give up on you or anyone else they consider to be a valid possibility. If you did kill Maggie, the police will eventually come up with what they need to get you."

"Thank you, Sam. I needed that. Gee, I'm so glad I came over." She paused for a moment and squinted. "Are you thinking I could have killed Maggie?"

Sam smiled. "Don't worry about it, Sarah. You and I both know you didn't kill Maggie, so the cops are not going to come up with anything else."

Sarah eyed him for several beats, and a little smile slid across her face. "I think you know something, Sam, something you're not telling me. I think you know more than just my word that the killer planted the evidence to implicate me. And I have a hunch you may have some idea who. I hope I'm right and you and the cops catch the bastard. By the way, the whole town is still talking about Paul killing his girlfriend. Isn't that amazing?"

"Yes, it is," Sam said. He walked over and took the check from her hand and put it in her purse. "You keep that and buy me a dinner sometime."

"You got a deal. And thanks again for your help, Sam, and for being my friend."

She got up and started to leave, but stopped and stood for a moment with her back to Sam. When she turned, the expression on her face told him she wasn't ready to leave quite yet.

"Sam, there is something I need to tell you. It's been gnawing at me."

Sam stood and waited, wondering what now?

Sarah walked over to Sam, stopped in front of him and took a deep breath. "A while back I drove over to see you. I knocked on the door several times and got no answer. I sort of instinctively tried the door and it opened. I walked in and called your name several times. I was about to leave when a thought crossed my mind—a thought I'm not proud of."

Sam smiled. "Yes, I remember forgetting to lock the door and coming home to find Henry cowering in the corner. You were curious to know what was in my notes."

She covered her face with her hands and nodded. "Yes, how did you know?"

"The yellow pad wasn't put back as I had left it. Also as I said, Henry was acting very strangely."

Sarah began to sob. "Oh, Sam I am so, so sorry. I—"

"Forget it, Sarah. No harm done, and you had the guts to tell me when you didn't have to. Now, your only penance is to apologize to Henry for scaring the crap out of him."

Henry, who had warily eyed her since she arrived, remained behind Sam.

"It's OK, Henry," Sam said.

Sarah leaned over and picked him up. "Goodbye, Henry. Give me a kiss."

Henry obliged by licking her nose twice. She put him down and left.

After Sarah left, Sam's thoughts turned to Jennifer. With all that had been going on, he'd had little time to think about her—maybe a good sign that their breakup might not be as painful as he had thought.

He was hurting when they parted company that night. He was sure he loved Jennifer and still thought so. But he'd come to realize that since leaving Boston, he had developed a fatalistic, or was it simplistic, attitude toward life. That old Spanish saying, *Que Sera Sera* had it right. Whatever will be, will be. It was a very liberating feeling. But at the moment, the prospect of life without Jennifer was not exactly liberating.

He opened his computer and went to work on his novel. For the first time in weeks he felt his writing flow, fleshing out his protagonist, Dirk, with each page. Dirk, his hero. He felt a growing simpatico with him and wondered if Dirk would feel the connection if he were real. Probably not.

Four hours later he closed down the computer. There was still plenty of work to do, but he knew it wouldn't be too long before he could type the words, "The End", first draft or not. No matter how many books he would ever write, he knew that tremendous feeling of accomplishment would never diminish.

His thoughts drifted back to the Maggie Robbins' case. The person most likely responsible for her murder was in the grip of the Miami police. If he and Diane were correct in their suspicions of Paul Robbins, she would have at least one and possibly two unsolved murders on her record. Robbins was a killer, either here or Miami. Which was it? He felt certain it was here.

Sam had been cooped up so long in front of the computer, he needed to take a walk. He headed toward the village, meandering through curving avenues with Spanish names and a potpourri of cottages nestled in thickets of brightly colored tropical foliage. He turned right on Ocean Boulevard, and walked up to where it curves, both right and left along the water.

Deciding he had strolled far enough, he turned and went back toward the village. As he walked past Donegan's Deck, someone called his name. "Samuel, my boy."

Only one person ever called him Samuel. He turned and saw Brewster, his actor neighbor sitting on the outside patio of the restaurant, a rustic village hangout where ninety percent of the clientele sat outside on the spacious wood deck facing the street.

Brewster was on his feet, hoisting his beer mug toward Sam. "Come over here, Sam and let me buy you a beer."

Sam grinned at the sight of Brewster attired in white flannel trousers, saddle shoes, paisley shirt with an ascot neatly knotted at the neck, in sharp contrast to the cut-offs and tank tops of the other male patrons. He admired Brewster's full head of white hair gleaming in the late afternoon sun. At the moment Sam could think of nothing he would rather do than join Brewster for a beer. And Brewster did add a bit of cachet to the place.

"Samuel, my friend, what a treat spotting you," Brewster said, welcoming Sam with a beer he had waiting for him.

Sam sat down and sipped his beer. "Brewster, you're a slow learner. I'm going to have to work on you. My name is not Samuel. My given name is Sam, and if you don't stop calling me Samuel, I'm going to call you Barnaby."

Brewster exploded with laughter, and began coughing and wheezing. Sam rose to help him, but he held his hand out and shook his head, reassuring Sam he was all right.

When the hacking subsided, Brewster replied in the rich baritone that sounded like he was reciting Hamlet—a role he had, in fact, played many times. "I'm sorry, my good friend, but you always strike me as more of a Samuel than just plain Sam, which you must admit sounds rather pedestrian." Again his hand went up to finish his thought before Sam could speak. "Which, dear boy, you are most definitely not."

"Thanks, Brewster." Sam winked at him and leaned forward. "You're not meeting a beautiful woman here, are you?"

Brewster looked off in the distance and sighed. "If I were, alas! There is little that I could do to satiate whatever lust may lurk in her loins." He turned back to Sam with a broad smile. "But I could regale her with charming repartee."

"Of that, Brewster I have no doubt," Sam said.

"And speaking of beautiful creatures, how is my wonderful Henry?"

"Henry's doing just fine."

Brewster finished his beer and pulled a pristine linen handkerchief from his pocket and dabbed his lips. "Sam, did you read about that Robbins' fellow you know, the one whose wife was murdered, has been arrested for killing his girlfriend in Miami?"

"Yes, I did," Sam said.

"Interesting," Brewster said as he beckoned for the check. "You know some people think he might have had something to do with his wife's death. Did you know that, Sam?"

"Yes, I've heard that," Sam said. He checked his watch and finished his beer. "Gotta go, Brewster. Are you heading back?"

"No, a friend of mine is picking me up here and we're going to have an early dinner at Ophelia's charming waterfront restaurant, where I'm sure a man of your impeccable taste and style has dined many times. Would you like to join us?"

"No thanks, but have fun."

Brewster smiled and nodded. "Go along. You probably have a date with one of your beautiful women."

Sam started to speak, but Brewster talked over him. "Oh, I see your comings and goings. The other day, a very attractive lady in a red convertible, and that stunning young woman with the strawberry colored hair. You're a lucky man, Sam. Enjoy your bachelorhood and your youth. And let this old man live vicariously through your adventures."

Sam studied Brewster for a moment and saw a handsome, dashing man underneath the old age, and realized that behind the façade of urbane joie de vivre lurked a man longing for his own youth.

"Brewster, something tells me that whatever adventures I might have, pale beside those that you have enjoyed."

"Well said, lad. But, alas! Past tense," Brewster said as Sam left.

The conversation with Brewster rattled around Sam's head on the walk home. It reinforced his growing conviction that you make the very most of each day, emphasize the positive and not worry over whatever negatives come up. Life is indeed short, or at least the prime of one's life is.

He turned onto his street and headed toward his cottage. Jennifer's Jeep was parked in front.

Sam walked over to the open Jeep where Jennifer sat. She gave him a little half smile, but said nothing.

"Hi Jen, how long have you been sitting there?" he asked.

"I just got here and spotted you coming down the road." Again, she hesitated, avoiding eye contact with him. "Uh, can we talk?"

"Sure," Sam said, with a casualness he didn't feel. "Come on in."

"Can we walk over to Dog Beach? The sun is so pretty in the west over the water," she said, still sitting.

He opened the door, reached in and helped her out. "Sure, let's go."

Neither said much on the walk to the beach, but Sam felt the tension in the air. He stole several glances at her, looking chipper in her Galt uniform, brown Bermuda shorts, Galt T-shirt, and white sneakers. She also looked tired.

There were only a few people on the beach. They found a quiet spot behind three large rocks. Sam watched Jennifer, trying to gauge her body language or anything else that might tell him what she was thinking. He saw nothing and waited for her to get around to the point.

"Sam, this has been a very difficult week for me. I hope I never have to spend another like it," she said.

"Well, I can only say I'm sorry for whatever part I have played in your cognitive dissonance." He arched his eyebrows like, how do you like that one?

She smiled. "All right, stop being Samish. Anyway, you and Patrick are very different guys, which is what has made this week so difficult."

He started to say something, but she waved him off. "Patrick and I have known each other for a long time. We have a history. You and I have had much less time together."

"Que sera," he muttered to himself.

"What?"

"Nothing."

She gave him a puzzled look and continued. "Well, I . . . oh hell, I'm not going to beat around the bush."

Here it comes, Sam thought and readied himself for life without Jennifer.

"Sam, you're a very complex person, probably more so than even you realize. You're smart, you're a thinker, and you have a sensitive side that I have found very appealing."

Sam gave her an "Aw, shucks" look and began digging at the sand with a stick he'd picked up. He wasn't sure where she was going with this, but starting out with the compliments was not a good sign. He continued digging, waiting for the "buts" to come.

"You're also a little flaky, Sam," she continued. "And God knows you can be independent." She leaned her head toward him, trying to get him to look at her.

He focused on his digging, muttering, "Emphasize the positive."

"Dammit it, Sam! Will you stop mumbling and look at me?"

He jumped as though stung by a hornet and dropped the stick. When he looked at Jennifer, there were tears in her eyes. "Jen, I—"

"Oh shut up and listen to me."

She puckered and her lower lip began to quiver. He watched her face, now contorted with tears and scrunched into a rubbery mask that he found irresistible. He started to speak, but she waved him off.

"I've been a jerk," she continued. "And I have just been through the worst week in my life, but the bottom line is that I cannot juggle two men, and I don't want to."

Sam threw away the stick and slid over to her. "And?"

She moved her body into him and put her arms around his neck. "Sam, if you will forgive me, I would like to blot out this week and take up where we left off. Can we?"

When she sniffled and puckered up again, Sam took her in his arms and held her. Neither said anything except Sam's whispered, "Yes." There was nothing else that needed to be said.

A breeze came up and Sam felt Jennifer shiver. "Come on, Jen," he said. "Now that virtue has triumphed, let's head back."

She reared back and pointed her finger at him. "There! That's what I mean about you. 'Virtue triumphs'," she said, mocking him. "You'll never change." She grinned and held his face in her hands. "And please don't."

"You neither," he said and taking her hand, led her back to the cottage.

After a brief but happy reunion with Henry, it was Jennifer's turn to lead Sam. She slid her arm through his and they went into the bedroom.

They lay on the bed with their heads on the same pillow, Jennifer cuddled into Sam's arms. "It's been a very long week, Sam. And toward the end of it when I began to miss you badly, I realized I had made a big mistake, and I hope you can forgive me for putting you through this. If it's any comfort, I feel like a jerk, and I know I'm lucky that you're still here."

Sam gently pulled her closer and kissed her. "It's been a tough week for me too sweetheart and I've missed you terribly. But I do want to congratulate you on your wise decision and for reaffirming my conviction that you are a woman of impeccable judgment."

After a moment of no response, she began to giggle, which accelerated into laughter that shook the room. She rolled over on top of him and nibbled on his ear. "That's the Sam I've been missing," she said. "And now, I'm going to ravish you."

"Sounds good to me," Sam said.

Their lovemaking was long and filled with tenderness, interspersed with conversation and laughs, along with creative ways to please one another. Eventually they dozed off, wrapped in each other's arms.

It was early evening by the time they were up and around again. They showered and had a drink on the porch. Together they fixed dinner and ate, listening to the soft sounds of Chet Baker's *Songs for Lovers*.

Jennifer left at eleven o'clock, a departure neither of them wanted.

"Sorry, Sam, but I've got this eight o'clock staff meeting, and I need to get home to get a decent night's sleep and do all the things a woman needs to do in the morning, always better done at home. I'll call you after the meeting."

Sam sat on the porch for a while after she left, reviewing their perfect evening and how easily they had slid back into things. Funny, when she arrived he had bad vibes, just as he did when she told him about the problem last week. He had tried to be casual about the whole thing, setting up defense mechanisms like "whatever will be will be" when inside he was hurting badly, afraid to admit it even to himself—especially to himself.

He had always tried to find something good out of problems, even if the good wasn't immediately apparent. If not for the trouble with Lisa, he would have never known Jennifer. And as painful as this past week had been, it made him acutely aware of how much he cared for her and how much a part of his life she had become.

"All's well with the world," he said and went into the house.

63

In late July Paul Robbins was tried and convicted for the murder of Gia Fuentes. He was sentenced to life in prison.

Sam had neither seen nor talked with Diane Lewis for some time. He had recently heard from one of the sheriff's people he had gotten to know that Lewis was not doing well. She was very down from having two unsolved murders on her record and was apparently becoming paranoid about either losing her job or, at the least, being demoted.

He called her, hoping to cheer her up but had no success. "Come on, Diane, let me take you out for a long, leisurely lunch, where we can just kick back and relax."

"Thanks, Sam. It's good of you to call, but I'm just not in the mood for any long, leisurely lunches. I'm not doing much of that these days. Oh, by the way, I've been meaning to call you. Frank Baumert was found dead two days ago in a Tampa motel room. The Tampa police think it was a drug deal gone bad. They found traces of cocaine on a table."

Sam wasn't surprised. "He have any money on him?"

"Nothing." She thanked him again for asking her to lunch, wished him good luck with the new book when it came out, and hung up.

Sam understood her frustration. She was a terrific cop who took her work seriously and was not accustomed to failure. She had in fact, been a shining star in the department and people there felt she was headed for bigger and better things.

She had not given up on Robbins easily. Sam refused to let her. Together they had marshaled all of the evidence they had, which they both felt was considerable and had taken it to the district attorney in Miami who would be trying Robbins. They had gone all the way to the state attorney without success. Miami refused to even consider that Robbins was in Sarasota killing Gump when Gia was killed. They had their man and that was that.

Diane had finally given up and moved on. The injustice of it all continued to plague Sam and not a day went by that he didn't think about it.

But in other ways, he had no complaints. He was nearly finished with the final draft of his book, the hectic pace of his life had slowed down—and most importantly, things were back on track with him and Jennifer.

64

Sam sprawled on his chaise lounge, still plagued by Paul Robbins having been convicted in Miami when he should be in prison for the Sarasota murders. Several weeks had passed but he still couldn't get Robbins out of his mind. He forced himself to think back on every conversation he'd had with and about Paul, when an idea hit him. He sprang off the chaise and made a phone call.

Two days later Sam sat opposite Paul Robbins in a small visitors' room at the Florida State Prison in Starke. He wasn't surprised at Robbins' appearance. His complexion was the shade of a Florida sky before heavy rain. His dull eyes stared blankly at Sam, and his hands shook when he set them on the table between them. He looked ten years older than when Sam last saw him. "Hello, Sam," he said softly, forcing a wan smile.

"Hello, Paul."

Paul put his hand up to his left eye as though trying to stop the tic in it. He noticed Sam staring at his other eye and pointed to the bandage over it. "I said something my cell mate didn't like."

"Is that how it is here?" Sam asked.

"Worse," Paul said and they both went quiet for a moment before Paul with forced cheer in his voice said, "Sam it's good of you to come. You're the person I have missed the most." He looked around the room. "You must have some pull. Except for conferring with our lawyers, inmates normally have to meet with their visitors behind a glass wall and talk over a telephone."

Sam nodded. "I'm a licensed private investigator." He smiled, "Plus it didn't hurt that the assistant warden here is an old friend of mine from Boston."

A tepid smile crossed Paul's face. "Means a lot, your coming to see me, Sam."

"Has Mark visited you?" Sam asked.

Paul frowned. "No," he said quietly.

"Has anyone?"

Paul shook his head.

They shared some awkward small talk before Sam said, "You know Paul, I certainly would never have thought you capable of murder, but I'll tell you something—and this may sound strange. If you were to commit a murder, I would have thought you'd be one of those people who would get away with it." Sam scowled and shook his head, "How could you have been so stupid?"

Paul sat up and shot him a look. "Stupid?"

"Yes. Stupid. Look, I'm not going to berate you for killing Gia. Your being in this hell hole is punishment enough. But I always thought you were a very intelligent guy, and now I realize you aren't at all. You had me fooled."

Paul straightened and shifted in his seat. "I am not stupid, Sam. I did not have you fooled."

"Of course you did, Paul. One of the things I liked most about you was your keen mind, and now, look at you. How could I have so misjudged you?"

Paul winced and glared at Sam. His eyes rose to Sam's and a strange look came over his face—an incongruous mixture of pride and embarrassment.

Sam studied his face and sensed he might have struck a chord. When Paul spoke he formed his words carefully. "Sam, you didn't misjudge me."

"Sure I did. You were really stupid, Paul, and I'm as disappointed in discovering that as I am in knowing you're a murderer," Sam goaded. "Hell, I would have thought that you, of all people, would have been clever enough to get away with murder instead of bungling it the way you did."

The grayness in Paul's face disappeared, replaced by an angry flush. "You really think I'm stupid, huh?" he repeated.

"Paul, how else should I think when I look at what you did? You get into a big, loud argument with your girlfriend, so violent that the neighbors had to come to the door. They see you with a torn shirt and scratches all over you, and Gia with a swollen face and black and blue marks. Then you leave your fingerprints all over the knife you used to kill her. Christ! A seventh grader wouldn't have been that dumb. How could I have so badly misread you?" He shook his head in disgust.

Sam sat back and watched the agitation building in Paul, struggling to contain his frustration and anger. Twice he tried to speak and both times he stopped.

Sam burrowed in. "That's your legacy, Paul. A murderer. And a stupid murderer to boot."

Paul took a deep breath and spoke in a firm voice. "Well, I have news for you, Sam. I am not stupid. In fact, I am pretty goddamn smart."

Sam snickered.

Paul leaned in closer and spoke in a half whisper. "I'm going to tell you something and then see if you think I'm so stupid. I did not kill Gia Fuentes."

Sam waved his hand at Robbins. "Come on, Paul. Get off it. Do you think I'm as dumb as you are?"

Paul closed his eyes and shook his head violently as if trying to shake away Sam's words. "I did not kill Gia Fuentes," he repeated.

"The police and a jury said you did, Paul."

"I know that, but I didn't." He paused and the hollow eyes burned into Sam, his face now so close, Sam winced from the foulness of his breath. "You didn't misread me, Sam. If anything I'm even smarter than you thought. I didn't kill Gia in the idiotic manner you think. No, I committed two murders in a scheme so brilliant that the murders would never be solved." He hesitated, waiting for his bombshell to sink in, and whispered, "I killed both Maggie and Larry Gump and got away with it. Stupid? Try brilliant, Sam. I was in Sarasota murdering Larry Gump the night Gia was killed.

"What you think was stupidity on my part was quite the contrary. I was once again setting up the perfect alibi." He paused again before asking, "Do you still think I'm stupid, Sam?"

Sam appeared stunned. "Not if I can believe what you're telling me."

"There's more," he said.

Sam waited.

Paul turned back to Sam and lowered his eyes. "I killed Maggie for a number of reasons. Do you want to hear them all?"

Sam's eyes closed as he tried to deal with the wave of emotion sweeping over him. "Yes," he whispered.

Paul nodded and continued. "She ridiculed me every chance she got. Told me I was a loser, and constantly compared her success with my failures. She cuckolded me by having an affair with a woman. She was going to change her will and cut me out of it. Yes, there were many reasons, Sam." He paused and struggled to contain his excitement.

"Why are you telling me this, Paul?"

"Because I won't have you thinking I'm stupid," Paul shot back. "I had committed the perfect crimes, and was very clever in how I set them up.

"The night Gia was killed she and I faked the argument and fight to establish my presence there in her apartment. Later that night when the pizza guy came, Gia played a recording of my voice to again establish my presence."

"While you were in Sarasota killing Larry Gump."

"Yes."

"And you arranged a similar alibi when you were in Sarasota killing your wife."

"Yes."

"Do you want to tell me exactly how you managed to have people believe you were in Miami when you were in Sarasota killing Maggie?"

Paul described the same scenario that Sam and Diane Lewis had figured out, but could do nothing about. Every detail was the same.

"Why did you charge the gas that night?"

"I was so tense and running on adrenaline, I simply forgot to bring my money clip. And I covered by reporting my credit cards stolen."

"And then did you plant the evidence that implicated Sarah Hastings?"

Paul lowered his eyes for a moment before responding. "Yes," he said. "I hated Hastings. I planted the nail, the perfume, and I wore a pair of size ten hiking shoes, the kind either a man or woman could wear."

Sam stared at him for several beats, wanting to say, 'And you would have seen an innocent woman go to prison for something she didn't do.' But he remained silent. "Then who killed Gia?" he finally asked.

"It's the same person I told the police about, that scumbag, Rick Perez. He had dated Gia until she discovered he was crazy. I mean really unstable. Crazy. He stalked her for a while, scaring the hell out of her—even threatened to kill her—twice. She was terrified of him.

"There was no doubt in my mind that he killed Gia and of course I told the police. They talked with him, but it was only perfunctory because they had their killer and were not about to rock the boat. If the cops didn't have me, and had taken him in and put him in a room for as long as it took, he would have cracked. He's weak and not very bright."

"Did you know him?"

"No, but Gia told me about him."

"Interesting," Sam said. "There's just one question rattling around, Paul. What about your fingerprints all over the knife that killed her?"

Paul was already nodding his head. "As I told the cops, I used the knife earlier in the evening to cut the lasagna that Gia had made. Knowing what a fanatic she was for cleanliness, I then wiped the blade with a wet paper towel and set the knife on the sink next to her rubber gloves. I'm sure he slipped on the gloves before picking up the knife."

He paused and waited for Sam's response. When none came, he continued. "So you see, Sam, I had gotten away with two perfect crimes. Do you still think I'm stupid?"

Sam couldn't believe what he'd been hearing. When he decided to visit Paul and play upon his fragile ego and his fanatical need for people, including and maybe especially Sam to respect his intellect, he had serious doubts that it would work. But everything he had heard and observed first hand about Paul told him it was worth a shot.

"Well, Sam, do you?" Robbins asked again.

"No, Paul I guess I have to reassess my opinion. Let's just say you were unlucky. When you got arrested for a crime you didn't commit you were in a box. You couldn't tell the police you weren't there to kill Gia because you were in Sarasota killing someone else."

"Exactly."

"Well, it is pretty ironic, isn't it Paul? You pull off two brilliant schemes to commit murder, and you get arrested for one that made you look like you're dumb as a post. I can see where that would gall a man like you."

Robbins' eyes came to life. "Yes, yes. Exactly. It's been tearing me apart."

"And that's why you had to tell me."

"Yes."

"I guess it's poetic justice, though, isn't it, Paul? You're going to rot inside here for a crime you didn't commit."

"I'm dealing with it, Sam. But remember, what they convicted me of was not premeditated murder. With good behavior I can be paroled in fifteen years, maybe less."

"Yes, I suppose that's a lot better than spending ten years or more on death row waiting to be executed." He paused, studying the despicable man he once thought of as a friend. "Of course you realize that I will be sharing everything you've just told me with the Sarasota police and they will move heaven and earth to have you extradited there to stand trial for premeditated first degree murder."

Paul glared at Sam with an expression like Sam had betrayed him. And then his demeanor changed. "Everything I just told you? I have no idea what you're talking about. I haven't told you anything."

"You son-of-a-bitch, you just confessed to two murders to gratify your sick ego."

"Is that why you came over here, Sam? To make up some silly story?"

"No, Paul. I came here because I knew how stupid you really are—stupid enough to tell me about all the slick, clever things you did to commit two murders. Stupid enough to allow your sick ego to do you in." He stood up, turned his head and said "We're finished here."

Paul shot Sam a puzzled look and turned to see Diane Lewis, the prison warden and two guards enter the room.

"We got everything, Sam. Right down to the last word," Lewis said.

Paul looked in disbelief from one to the other, before turning a hard stare at Sam. "You rotten bastard. You're wearing a wire."

Sam smiled broadly. "Yep."

65

Two days later Sam sat in State Attorney Stanley Cramer's office along with a glum Diane Lewis and Sheriff Richard Ennis. "Goddamn it, Diane, when I called you with my brainstorm to visit Paul wearing a wire to try and goad him into bragging about murdering Maggie and Gump, you people said that wire tapping is perfectly legal if it's critical to the solving of a murder—or any crime," he said.

State Attorney Cramer spoke up. "That's absolutely correct, Sam, but we also knew that Miami would be within their rights to refuse having him extradited to Sarasota. They will fight us on this and they will probably win."

Sam looked from one to another, letting his gaze rest on Lewis. She lowered her eyes.

Cramer continued. "Robbins had a fair trial, and while they acknowledge that our use of a wire was legal they can't and won't use that as a basis for remanding him to us. Robbins could have just been ranting."

"But you could try him for Maggie's murder," Sam said. "They have no jurisdiction on that one."

"That's right and that's what we have to decide. Is it worth going through the expense of a trial? Also, no trial is ever a slam dunk. You never know what can happen. We have the tape, but that's not necessarily a sure thing in a trial." He turned to Diane. "As far as you and your people are concerned, your record is clean on both these murders. I'm satisfied and so is Sheriff Ennis. Right Dick?"

"Damn right," Ennis said.

"So where does that leave us?" Sam asked.

"We're not going to fight Miami. We're going to leave him there," Cramer said.

"But the son-of-a-bitch will be out in fifteen years," said Sam.

Cramer smiled. "Although this tape won't technically have any legal jurisdiction over a parole board's decision, knowing how these boards operate, I can almost guarantee you that Mr. Robbins is in for a rude awakening if he thinks he will be paroled."

Sam looked to Lewis for her take on all this.

This time she responded. "Sam, as you may know, we have what's known in law enforcement as a "Hold" on Robbins, which means that if and when he is released for Gia's murder, we have a "Hold" to bring him to Sarasota and put him on trial for his wife's murder. Either way, Mr. Robbins is in for a very long haul."

The sheriff spoke up. "And if we get him, the charge is first degree, premeditated murder."

"And we go for the death penalty," Cramer added.

"And Perez?" Sam asked.

"He's Miami's problem, not ours," said Lewis.

* * *

After leaving Lewis and the others, Sam called Jennifer from his cell phone and learned that she was out of town until tomorrow. At home the events of the last couple of nights caught up to him. No longer able to keep his eyes open, he went to his bedroom, lay down and fell into a deep sleep.

When he finally awoke he turned on a light and checked his watch: ten o'clock. He'd been sleeping for nearly seven hours.

Now wide awake, he decided to take a walk. He slipped on a pair of shorts and sneakers and sauntered up the street a few blocks and circled over to the beach.

Not a soul in sight. The summer night was a balmy seventy-five to eighty degrees with a full moon and not a cloud in the sky. He walked in silence, listening to the water rippling and lapping against the shore. A breeze came up and gently whistled through the trees rimming the beach.

He had been walking for about twenty minutes when he noticed an object about the size of a very large rock that appeared to be moving. He walked closer and, silhouetted against the moonlight, moving ponderously up the beach, was a sea turtle. Sam's heart skipped a beat.

The turtle, moving with a sense of purpose, dragged its way across the sand, emitting an audible grunt after each labored intake of breath. Sam couldn't believe his eyes. This valiant creature was about to complete a journey that probably began hundreds, maybe thousands of miles ago. He walked slowly behind her, being careful to keep a respectful distance.

Sam, watching in awe as she moved along the sand, was suddenly overcome with an odd sense of privilege at what he was about to see. How many years had these turtles been hauling themselves ashore at this very spot? Thousands? Millions? How many times had this particular turtle found her way here?

He continued to keep his distance, halting whenever the turtle stopped to rest. Finally, after about forty-five minutes and a distance of maybe fifty yards she stopped.

Sam moved in closer and watched, still staying behind her. Digging with her hind feet and using her back flippers like shovels, she dug a hole about a foot deep. Her grunting intensified as she sat and deposited her eggs in the hole.

Sam hadn't thought about the animal actually making sounds, and he found a kind of mystical magic in what he was sharing with her. At that moment, he understood what motivated the sea turtle people and why they cared.

He watched as she filled in the hole, leaving a small mound as testimony to her efforts, then turn and slowly make her way back toward the sea. After another forty-five minutes the weary turtle reached the water and floated away into the darkness. Sam knew he would never forget what he had just witnessed.

He stood for a moment on the beach, listening to the ebb and flow of the gentle surf, reveling in the tranquillity and beauty of where he stood.

As he walked across the beach toward home he looked up and spotted something he'd not noticed before. A few blocks away, a giant building crane stood silhouetted against the clear sky.

* * *

On the other side of the state, Rick Perez stood under the flashing neon lights of the Miami bar he'd just left. He waited for the steady traffic stream to abate before staggering across the street to the parking garage. A car nearly hit him before he reached the other side.

"Asshole," the driver screamed. Rick gave him the finger and disappeared into the garage, still muttering about the bartender who ordered him to leave the place.

The idiot tells him he's had too much to drink. Only had five or six rum Cokes—maybe more. Who counts?

He found his car and fumbled for the keys. Inside the vehicle his mind returned to his thoughts in the bar. He hadn't thought about much else since that awful night when he went to see Gia.

Bitch called him names, told him what a loser he was. Rick closed his eyes, and shook his head, trying to dislodge the words that wouldn't go away. "Get the fuck out of here, you creep." And then she laughed at him, made fun of him, and called him a loser.

He wasn't sorry he killed her. She deserved it. Bitch.

He navigated his car down the winding ramps and into the street. Struggling to keep his eyes open, he reached the ramp taking him up to I–95, where he lurched his car onto the highway. The last thing he heard in his troubled life was the impact of an oncoming ten wheeler.

66

The next day Jennifer called Sam about four P.M. "Hi, Sam. This is Jennifer. I'm back. What are you doing tonight?"

He smiled at the sound of her voice. "Not a thing. In fact I've been sitting here thinking about you. Come on over and I'll make dinner."

"You got a deal," she said. "Be there in forty-five minutes."

An hour later Jennifer arrived. He watched her climb out of the Jeep, throw him a wave and a smile and stride toward the house wearing a white polo shirt, khaki Bermudas and sneakers, and her hair drawn back in a pony tail.

"Sorry it took so long to get here," she said. "The traffic coming over the bridge was terrible. Anyway, here I am." She held out both arms. Sam moved in between them and they hugged.

"Hmm, you smell good," he said.

"Thanks. It's one of the little touch ups I added before coming over. Where's Henry?"

"He's back in his room nursing his wounds, sulking. He had another little run-in with his cocker spaniel buddy and got nipped on the nose again. Henry's a lover, not a fighter."

He made them each a gin and tonic, and after he filled her in on the details about Robbins they sat on the porch, inhaling the sea air carried by the breeze coming off the Gulf.

"How about if I put a couple of steaks on and open some wine while you make one of your super-duper salads?"

"Can't think of a better idea," she said. "I've been looking forward to this—a nice intimate dinner with you."

A horn tooted and segued into a rendition of "Deep in the Heart of Texas." Sam and Jennifer looked out and saw Jimbo pull up in a block long, early seventies Lincoln Continental.

"Better make that three steaks," Jennifer said.